THE HOUSE
IN THE PINES

THE HOUSE
IN THE PINES

A NOVEL

ANA REYES

DUTTON

DUTTON
An imprint of Penguin Random House LLC
penguinrandomhouse.com

Copyright © 2023 by Ana Reyes
Penguin Random House supports copyright. Copyright fuels creativity, en-
courages diverse voices, promotes free speech, and creates a vibrant culture.
Thank you for buying an authorized edition of this book and for complying
with copyright laws by not reproducing, scanning, or distributing any part
of it in any form without permission. You are supporting writers and allow-
ing Penguin Random House to continue to publish books for every reader.

DUTTON and the D colophon are
registered trademarks of Penguin Random House LLC.

LIBRARY OF CONGRESS CATALOGING-IN-PUBLICATION DATA

Names: Reyes, Ana, 1982– author.
Title: The house in the pines: a novel / Ana Reyes.
Description: New York: Dutton, an Imprint of
Penguin Random House LLC, [2023] |
Identifiers: LCCN 2022019074 |
ISBN 9780593186718 (hardcover) | ISBN 9780593186725 (ebook)
Subjects: LCGFT: Thrillers (Fiction). | Novels.
Classification: LCC PS3618.E9377 H68 2023 | DDC 813/.6—dc23
LC record available at https://lccn.loc.gov/2022019074

International Edition ISBN: 9780593473719

Printed in the United States of America

1st Printing

BOOK DESIGN BY ELKE SIGAL

For Bonk, Mom, Dad, Bubba, Brian, and Hilda

THE HOUSE
IN THE PINES

PROLOGUE

D eep in these woods, there is a house that's easy to miss.

Most people, in fact, would take one look and insist it's not there. And they wouldn't be wrong, not completely. What they would see are a house's remains, a crumbling foundation crawling with weeds. A house long since abandoned. But look closely at the ground here, at this concrete scarred by sun and ice. This is where the fireplace goes. If you look deeply enough, a spark will ignite. And if you blow on it, that spark will bloom into a blaze, a warm light in this cold dark forest.

If you come closer, out of the cold, the fire gets stronger, blows smoke in your eyes, tumbling smoke with a burning-pine smell that sweetens to the smell of perfume, then softens to the smell of your mother's coat. She's murmuring in the next room. Turn around and here come the walls, shyly, like deer emerging from the trees. Frozen concrete becomes an area rug. Take off your shoes, stay a while. Outside the wind is rising, and there comes a clacking, a close, rapid chatter. It must be the windows in their sashes. A light snow sifts from the sky, blanketing this cozy home. Tucking it in for the night. "Goodnight little house, and goodnight mouse." Remember? For once, there is no reason to get up, no one to chase or run away from. From the kitchen comes the smell of home, the sounds of a sauté. This is how the world was once, before the first colic, the first scald, the first getting lost. And this is why you do it. "Goodnight nobody, goodnight mush. And goodnight to the old lady whispering 'hush.'"

Get a good night's sleep, because when you wake, this house will be gone.

ONE

M aya didn't know it yet, but the video had already begun to circulate on social media. A grainy six-minute stretch of security footage that was strange and unsettling enough to garner several thousand views the day it went up, but not quite lurid enough to go viral, not ghastly enough to inspire repeat viewings. Not for most people, anyway. But for Maya, its existence would upend all that she'd been building for herself these past few years, this sometimes sloppy but mostly solid life that she shared with Dan, who snored quietly beside her in bed.

She hadn't yet seen the video because she was avoiding all screens, not wanting their blue light to keep her awake. She had tried everything to sleep: Benadryl, melatonin, counting backward from a hundred down to one. She had turned the clock around, taken a bath and some cough syrup, but none of it helped. This was her third sleepless night in a row. She had moved in with Dan earlier this month and could easily draw from memory the shape of every water stain on the ceiling. The branching lines of every crack.

Turning onto her side, Maya reminded herself to get curtains. The space heater at the foot of the bed clicked on, a white noise she usually liked, but now the rattle of its metal grille grated on her. Kicking off the covers, she got out of bed and pulled on a flannel shirt over her underwear. The apartment was cold, the central heat only partially effective, but her skin was damp with sweat.

The chilled wooden floor felt good on her feet as she made her way down the dark hall, passing the second bedroom, empty now except for the exercise bike that she and Dan had bought off Craigslist. She'd never done much to decorate any of the apartments she'd shared with the various roommates she'd had since college—no posters, no pictures in frames, not so much as a throw pillow—but lately she'd begun popping over to T.J. Maxx after leaving work at Kelly's Garden Center just across the parking lot and heading straight for the home décor section. Buying end tables, area rugs, and other things she couldn't really afford.

Maya had plans for this place. She was determined for it to feel like home.

It was just before dawn, a gray, wintery light settling over other recent purchases in the living room: The coffee table to replace the one Dan's roommate had taken when he left. New shelves for the many books she had brought, added to all of Dan's. A new-to-them couch, dark green velvet. And hanging on the wall above it, the one decorative item she'd brought with her, the only art she'd held on to for the past seven years.

A Mayan weaving about the size of a bath towel. A tapestry of red, yellow, green, and blue, threaded into interlocking rows of symbols resembling flowers and snakes. This was more than a decoration to Maya. She didn't know what the symbols stood for exactly, but she knew that somewhere in the mountains of Guatemala lived people who could read them. She passed by the tapestry in the dark on her way to the kitchen.

The sink held the night's dirty dishes, plates splattered with Bolognese. She loved cooking with Dan in their new kitchen, and the food had been fragrant with garlic and fresh tomatoes, but it hadn't tasted right. Or maybe she just wasn't hungry.

Or maybe her stomach had been clenched like a fist. Dan had asked if anything was wrong, she had told him she was fine, but she wasn't. Opening a cabinet, she pushed aside a few coffee mugs, tumblers, and wineglasses until she found what she was looking for. A shot glass, a single ounce. That's all she would have, she told herself, and the photo strip magneted to the freezer reminded her why.

The photos were from last Halloween, taken in a photo booth at the bar where they'd spent the night dancing with friends. Maya had gone as "Fairy Witch," a character she'd invented while scouring Goodwill for a costume at the last minute. She wore a glittery pair of wings, a pointy black hat, a blue dress with sequins on the collar, and somehow this had landed her second place in the costume contest.

Dan was Max from *Where the Wild Things Are*. It had been difficult to find a gray onesie large enough to fit his hearty frame, let alone one that was ethically produced, but Dan had started looking well in advance. Then he'd sewn a furry tail onto its seat and made himself a crown of recycled gold card stock.

The two of them looked like opposites in a lot of ways; she was petite and surprisingly athletic-looking for someone who'd never played sports, while he was tall and looked like he loved to eat, which he did. He was blue-eyed and fair with a short chestnut beard and glasses, while she was olive-skinned and ethnically ambiguous. People had always guessed that she was Indian, Turkish, Mexican, or Armenian. She was, in fact, half Guatemalan, a quarter Irish, and a quarter Italian. Thick black hair and high Mayan cheekbones met the round chin and upturned nose of the Irish on her face. She and Dan might have looked like opposites, but if you looked closely, you'd see that there was something in each of their postures—a slight leaning down on his part toward her, and an upward tilt to her stance as if to meet him halfway. They looked happy. And she looked drunk—not quite sloppy, but close.

She took out a bottle of gin from the freezer. White vapor swirled from its neck as she twisted off the cap and filled the tiny glass up to the brim, raised it—*Cheers!*—to their mugging faces, and made herself a promise: Tomorrow morning, she would tell Dan the reason that she hadn't been herself these past few days, the reason she couldn't sleep or eat. She would tell him she was going through Klonopin withdrawal.

The problem was that Dan didn't know Maya had been taking Klonopin in the first place. When they met, she had already been taking it every night for sleep. No huge deal—once upon a time, she'd even had a prescription—why mention any of this to someone she was dating?

Prior to Dan, she hadn't dated anyone for longer than a month. But then one month with Dan stretched into three, and before she knew it, two and a half years had passed.

How to explain why she'd waited so long? Or why she was on it in the first place?

And what would Dan think if he knew that the pills came not from a pharmacy but from her friend Wendy?

Maya had rationalized her dependence in so many ways, telling herself it wasn't a lie, just an omission; that she kept the pills in an aspirin bottle in her purse for convenience, not to hide them. All along, she had planned to quit, and then, she assured herself, once her habit was safely in the past, she would tell him.

But now she had run out of the little yellow pills, and Wendy, a friend from college, wasn't returning her calls. Maya had tried a dozen times, texting, emailing, and finally calling. The two had remained close for a few years after graduation, largely because they'd both stayed near BU and both liked to party. They rarely saw each other during the day but drank together several nights a week. But now that Maya had cut down on drinking, they saw each other less and less; looking back, she realized their monthly brunches had become literally transactional: fifty dollars for ninety milligrams of Klonopin.

Could this be why Wendy wasn't returning her calls?

As Maya's withdrawal got worse—insomnia, the fiery feeling in her brain, the sense of crawling ants on her skin—she wondered if Wendy had known just how hellish it would be.

Maya hadn't known. The psychiatrist who'd prescribed it to her seven years ago, Dr. Barry, hadn't said anything about addiction. He'd told her the pills would help her sleep, which they had—but only for a time. As the months passed, she'd needed more and more to achieve the same results, and Dr. Barry was always happy to oblige, upping her dosage with a flick of his pen—right up until Maya graduated college and lost her insurance. Once she could no longer pay for her sessions, she found herself cut off, and only then did she realize that she couldn't sleep anymore without pills.

Luckily for her, Wendy also had a prescription and didn't much trust the mental health establishment. She didn't take any of the meds her doctor prescribed, preferring to sell them or trade them for other drugs. Maya had been buying her Klonopin from Wendy for the past three years, ever since she graduated college. Telling herself all along that she would quit. She hadn't expected going off to be easy, but the severity caught her off guard, and Googling her symptoms hadn't helped. Insomnia, anxiety, tremors, muscle spasms, paranoia, agitation—she could handle those. What scared her was the possibility of hallucinations.

It took all her will to recap the gin and return it to the freezer. She went to the bathroom and took a swig of Ny-Quil, wincing as the syrup went down. Her reflection winced back at her, ghostly in the light spilling through the high frosted window. Her skin was pale and clammy, her eye sockets like craters. Withdrawal had taken her hunger, and Maya saw that she was losing weight, the bones of her cheeks and collarbones more pronounced. She forced herself to unclench her jaw.

In the living room, she sank into the couch and peeled off her sweaty flannel shirt. She turned on the reading lamp and tried to lose herself in a book, a mystery she'd been enjoying up until now, but found herself reading the same paragraph over and over. The quiet felt loud. Soon the street outside would ring with the voices of commuters to the Green Line, people getting into cars parked along the curb and doors slamming.

She heard footsteps and turned to see Dan emerging from the darkness of the hall. He looked half asleep, hair sticking up from his pillow. He'd been up late, studying for his third-year law school exams.

They were both twenty-five, but Dan was doing more with his life, or at least that's how it felt to Maya. Soon he would graduate, take the bar, and start looking for a job, tasks she didn't envy. What she envied was his faith in himself. He wanted to be an environmental lawyer, a goal he'd been working toward for as long as she'd known him, while she'd worked at Kelly's Garden Center, tending to customers and potted plants, ever since graduating from BU.

It wasn't that she thought the job was beneath her, but sometimes she worried that Dan did, or that he looked down on her apparent lack of drive. Early on in dating, she had told him that she wanted to be a writer, and he'd been supportive; he'd brought it up occasionally, asking when he'd get to read her work. But the truth was that Maya hadn't written anything since senior year of college.

And lately he'd stopped asking, as if he'd stopped believing she would ever follow through.

He squinted at her through the gloom. Maya sat on the couch in her underwear, while he wore sweatpants, wool socks, and a long-sleeved shirt. "Hey . . ." he said groggily. "You all right?"

Maya nodded. "I couldn't sleep."

But Dan wasn't stupid. He was, in fact, extremely smart—this was part of why she loved him. He knew something was wrong, and she wanted to tell him—she had promised herself she would—but now was obviously not the time. (Again.) Rising from the couch, she draped the itchy flannel around her shoulders and crossed the living room to lay a hand on his arm. "I was just about to go back to bed." She looked up into his tired eyes, then past him to the bedroom.

It was hard to say when the bedroom had gotten so messy. Neither of them was naturally tidy, but they managed to keep the living room and kitchen neat. As guests never had any reason to go into the bedroom, though, Maya and Dan left clothes on the floor and dirty mugs, wineglasses, and books strewn around, and lately it had gotten worse.

The mess had never bothered her, but now the room felt disturbingly like the inside of her head.

She lay down and closed her eyes, and Dan made a sound like he might say something. She waited. She waited until his breaths were slow with sleep.

———————

The dream began right away. One moment Maya was listening to Dan's breath, the next she was on her way to Frank's cabin. Awake, she had forgotten this place, but asleep, she knew the way by heart: down a narrow path through the woods, then over a bridge to the clearing on the other side. The cabin was in the clearing, ringed by a wall of trees. Two rocking chairs sat empty on the porch. The door was locked, but asleep, Maya always had the key.

She went inside, not because she wanted to but because she had no choice. Some part of her—the part of her that dreamed—insisted on returning here night after night, as if there were something she was supposed to do here. Something she was supposed to understand. A fire crackled warmly in the tall stone fireplace. The table was set for two. Two bowls, two spoons, two glasses yet to be filled. Dinner simmered in a pot on the stove, some kind of stew. Cooked meat and rosemary, garlic and thyme—it smelled delicious—and she felt her body begin to relax, to slow down, even as terror sprouted in her gut and wrapped its tendrils around her heart.

It didn't feel like a dream.

She knew Frank was here. He was always here. The

stream gushed softly in the window, a peaceful sound, but Maya knew better. There was danger here, lurking just beneath the surface of things, woven into the fabric of this place. Danger in its coziness, its warmth. Danger even in the sound of the stream, its gentle gurgle—it was getting louder. The sound of water rushing over stones. Rhythmic and insistent, it grew louder and more pronounced until it seemed to be talking to her, words surfacing from the white babble but disappearing before she could catch them.

Maya listened, trying to understand, until she realized that it wasn't the river that was talking to her. It was Frank.

He was standing behind her, whispering in her ear. Every hair on her body rose. Her heart thrashed and terror shrieked in her ears as she slowly turned around.

Then she opened her eyes, drenched in sweat.

It was rare that she remembered her dreams upon waking, and when she did, the impression was usually vague, but in the days since she had taken her last Klonopin, her sleep had grown exponentially more fractured, and her dreams more vivid. They left behind a fog of dread. She reached for the clock and turned it to face her. 5:49. Careful not to wake Dan, she rose once more from the bed, grabbed her laptop from the desk, and tiptoed to the living room.

She pulled up a playlist of soothing nature sounds and her mom's German chocolate cake recipe. Tonight, she and Dan were driving the two hours to Amherst for his mom's birthday. Normally Maya would have looked forward to this—she liked his parents and had offered (before she ran out of pills) to bake his mom a cake—but now she wondered how she would make it through dinner, just the four of them, without his parents realizing that something was wrong.

She wanted their approval. The first time she met them, Dan's father had thought it would be fun to speak to her in Spanish, which was awkward because Maya's Spanish was embarrassing. She sounded like any other English speaker who'd studied the language in high school, her vowels too long, her verbs the wrong tense, while Dan's father could roll his r's. *Sorry*, she'd said to him in English; she'd been trying to redeem herself in Dan's parents' eyes ever since.

Like their son, Greta and Carl were smart. Intellectuals. She was a photojournalist, and he was a fifth grade teacher and multilingual poet. Maya wanted them to like her, but beyond that, she wanted to be like them. She didn't plan to work at Kelly's Garden Center forever. She wanted to tell them that her father had been a writer too, even if her mom worked in the kitchen of a luxury rehab center, baking bread.

But then Dan's parents might have wanted to know more about her father, who died before she was born. Telling people this always led to a moment of awkwardness as everyone searched for the right thing to say, and the last thing she wanted for tonight was more awkwardness.

She would simply tell them that she was feeling under the weather. This was true. She would cover up the dark circles beneath her eyes and try not to fidget. She would smile, not too widely or too small, and no one would know how little she'd slept.

Rubbing her temples, she tried to focus on the waterfall

sounds coming from her speakers. She wrote down the ingredients they needed. Shredded coconut, buttermilk, pecans. Then, lacking the attention span for a book, she went to YouTube and scrolled through the many channels she subscribed to. She needed something to distract herself from the craving gnawing on her brain, something designed to grab her attention and hold it.

But Maya wasn't on social media of any kind. Her friends saw this as an eccentricity, Dan claimed to find it refreshing, and she'd managed to convince even herself it was some kind of stance, some statement she was making. Maybe it was, to some extent, but the truth was more complicated and not the kind of thing Maya should be thinking about right now, her anxiety already at a ten.

She watched a short video about a cat who'd raised an orphaned beagle as its own, then one of a Boston terrier with a talent for skateboarding. She had no profile picture, no identifying information of any kind online, but of course that didn't stop her from receiving targeted advertising and recommendations.

Later she'd wonder if this was why the video popped up in her feed. "Girl Dies on Camera." Of course she clicked. According to its caption, the grainy, six-minute video was security footage taken from a diner in Pittsfield, Massachusetts, Maya's hometown. Despite looking like it was from the 1950s, the diner must have been relatively new, as she didn't recognize it. A row of shiny booths, mostly empty, lined a wall of windows. It looked to be the middle of the day. The video was in color, but the quality was low, everything washed out. The black-and-white checkerboard floors. Pictures of classic cars on the walls. The only customers were a family of four and two elderly men drinking coffee.

The camera was aimed at the front door in order to catch a criminal bursting in with a gun or running out with the cash register, but this wasn't what the camera caught. Instead, when the door opened, it showed what looked like an ordinary couple, a man in his thirties and a slightly younger woman. The woman looked a little like Maya, with a round, open face, high forehead, and wide, dark eyes.

The man was Frank Bellamy.

Of this, Maya had no doubt. She hadn't seen him for the past seven years, but there was no mistaking the small chin and slightly crooked nose. The easy walk and disheveled hair. The video erased any signs of aging on his face, making him look exactly as she remembered. As if no time at all had passed. She watched the couple seat themselves in a booth and pick up their laminated menus. A waitress came over with water and took their orders without writing them down.

What happened next looked like a normal conversation between Frank and the woman, except that Frank was the only one talking. The woman listened. She was tilted toward the camera, her face visible, while he was tilted slightly away, so that the camera saw only his right ear, cheek, and eye, and the edge of his mouth as he spoke.

Cold tentacles circled Maya's lungs.

A lot of viewers probably stopped watching at this point, as the video was five minutes in and almost nothing had happened. Not even its clickbait title was enough to hold most peoples' attention beyond a certain point. Whoever had posted the video might have chosen to edit out this long, one-sided conversation that Frank had with the woman, but then maybe it was needed to show how what happened next truly came out of nowhere.

Maya leaned in closer to the screen, trying to read the woman's face. The woman appeared only vaguely interested in whatever Frank was saying, her face slack, providing no clue to her thoughts. Frank could have been telling her a story, one without humor, apparently, or any element of surprise. Or maybe he was giving her instructions of some sort. Or directions to somewhere far away.

She could have been a student at the back of a lecture hall on a drowsy summer day. Still in her puffy yellow coat, she focused her dark eyes gently on his face, resting her elbows on the table. Maya saw in the time bar that the video had only twenty seconds left. That was when it happened.

The woman rocked back and forth in her seat. She hinged forward at the waist, eyes wide open. She made no attempt to break her fall, forearms resting on the table as her face crashed down. The suddenness would have been comical in other circumstances, like a clown face-planting in a banana cream pie, only here there was no pie and no laughter. Just a slight, stunned pause before Frank rushed over to the woman's side of the booth, slid in beside her, and began to say something, probably her name. Now that he was facing the camera, it was easy to see his fear and surprise.

When he pulled her to him, the woman sagged with

dead weight over his arm. The video ended just as the waitress hurried over. But in the moment just before it ended, Frank's eyes rose up to the camera, directly into it, and it felt to Maya like he was looking right at her.

She closed her laptop with shaking hands.

The video had been posted less than three days ago and already had 72,000 views. Frank had every reason to think she would see it, which meant she had every reason to be afraid. After all, this wasn't the first time Maya had witnessed someone drop dead in his presence.

TWO

Aubrey West, Maya's best friend in high school, had fallen over dead on a bright summer day shortly before Maya left for college. Aubrey's death hadn't been caught on video but had garnered attention nonetheless. TV coverage, newspaper articles, gossip. A healthy seventeen-year-old dropping dead out of nowhere. *If it could happen to her,* people thought.

Like the girl in the video, Aubrey had been having a conversation with Frank when it happened. And Maya had been convinced that Frank killed her. She couldn't explain how he'd done it (even if she did have a sense of why), and in the end, because she lacked proof (and eventually confidence in herself, her own perception, her own sanity, even), she had no choice but to move on.

Or try to, anyway.

Maya had always liked a good buzz, ever since the first

time Aubrey swiped a pint of her mom's vodka and they drank it stirred into Sunny D. But drinking was different then. She and Aubrey sought out highs of all kinds as teenagers but saw themselves as separate from the burnouts at school, the kids who snuck out to the parking lot between classes and slouched at their lockers with red eyes. Maya got all A's without trying, and Aubrey, though her grades never reflected it, was smart in her own way. She understood people, saw through their acts. Her family had moved around a lot when she was little, so she had a lot of practice when it came to making friends, but one thing she hadn't learned was how to keep them.

She was the new girl when Maya met her in ninth grade English, mysterious and intriguing to all, especially the boys, with her green eyes and sly grin. Maya was only one of many new friends Aubrey had made in her first few weeks of school, but out of all of them, their friendship was the one that lasted. The one they both cultivated.

They'd been paired up for a report on Emily Dickinson and bonded over poetry. Poetry was part of why they worked, the shared ability to be swept away by a beautiful line. But it was also that neither quite belonged—Aubrey, the perpetual new girl, and Maya with her nose in a book. She looked Hispanic but had grown up with a single white mom and knew very little about her family in Guatemala. She didn't feel she fit in with the other Hispanic kids, while not being white meant she stuck out in Pittsfield.

Maya spent most of her time reading and making up

stories. She was more popular with teachers than with her peers, but she was okay with that. She was going to be a writer, just like her father had been. She was going to write books and be famous. She was going to leave Pittsfield behind.

She got into almost every college she applied to and chose BU because of its creative writing program and because of the scholarships she was offered. But the week before she was supposed to start, Aubrey died.

And Maya's life was divided into a Before and an After.

She lost her closest friend. Saw it happen before her eyes, yet to this day sensed that there was more to the incident than what she saw. Like watching a magic trick and understanding that it was an illusion, but not knowing how the magician had pulled it off.

It didn't make sense. Aubrey was healthy, didn't have any preexisting conditions. Her parents had an autopsy performed, but that didn't answer anything, and the medical examiner eventually labeled it "Sudden Unexplained Death"—the name for when someone drops dead for apparently no reason. It was often blamed on an arrhythmia of the heart or a certain kind of seizure.

Only Maya felt sure that it was Frank.

There was no weapon, no poison, no contact of any kind. No bloodshed or wounds on Aubrey's body. Maya couldn't prove it—couldn't explain it, even—but she insisted that he had deceived them all somehow.

Maybe if she'd had a shred of evidence, the police would

THE HOUSE IN THE PINES

have taken her seriously. But as it was, they questioned Frank and, finding no reason to keep him, let him go—with a warning to Maya about false accusations. They said she could ruin a man's life that way.

Her mom had more patience for Maya's suspicions, but when they failed to add up, she began to worry about her daughter's mental health. Mental illness ran in the family like a curse, and at seventeen, Maya was right at that age when it could strike.

This was how she wound up under the care of Dr. Fred Barry, who Maya's mom had found in the Yellow Pages.

Within an hour of meeting her, Dr. Barry diagnosed Maya with brief psychotic disorder. Grief could bring it on. He said her fears about Frank were delusional but assured her that she wasn't the first to react with magical thinking to a death so sudden and unexpected. Less than two out of every hundred thousand people suddenly drop dead for reasons that can't be explained by an autopsy.

Some cultures blame such deaths on evil spirits. The mind will always try to explain what it can't understand—it will make up stories, theories, whole belief systems—and Maya's mind, Dr. Barry said, was of the type that saw faces in clouds and messages in tea leaves. Patterns where others saw none. It meant she had a good imagination—but one that could trick her.

The antipsychotics dulled the certainty burning in her gut that Frank had deceived them all somehow, but the feeling never went away completely. It came over her sometimes, a dark crawling. The horrible conviction that Dr. Barry was wrong, even though everyone believed him, and that Frank had, in fact, murdered her best friend.

And with that conviction came fear. Maya was a loose end for Frank, a witness to whatever it was he had done. If he was a killer, she had every reason to be afraid, and the fact that she didn't know *how* he'd done it made it worse, a dreadful uncertainty that kept her from moving on. But over time she learned not to talk about her suspicions with Dr. Barry, or anyone else for that matter. She couldn't stand it when people looked at her like she was crazy. Satisfied that she was no longer delusional, Dr. Barry pronounced her cured, if a little anxious, and swapped out her antipsychotics for Klonopin.

It worked. The Klonopin dulled her fear and knocked her out at night.

Alcohol helped too. All through college, she was black-out drunk several nights a week. She still managed to get A's and B's, but that was just the easy classes she was taking, overcrowded lectures where no one knew her name and it didn't matter if she was hungover. She kept telling herself she was having fun, and maybe she was; it was hard to remember. There were enough embarrassing pictures of her online dancing on tabletops, always a drink or a shot in hand, to suggest she was having the time of her life.

After college, she was happy to take the job at Kelly's Garden Center. And though every now and then she would sit at her desk to write, she never made it past the first page of anything. The problem was that she no longer liked being alone with her thoughts. She had been working at the garden center and sharing an apartment with her friend Lana for over a year when she met Dan.

They met at a party, at the hour when everyone was either dancing in a sweaty clump, slurring too loudly in the kitchen, or sprawled on the host's bed, doing coke. Maya had assumed that she and Dan were both high when they started talking while in line for the bathroom—how else to explain that they were still talking at breakfast the next morning, seated across from each other at Maya's favorite Mexican restaurant?

Over huevos rancheros and cinnamon-spiced café de olla, they talked about everything, but what Maya remembered most was learning that Dan, like her, had read a children's version of *The Iliad* as a child, and been obsessed with Greek mythology ever since.

Maybe it was the intimacy of being with someone who loved the same stories. Or maybe it was that, in talking about such stories, they were really talking about themselves. It had been years since Maya had spoken to anyone of the central trauma of her life, and while she certainly hadn't spoken of it then, she found a certain comfort in Dan's tenderness toward Cassandra, the woman cursed to utter a truth no one would believe.

It wasn't until their third or fourth date that Maya realized he hardly drank—had, at most, two drinks at a party—and didn't use drugs. This meant that their first conversation had not, in fact, been cocaine-fueled, at least not on Dan's part, which felt significant.

It also meant that he was utterly lucid around her, unlike most of the men she had dated, who, in retrospect, had been more like drinking buddies. The thought of all that sober attention on her was nerve-racking, but over time—over brunches and dinner tables, long talks and increasingly cozy silences—Maya found herself wanting to be lucid around him too, so as not to miss out on their time together. Their bike rides along the Charles River. The *Iron Chef* marathons on the couch. The messy, elaborate meals cooked together in his kitchen.

Spending all that time sober hadn't been easy for Maya at first. Sometimes, out of nowhere, memories like long-sleeping leviathans would stir, threatening to rise up and swallow her whole. Aubrey collapsing on the ground. The dark glitter of Frank's eyes. The terror of knowing that none of Maya's efforts to stay under the radar would mean anything if he decided he wanted to find her.

This wasn't all that haunted Maya these days. After nearly a decade of constant inebriation, she found that she had forgotten how to handle day-to-day struggles, like going to the RMV or winding down for bed at a reasonable hour. It felt strange, when frustrated, not to get drunk.

Sometimes she caught herself snapping at Dan for no reason and hating herself for it. Afraid of pushing him away, she did her best to hide her anxiety, the air itself suddenly raw and jagged, and never mentioned the cold sweats that woke her at dawn, or the insomnia that kept her from sleeping in the first place. But eventually all that subsided, helped along by the Klonopin she took in place of the vodka or gin she normally would have used to knock herself out.

She took Klonopin during the day sometimes too, in upward-creeping doses as her tolerance grew. What mattered to Maya was that the old dread wasn't nearly as pervasive as she'd feared. Most of the time, her thoughts left her alone, or maybe it was just that enough time had passed. She ate well and exercised, rarely having more than a single drink per night (along with a few pills from the aspirin bottle, which she kept in her purse so that Dan would never accidentally take one, thinking it was aspirin).

And these days, when Maya thought of Aubrey or of Frank, or dreamed that she was back at the cabin, she comforted herself with the words of Dr. Barry, who had assured Maya that there was nothing she could have done for Aubrey. Nothing that anyone could have done. No one whose fault it was. Not even Frank.

This was what Maya told herself every time the phone rang and she didn't recognize the number, or she heard footsteps behind on her a dark street. But how could two women drop dead for no apparent reason while talking to the same man?

THREE

So, what exactly am I looking at here?" Dan had his glasses on but seemed bewildered by the video on Maya's computer, and the situation in general. He'd woken at seven to find her pacing the living room, and now, rather than explain herself, she was showing him a video.

"Frank Bellamy," she said as, on her screen, the couple entered the diner.

"Who?"

She and Dan had gone over their respective dating histories early on, but Maya hadn't told him about Frank. She had tried to force him from her mind, along with the rest of that summer, the summer she either witnessed the murder of her best friend or lost her mind completely. "I met him after high school," she said. "We sort of dated." The relationship had lasted all of three weeks, ending the day Aubrey died—

or, more accurately, *changing* that day into something else, a fear that warped every aspect of Maya's life.

Dan raised an eyebrow and smiled sideways at her. "What is this, cyberstalking? Should I be jealous?"

"Just watch." She wanted his unbiased eye. Dan was sailing through law school, as he was good at picking up on details that others might miss and understanding how they fit into a story.

"Tell me if you notice anything . . . off about Frank," she said.

Dan's smile faded as he took in her expression. He turned back to the video, settling back on their couch while Maya perched beside him, bare legs tucked beneath her. She couldn't believe she was showing him this video.

She wanted, on the one hand, to forget Frank, as she had all but managed to do until a few hours ago. She wanted to reassure herself that she was imagining things, seeing connections where there were none. It would have been easy to have hidden the video, not just from Dan but from herself as well, and gone on acting like her biggest problem was running out of Klonopin.

But then Maya thought of the dead woman's face, not so different from her own, only younger and probably more innocent. How improbable that both she and Aubrey, seven years apart, would drop dead in Frank's presence. She had to imagine, or at least hope, that Dan would find it suspicious.

"She looks like you," he said.

There was no denying Frank had a type.

"Bit of a rambler," he said.

"He was a real storyteller . . ."

The woman on-screen pitched forward. "What the hell?" Dan watched Frank shake the woman by the shoulders, shouting without sound. "Wait," Dan said. "She's not . . ."

"Yes!" Maya hugged herself, squeezed the ends of her sleeves in her fists. "I looked her up. Cristina Lewis. She was twenty-two."

"I don't get it. What happened?"

Maya slowly shook her head. "I don't know. But I think he . . ." She almost couldn't say it after so long; she'd buried the words deep. "I think he did it."

Dan's eyes went wide. "Did what? Killed her?"

She nodded.

"How?"

"I don't know."

He waited for her to go on. She swallowed. "Do you remember when I told you about my friend Aubrey?"

"Of course. The one who died." He spoke gently, knowing this was hard for her.

Maya had told him about Aubrey, and that she was dead, but she hadn't answered the one question everyone has upon learning someone's died: How did it happen? Maya hadn't wanted to talk about it then, but now she had to. "Aubrey died," she said, "just like Cristina. She just . . . tipped over. I saw it happen."

The incredulity on Dan's face was encouraging. "What did the medical examiner say?"

"There's this term for when they can't figure out what

killed a person. *Sudden unexplained death.* It's extremely rare and almost always happens when the person is asleep. They just never wake up."

"Wow. That's . . . terrible."

"But here's the thing. Aubrey was awake when it happened. And she was talking to Frank."

Dan leaned closer to the laptop screen, rewound the video, and rewatched the part where Cristina died. Then he watched it again while Maya watched him, hoping he would catch something she'd missed.

But when he spoke again, he sounded perplexed. "So how did he kill her?"

It's like he has some kind of power . . . That was what she'd said to the police when she was seventeen, but now she knew better. She had to sound rational. "I never figured it out," she said, "but if anyone was capable of it, it was Frank."

Dan furrowed his brow. "The police didn't question him?"

"They let him go." Her shoulders sagged.

"Okay . . . and what about Cristina Lewis? What do you know about how she died?"

She heard the doubt creeping into his voice and tasted the old anger that had seized her whenever anyone—the police, Dr. Barry, her mom—didn't believe her. "Here," she said, pulling up a *Berkshire Eagle* article on her computer. "This is all I could find." She watched him read the article, knowing it wasn't going to help.

The article said that Cristina was from Utah, had been

a painter, and worked as a ticket seller at the Berkshire Museum. Either her death was truly as inexplicable as it appeared, or not everything was being shared with the press.

After laying out what had happened—an account no different from what the video showed—the article included a quote from her grieving boyfriend, Frank Bellamy: "I just can't wrap my head around it. I wish there was something I could have done."

It wasn't his words that upset Maya but the fact that the article presented him as a *witness.*

"Says here the death isn't being treated as suspicious," Dan said. "The police would've questioned Frank since he was there."

Maya scoffed. "That's what happened last time."

Dan looked at her. Her clenched posture and sweaty temples. The heavy bags under her eyes. "Are you all right?"

"Yes," she said, "I'm just frustrated."

He seemed unconvinced. Concerned, even.

"What's going on?" he asked. "Something was off even before you saw the video."

She could have told him then about the Klonopin. But Dan didn't believe her about Frank. He was trying, but he didn't. Telling him she was going through withdrawal would only make things worse. "It's just seeing that girl die . . ." She trailed off.

"I can imagine. It must've been so hard to lose your best friend."

Her eyes watered. She looked away. Anyone else might have seen how upset she was and humored her. But unlike

THE HOUSE IN THE PINES

her, Dan had no problem telling people what they might not want to hear. She wouldn't change this about him, but it hurt. There was no one whose opinion she trusted more, and if he didn't believe Frank could have killed Cristina, then he was probably right.

Maya was probably being paranoid.

FOUR

S he knew the cake would be delicious. Deeply chocolatey, topped with pecans. It would be beautiful on the cake stand she had bought for this purpose. She wanted to impress Dan's mom, an acclaimed photojournalist. The cake had to be perfect, and it would be because Maya had learned to bake from her mom, Brenda Edwards, who had learned from her own mother, and so on, a line of women who'd been stress-baking for years before anyone coined the term.

Growing up, Brenda had a sister named Lisa whose behavior had prompted the baking of many desserts. As children, the two were best friends or they were enemies, depending on how Lisa was feeling. She had a way of warping her surroundings to fit whatever mood she was in. She could turn a boring shopping trip into an adventure, or a trip to the beach into a hellish ordeal.

Wherever Lisa went, doors were slammed and voices were raised. The only constants in her life were her parents, her three brothers, and Brenda, and out of all of them, Brenda was the one who knew her best. The one who would blame herself most for what happened.

Lisa was fifteen when she began to suspect that breezes off a nearby lake were blowing in through her bedroom window and poisoning her with toxic fumes. Brenda, who was two years younger, believed her at first. And to be fair, Silver Lake, which was less than two blocks from the house, had been notoriously contaminated for over a century. A cotton factory in the 1800s was the first to pollute its water, followed by a hat factory and two oil spills. In 1923, the surface of the lake broke out in flames—and that was all before GE dumped PCBs into it.

Lisa's suspicions didn't come out of nowhere, but over the next few weeks, they spiraled into obsession, the first of many obsessions she'd have in her life. She stopped bathing, convinced that the lake's noxious waters had seeped into their water tank. She wore a gas mask everywhere she went, even though her parents begged her not to. She had fought with them all her life, but as time went on, the fights got worse. She told her parents and siblings that they would all die unless they moved to a different house.

By the time she was sixteen, it seemed obvious that the problem wasn't Silver Lake. Something was wrong with Lisa, but no one would name it. This was back when few people talked about mental illness, not to mention that Lisa's parents—Maya's grandparents—were experts at avoidance. The only place either spoke openly was in the darkness of a confessional booth at church.

Lisa never got the help she needed, and instead evened herself out with vodka and pot and eventually speed. The rest of the family put up with her until she was eighteen, at which point she moved to California with a much older man.

She was dead at twenty-one.

Maya was too young to have met her, yet even in death, her aunt Lisa was a major presence. A cautionary tale. One whose guilt followed Brenda around. So when her daughter, at the age of seventeen, started saying things that didn't make sense, Brenda called a psychiatrist. Then she forced Maya to take the antipsychotics Dr. Barry prescribed, and to this day, Maya hadn't fully forgiven her.

She hadn't seen her mom in over a year, but Maya thought about her every time she baked. It was her mom who taught her to be precise. Precision took focus. Brenda's careful cups of flour had distracted her from her sister's screaming and suicide threats. She taught her daughter how to pour her attention into the batter, and this was what Maya did now. She turned the mixer on high, sent her ingredients swirling, and stirred in three yolks. She beat down the images bubbling back up.

Dan hadn't believed her, but she didn't want to resent him. She'd rather rewind to before she saw the video—to yesterday—when finally, after almost seven years, she'd lulled herself into thinking that maybe her mom was right: maybe Maya *was* just like Aunt Lisa, unable to see beyond her own delusions. *The unwell mind*, Dr. Barry had said, *is rarely capable of recognizing its own illness.* The words had comforted Maya over the years, because if she was delusional, then she wasn't in danger; Frank hadn't really killed Aubrey.

The video had shattered that comfort, and Maya was right back to being seventeen, the only witness to a murder. The difference was that now she understood there was nothing she could do about it. She knew better than to go to the police—she'd tried that. She had tried telling Dan. What else could she do?

Sliding the cake pans into the oven, she got started on the frosting, toasting pecans and simmering milk. She folded in shredded coconut, tasted it, and, for once, didn't enjoy another heaping spoonful. With the frosting done, she had nothing to concentrate on until the cake came out of the oven.

She went back to the freezer. She'd been so good lately, so moderate, and now here she was, not even noon, pouring her second shot of the day. But then, wasn't this kind of an emergency? That video would have been a crisis under any circumstance. When she was strung out and sleep-deprived, it was intolerable.

And then there was dinner with Dan's parents.

Maya burned her hand taking the pans out of the oven. She ran the burn under water and didn't mind the sting. It brought her back into her body. She counted her breaths. Told herself it wasn't worth it to dwell on the video, or on Frank. Especially not as she was going through withdrawal.

"God, it smells amazing in here," Dan said as he stepped in from the cold. His eyes landed on her hands beneath the water. "Did you burn yourself?"

"Not too bad."

He looked concerned but didn't say anything as he knelt to untie his shoelaces. He must have been tired of asking if she was okay.

"How's the studying going?" she asked.

"It's going," he said, but his tone was pained. He was a major procrastinator, cramming weeks of studying into his last three days before finals. He spent the day with his books while Maya tidied the bedroom and watered the plants. She and Dan were planning to get a dog, which meant they needed to get rid of their firestick plant and its toxic sap. She snapped a picture of the three-foot-tall succulent with its orange- and crimson-tipped stems, then sent it around to a few friends to see who wanted it.

She also sent a picture to her aunt Carolina, whose love of plants had inspired Maya's own. Tía Carolina lived in Guatemala City and Maya had met her only once, but they had kept in touch over the years. She was Maya's only connection these days to the country her father was from.

She tried to read afterward, but soon gave up and went for a walk to avoid pacing around the apartment. She paced instead through her neighborhood, past other buildings like the one she and Dan lived in, with metal fire escapes zagging up the walls, and brick town houses with concrete stoops. She took Commonwealth Avenue all the way to Boston University, where she had gone to college, passing convenience stores and a shawarma café she used to frequent, then continuing on to the icy Charles River. With every step alongside the river, joggers and cyclists speeding by, she tried not to think of Frank.

When she got home, it was almost time to go, and Dan was stressed. He'd agreed to this visit with his parents weeks ago, not anticipating how much studying he would leave until the last minute. Maya poured herself a teacup of gin and drank it in the shower. She'd banished Frank from her thoughts before and could do it again. She would not think of him, nor Aubrey, nor Cristina.

She rarely wore makeup, but tonight she wore concealer like a mask. She wore her nicest sweater, cream-colored cashmere, with brown corduroys and low-heeled boots. She covered her cake with the stand's bell-shaped glass cover, threw some clothes and a toothbrush in her backpack, and stood waiting by the door while Dan looked for his keys.

"Found them," he said, rushing in with mismatched socks.

Dan drove. Each of them was lost in their own worries as they left the city for the state's forested interior. Amherst was two hours to the west. Maya's hometown of Pittsfield was just an hour beyond that, but the two towns felt very different. Pittsfield had once been a bustling metropolis, but those days had ended before Maya was born. The city had never really recovered from losing GE in the '70s and '80s.

Amherst, on the other hand, bustled with young people from the five colleges in the area. Even with the students gone for winter, its downtown seemed livelier than downtown

Pittsfield. There were no empty storefronts. Young families and professors walked in and out of coffee shops and farm-to-table restaurants. The independent movie theater advertised a movie Maya had never heard of.

The house Dan grew up in was large and contemporary-looking, with sharp angles and floor-to-ceiling windows shaded by hedges. There was more snow here than in Boston, draping the lawn with a thin white sheet. Dan's father came to the door as they got out of the car.

Carl, a heavier and blonder version of Dan, was a fifth grade teacher and locally famous poet. Apparently, his students loved him, and Maya could see why. He shared Dan's openness and warmth. His smile was enormous as he greeted his only child. He shook Maya's hand, then led them through the high-ceilinged foyer to the kitchen. "What can I get you to drink? We're having daiquiris, Greta's favorite, but there's also wine and sparkling water."

"A daiquiri sounds great," Dan said as he hid the cake at the back of the fridge.

"I'll have one too," said Maya. "Thanks." She was doing her best to seem happy and relaxed as her withdrawal amplified the buried anxiety in her gut along with the usual anxiety of wanting to impress Dan's parents. It wasn't just that she loved their son, but that they appeared to have everything she dreamed of for herself. They were comfortable and successful in their fields. They were paid to think. They exuded contentment.

She began to relax the moment Carl handed her a drink. She knew from her doomscrolling that alcohol and Klonopin acted on many of the same brain receptors, which explained why they felt so alike. She exhaled. Tried not to drink too fast. The house was warm and smelled like rosemary, garlic, and roasted meat. The furniture was eclectic. The art on the walls was from around the world: framed photographs likely taken by Greta in what looked like Morocco, a mosaic of tiles, several masks.

Greta came downstairs in a silk tunic and linen pants. Tall and elegant, she held herself like someone who did a lot of yoga. She was older than Maya's mom by at least a decade, her loose curls more silver than black, but she seemed less tired. "Danny," Greta said, kissing her son's cheek, then hugging him tight. Maya rose to greet her, and Greta kissed her cheek too. She smelled like rose water. "Thank you for coming."

"Happy birthday," Maya said.

Dinner was roasted leg of lamb with rosemary, salad, and fingerling potatoes. Maya sat beside Dan at the table and cringed when Greta sat across from her. Greta was sharp and absorbed the world with her eyes. Maya shrank from her gaze.

She was grateful when Carl opened a bottle of pinot noir. All she had eaten was a small plate of leftover spaghetti and a taste of frosting, so Maya really felt the wine, especially after the daiquiri. The alcohol loosened the vise around her head. It softened the edges of her thoughts, and she almost felt normal as the conversation settled into an easy dynamic with Greta at the helm. They talked about an upcoming eclipse she planned to photograph, and eclipses in general, and Maya couldn't think of anything to say, so she listened, and was actually relieved when Greta turned to her to ask, out of the blue, if she'd read Isabel Allende.

Here was something Maya could talk about, which she hoped Dan's parents would take as evidence that she was well-read, rather than as a given. Tonight was going better than expected. This was, in fact, the best she'd felt in days, so the moment Maya saw someone else refill their wineglass, she did the same. And her laughter grew genuine instead of nervous as Carl told a funny story about Dan's fourth Halloween.

Dan had wanted to be a pumpkin that year, a costume that his parents couldn't find in any store, so Carl had made him one.

"And to be fair," Greta said, "it was a good costume! Very creative."

"She's being nice," Carl said. "The wire frame collapsed halfway through trick-or-treating and everyone thought he was a carrot!"

Maya and Greta laughed. Dan had heard this one before. He seemed tense, she thought, like he was thinking about finals. Or maybe something else was bothering him.

Maybe she was tipsier than she thought.

Outside the wind picked up. The windows rattled in their frames.

"It's a good thing you're spending the night," Greta said. "Sounds like a storm is coming."

A hush fell and Maya looked down at her plate. Most of

the food was still there. She speared a piece of lamb with her fork.

"The birdhouse," Carl said suddenly.

Maya looked up, confused, to see them all staring out the window at her back, apprehensive. Her scalp tingled as she turned to look, and as she did (her head too heavy, moving way too fast), she understood her mistake.

That last drink had been a terrible idea. Maya hadn't realized how drunk she was until she was in motion, and now the full force of two glasses of pinot noir, the rum daiquiri, and a teacup and two shots of gin hit her like a tsunami. Her eyes struggled to focus on what everyone was looking at. The birdhouse. The wind had blown it off its branch, and now the tiny house rested in a tangle of twigs that had broken its fall. But the wind was going strong, the twigs shaking, and any second the birdhouse, with its carefully crafted windows and gabled roof, would fall and smash open on the frozen ground.

Maya felt like she was inside of it. The room tilted. The floor swayed and she curled her fingers around the edges of her seat to keep from falling.

"I'll go see if I can save it," Carl said.

He left, and then it was just her, Dan, and Greta with her excavating eyes. Two very smart people who could probably tell by her weaving that she had the spins.

"Hey," Dan said softly. "You doing all right?"

Maya nodded, looking down at her plate. She could feel him beside her and Greta across from her, watching.

(Judging.) Maya couldn't look up. Nausea surged from her stomach through her chest to her throat.

"Can I get you a glass of water?" Greta asked without warmth.

Maya shook her head. She needed to get to the bathroom. "I'll be right back," she said as she got up. The thought of vomiting in front of Greta at her birthday dinner was so horrible that Maya broke into a clumsy run and was almost out of the room when her gag reflex kicked in and her mouth flooded.

She covered her mouth, but some of it seeped from between her fingers and splatted on the floor. No one said anything as she hurried away down the hall. The bathroom was at the bottom of the stairs. Closing the door behind her, Maya sank to her knees and heaved. It was all coming up. The wine, the lamb, the frosting, everything she wanted to keep down. Aubrey's body falling on the steps. Cristina pitching forward on her face. Frank looking up into the camera. Their motions synced in Maya's mind as she threw up. She had hidden Aubrey's murder in a box inside her head, but Frank was still out there killing. Even as the wine burned its way back up her throat, Maya had never felt so sober.

She gargled cold water, then stood paralyzed at the sink, too mortified to return to the table. Her clammy face stared back at her, shivering as sweat poured from her body— different from the sweat of exercise. Thicker. Cold. The mirror confirmed that there would be no more pretending she was okay.

FIVE

Maya drives with the windows down, letting the summer air rush in and steal their voices as they sing along with Tender Wallpaper's cover of the murder ballad "Two Sisters." The air conditioner is broken, but the CD player works, and she and Aubrey hurl their voices as if auditioning for a musical. They wear bathing suits beneath their shorts. Sneakers and tank tops, towels in the back seat. Aubrey dabs sunscreen on her lightly freckled face, her cherry-black hair flying around her head while the world blurs by, leafy and many shades of green.

When they arrive at the shoulder in the road, Maya parks her mom's car behind a Harley-Davidson. The air is cooler than in town. Maya and Aubrey follow a trail through the woods, slapping at mosquitoes.

Usually their silences are of the kind shared by good friends after many years—as easy as being alone. But today's silence feels different. Chilly. Maya gets the sense that

Aubrey is upset about something and has been for the past few weeks. She's noticed a snippiness to Aubrey's tone, an occasional meanness to her laughter. Maybe Maya's imagining it, but she doesn't think so, and it pisses her off that Aubrey won't just say whatever's on her mind.

"So," Maya says, just to say something, "who's the scarf for?"

Aubrey, ahead of her, doesn't look back. "It's a secret."

Until half an hour ago, Maya hadn't even known that Aubrey knew how to knit. But when she arrived to pick Aubrey up, Maya found her sitting on the porch of her duplex, knitting a scarf. Her hands moved with graceful, practiced ease, the lime green weaving unfurling from her needles.

Maya had thought they knew everything about each other.

They arrive at the waterfall a few minutes later. The deep, dark pool glitters like peacock feathers. Rainbows hover in the spray off the rocks. The place is usually crowded in summer, but today it's just Maya, Aubrey, and a couple of middle-aged bikers. The woman, covered in tattoos, reclines on a boulder while the man wades in the shallows, his long gray ponytail dipping into the water as he leans down to wet his arms.

The girls step out of their sneakers and shorts, leave their belongings on the rocky shore, and go in up to their knees. The water's so cold it feels sharp.

"One!" Aubrey says, challenging Maya to dive in with her.

"Oh, no way—"

"Two!"

Her whole body begs her not to do it, but Maya won't be the last one in. *"Three!"* she shouts before plunging deep into the pool, where it's even colder and darker and thunderous from the falls.

Her skin tingles as she bursts back up and looks back to see Aubrey, still standing, still dry. Laughing. Maya splashes her in outrage, and Aubrey shrieks, then drops silently down, disappearing with a faint ripple.

When she reappears, she's in the middle of the pool. She's the better swimmer, more comfortable in water. She floats on her back, looks up at the sky, the copper amulet she wears glinting on her chest. The amulet is etched with the supposedly magic words *SIM SALA BIM*, though Aubrey swears she doesn't believe in magic. She just loves it. She just wishes it were real.

Maya will miss her, even with the way she's been acting. Aubrey is staying in town after this summer, working as a waitress and taking classes at Berkshire Community College while Maya moves to Boston and attends BU. Reminded of what little time they have left, Maya sighs, paddles over to Aubrey, and floats beside her.

"You know what we never did?" Aubrey says.

"What?"

"We never jumped off the waterfall."

"Why do you say it like that? Like we'll never have another chance?"

"Who knows?" Aubrey shrugs. "Maybe we won't."

"Boston is, like, three hours away. I'll be home all the time."

Aubrey turns to Maya, treading water, and Maya sees that Aubrey's mood has shifted. Her smile is lively and mischievous. She points with her eyes at the high rocks at the top of the waterfall. "Let's do it now."

"You're crazy."

"People do it all the time. Little kids even."

Maya can't argue with this: last time they were here, all the children of a large family had jumped off, one after another, and the littlest one couldn't have been more than eight. "But what if—"

"We'll be careful."

Maya's mom works as an EMT, so she's heard horror stories of people killed or paralyzed doing things like jumping off waterfalls.

"What are you scared of?"

"Isn't it obvious?"

"Fine. I'll do it myself."

Aubrey turns and glides away.

Maya glances back at the shore. The biker couple has left. The sunbaked rocks are inviting, but Aubrey's excitement is contagious, and suddenly it seems like maybe Maya was only imagining that something was wrong. She's often been accused of being sensitive. She turns and paddles after her friend.

Cold spray from the waterfall strikes her face as she gets closer. Aubrey says something to her, but her voice is lost beneath the drum of water on water. *"I can't hear you!"* Maya shouts back. Aubrey shakes her head—*Never mind*—but Maya doesn't need to hear the words to hear the supportive tone. Here at the base of the waterfall, she sees the natural path around the side of it, reinforced by all the people who have come this way. Her nervousness turns to exhilaration as she climbs, the white cascade at her side like some breathtaking deadly beast. She doesn't feel cold anymore. She grips the wet stones with her hands.

Her heart beats faster as they reach the top and Aubrey steps out on the enormous boulder that juts, diving-board-like, over the pool. Maya stays several feet behind her. She feels like the high diver at a circus, looking down a crazy-long ladder at a tiny pool.

She can't do it. She'll just have to climb down and is already inching that way when Aubrey looks back over her shoulder. Her face is kind. Eyes bright with excitement. She reaches out her hand. The waterfall roars in Maya's ears. She can't do it, but then she does. She steps tentatively forward and takes Aubrey's hand.

Together they look out over the forest, the water crashing at their feet, and then they look at each other. This isn't the first time they have done something dangerous together. But it might be the last.

"*One!*" Aubrey says.

"Are you kidding me? You think I'd fall for that twice?"

But Aubrey's smile is genuine. "Two." Her voice is lost beneath the clamor of the falls; Maya reads the word on her lips.

They clasp their hands tighter. Raise them in the air.

"*Three!*"

They yell it at the same time, then step hand in hand over the edge.

SIX

Maya woke with a shrieking headache and a sour, leathery tongue.

She didn't know where she was at first. The moon shone through slats in the blinds, illuminating a room that looked like it belonged to a teenager. Sonic Youth and *Blade Runner* posters, comic books on the shelves. Glow-in-the-dark stars on the ceiling. This had been Dan's room. The night came rushing back. She had vomited. In front of Greta. On her birthday. Then she'd stood in the bathroom for twenty minutes, too embarrassed to return to the dinner table.

She had decided to tell them she had the flu.

Some kind of stomach bug, hopefully nothing contagious, she'd said to Greta, and Maya had certainly looked sick enough, hollow-eyed and pale. She'd watched the wariness on Dan's face give way to concern. Carl had offered ginger ale for her stomach—but it was impossible to tell what Greta thought behind those all-knowing eyes, looking out, always, for her son's best interest.

Maya didn't blame her. She almost wished Dan hadn't believed her, that he had called her out for drinking too much. But instead he had laid a hand on her forehead, checking for fever. He had brought her water and Pepto Bismol. He slept beside her now, his breath the only sound in the dark room.

She'd promised to be honest with him. Now she had to be honest with herself. She'd never been delusional, and the longer she went without pills, the clearer it seemed that she could have stopped Frank. But she hadn't, so Cristina died. And no amount of drinking would make Maya feel okay about that.

If she had been the one to die, Aubrey would have proved that Frank killed her. The truth was that she was smarter than Maya. She might not have worked as hard in school, but Aubrey was perceptive beyond her years.

Most of the friends Maya had made since were like Wendy—friends who didn't know her very well. People who went to the same parties but who she'd never sat with in silence. Now that she'd cut back on drinking, Maya hardly saw those friends, and it occurred to her that she didn't miss them.

She missed Aubrey. She missed her laugh. Maya thought of her every time she read a good poem and wanted someone to share it with. Every time she had the urge to try something adventurous, like trapeze lessons. Aubrey had been fearless. She'd been quick. She never would have let Frank get away with killing her best friend.

Maya knelt beside Dan and whispered his name.

She had dressed and stuffed her clothes from last night into the backpack she wore over one shoulder. The light was thin and blue, the house quiet. Dan blinked a few times as he woke.

"Hey," she said.

". . . what's going on?"

"I'm going home for a few days."

"What?" he asked, half asleep.

"Pittsfield, I mean, my mom's house."

Dan rubbed his eyes. "Okay . . . why . . . ?"

"I want to take care of some things." She wouldn't lie. "I have my ticket. I'll just walk to the Peter Pan station up the street. My bus leaves in forty-five minutes."

Lying in the dark for five hours, thoughts spiraling, Maya had decided this was the easiest way. Better to slip out before everyone was awake than to continue her flu charade. She wasn't going to fall back asleep anyway. It wasn't just withdrawal keeping her awake now. How could she sleep knowing Frank had killed again?

She'd already bought the bus ticket on her phone and located a station close to Dan's parents' house.

He propped himself up on an elbow. "You haven't been to see your mom in—what? A year?" He squinted at her. "What is this about?"

Tell the truth. She looked down. "The video."

He hadn't believed her yesterday and she didn't expect him to believe her now. She expected him to be dismissive, frustrated with her, but instead he took her hand and held it to his chest. He looked at her with kindness, his eyes focusing on her as he got his bearings. "I get it, Maya. I get why you're upset."

"You do?"

"Of course. Two people have dropped dead around this guy. It's creepy as hell. When you first told me about it, my instinct was to insist there was a logical explanation. Try to make it less scary."

Her eyes stung with relief. He did believe her. "Thank you . . ." she whispered. She leaned her head against his, eyes closed. Grateful. She told him her plan: "I haven't been able to find much online, so I thought I'd go to the diner. Talk to someone who was there when Cristina died—maybe the camera missed something. I could talk to her coworkers at the museum—they might know about her relationship with Frank."

Maya could have gone on, but Dan's eyebrows were halfway up his head. He wasn't on board with this.

"If I don't stop him," she said, "he's just going to keep doing it."

"Doing what? I'm sorry, but I still don't understand what you think he did."

Maya deflated. She had misunderstood. Dan didn't believe her; he was just being supportive. "I don't know either," she said. "That's what I need to find out. I need to prove it so I can go to the police."

"I'm worried, Maya."

"What would you do," she asked, "if someone killed Sean?" Sean was his closest friend, a hearty rock climber who it was impossible to imagine anyone killing.

"I'll tell you what I wouldn't do," Dan said. "I wouldn't go to the police, not based on anything you've told me, or anything we saw in the video."

Maya's head throbbed with wine and bitterness. "Okay, what do you think happened?"

Dan thought about it for a moment. When faced with an inexplicable death, everyone had a theory; no one was immune to the need to understand. He'd thought about it more since yesterday, when she told him, and his theory now was that Cristina had likely overdosed on something. The *Berkshire Eagle* article had said her death "wasn't being treated as suspicious," ruling out any evidence of foul play.

What hadn't been ruled out—what seemed most likely, Dan said—was that Cristina had succumbed to the same fate that had claimed so many in towns like Pittsfield. OxyContin or heroin, maybe fentanyl. This would explain the look on her face. She wouldn't be the first person to nod off in public: every gas station, bar, and public restroom in that part of the state posted signs for what to do if someone overdosed. The police carried Narcan.

What made it strange, he conceded, was the coincidence of both Cristina and Aubrey having died around Frank. Undeniably eerie—but then Aubrey's death, though rare, hadn't been suspicious either. Dan's opinion—laid out, Maya thought, as if she were a jury—was that she should cancel her ticket, sleep on this plan for a few days, get over her stomach bug, take care of herself.

This would have been a good time for Maya to confess there was no stomach bug, that she had drunk too much to cope with running out of pills he hadn't known she was on. But she had a bus to catch. And the last thing she needed was Dan questioning her mental health. "If Frank's not dangerous," she said, "what's the harm in me going out there for a while? Seeing my mom? I'll take a sick day at work. I haven't taken one all year."

Dan made a sad face.

And she remembered the dog. They had an appointment at a pet adoption center the day after Dan finished finals, and had been looking forward to it for weeks, spent hours talking about names. How could Maya have forgotten? Her shoulders sank. "I know the timing isn't great," she said, "but this is something I need to do. I should be back in time for our appointment."

Dan sighed.

She glanced at the clock. 6:23 a.m.

"Take care of yourself," he said, with a resigned quality to his voice that made her ache.

She held back tears just long enough to kiss him goodbye.

———————————

Maya's boss was understanding when she said that she was sick. She'd been working at the garden center for three years, after all, and was good with both plants and customers. She would have liked her job if she was paid enough and had insurance, but as it was, her boss was the one person Maya felt okay about lying to. She checked her bank balance and saw that she could afford to miss three days of work, four if she was frugal.

She spent the two-hour bus ride on her phone, searching for Frank. She drank water from a bottle she'd splurged on at the station, hangover in full swing, stomach lurching each time the driver braked. A muscle beneath her left eye twitched. Frank had somehow avoided leaving any digital trail.

The last time she saw him was when Aubrey died. It was later that day, just as Maya was leaving the police station after having been questioned for four hours. Frank had been released from questioning before she was—she saw him in the parking lot as he was getting into his car. A free man. Maya had frozen in terror. Her mother, who was walking beside her, asked what was wrong, but Frank had driven off by the time Maya found her voice. And to this day, Brenda hadn't seen him.

For her, he existed as the object of her daughter's delusional obsession, the human version of Silver Lake. But for Maya, he was real. Her stomach clenched every time she saw someone who looked like him, which was often. Frank was average-looking, slight of build with a small chin, dark hair, and pale skin. It seemed half the men in Boston could pass for Frank. And it would be so easy for him to kill her—he wouldn't have to show up at her house in the middle of the night or lock her in his trunk.

He could kill her in public, in daylight, and get away

with it. What happened to Cristina was exactly the fate Maya had feared, which was why she had to protect herself. She had to figure out his secret. She was smarter than she'd been at seventeen. Less vulnerable. She would keep her distance until she knew how to keep herself safe.

The bus wound deeper into the woods. She suspected that Frank had tried to contact her over the years, but as with almost everything else about him, it was impossible to know for sure. She never once answered a phone number she didn't recognize, never opened an email from someone she didn't know, yet to this day, when she entered her name into Google, the first suggested search result to pop up was "Maya Edwards + Aubrey West."

Hot air rushed from the vents. Still unable to find anything on Frank, she looked up Cristina Lewis. Like Frank, Cristina wasn't on social media, and her name was common: Maya waded through pages of Google results before finding the right Cristina Lewis on a list of artists who had done residencies at MASS MoCA.

She clicked on her name and was brought to her site. The design was minimalist, a light blue page with one of Cristina's paintings taking up a third. Maya held the phone close to her face. The painting was of a vast white desert beneath an empty sky. An alien planet, a place without life, cracks running through its parched surface, but the painting's title—*Bonneville Salt Flats*—suggested that it was, in fact, planet Earth.

There was no denying Cristina's talent. The cold, spare beauty of her work. It was all about the light, the way it speared down from a sun that wasn't in the painting. Cristina's name appeared, all lowercase, at the bottom of the website, along with her email address. Nothing else to click on.

Maya ran a reverse image search on the painting and found a public Facebook page dedicated to Cristina's memory and to "keeping her art alive by sharing it with the world." The group had eleven members, but the only one who'd posted was the administrator, a man named Steven Lang.

His profile picture showed a heavyset bald man in his thirties. Standing beside him on a snowy hiking trail was Cristina. She was a foot shorter than he was and looked even smaller in her puffy yellow coat. Anyone might mistake her for Maya at this distance.

Unlike Maya, Steven didn't seem at all concerned about online privacy. She quickly learned that he had worked with Cristina at the Berkshire Museum, though she couldn't tell what he did there. She tracked down his email address within minutes.

Hi, you don't know me, but my name's Maya and I saw the video of Cristina. I'm so sorry for your loss . . . I'm trying to get some info on the guy she was with when it happened, Frank Bellamy. Wondering if we could chat sometime? She hit send, then settled back into her seat and waited. She closed her eyes, hoping to fall asleep, but soon gave up and stared at the bare, frosted trees rushing by.

SEVEN

Maya, on her knees in the backyard, gasps for breath, overcome by hilarity. The sky screams blue. The air tastes like grass. She can't recall what is funny, which is, in itself, uproarious, and she can't stop, and it's terrifying, but when Aubrey says the word—the one that has them rolling in the grass—the fear goes away.

"Cha—cha—" Aubrey can't get it out. Tears river her face.

Laughter flares from Maya's throat. "Oh my god," she says, "oh my god, oh my—"

"Chort—"

"Stop!" Maya shrieks. "Stop!" She slaps the hard earth. *"Chortle!!"*

And they collapse.

How long have they been laughing? A minute? An hour? A year? "Chortle!" Maya shrieks. "I can't believe it, I can't believe . . ." She can't believe what? "I can't believe that's a word."

"Me neither," Aubrey says. "I can't believe . . ." She trails off, not laughing anymore, and Maya raises her damp head from her forearm, peers out from the unkempt curtain of her hair to see Aubrey petting the grass. Stroking it like a fine fur coat. "It's so soft," she says.

Maya rolls onto her back and snuggles in. She sweeps her limbs in a slow-motion snow angel and feels every blade of grass that brushes her skin. "I can't believe *any* of it," she says. She wears her usual cutoffs and an oversized zebra-print button-down from Goodwill that she'd thought would be fun for today. "The sky," she says. "The sky!" Her sunglasses, oversized and rhinestone-studded, are also from Goodwill, and it's a good thing she's wearing them, because her pupils are enormous and the sun is sending out waves. She sees them rippling across the sky, and it reminds her of a long-ago science lesson. "Do you remember," she asks, "what Mr. Murphy said about the sun and electromagnetic waves?"

"Not really."

"Me neither," Maya says, even though she does. "But now . . . I feel like I *get* it. You know?" She turns her head to look at Aubrey, and Aubrey stares back from behind her own shades, aviators with dark green lenses. They often shop at Goodwill together.

"You do?"

"Yeah," Maya says. "It's like space is made of water, just one big ocean, and the sun is a pebble tossed onto its surface . . . It sends out ripples in the water." She raises her arms, wriggles her fingers, and feels the ripples.

"Wow . . ." Aubrey says. "Sage really came through this time, huh?"

Maya giggles, recalling the last time they got acid from the aging hippie cashier who works at Big Y, where Aubrey works as a bagger. Sage, with his graying, patchouli-scented ponytail, is in love with Aubrey, so the acid's always free, but the last batch had been so weak, they'd wondered if it was as fake as his name. "*This* shit," Maya says, "is definitely real."

"*What* shit?" her mom asks.

Maya's fingers freeze mid-wriggle. She squeezes her eyes shut as if this will make her invisible.

"You want to tell me what's going on here?"

Her mom's going to kill her for this. But only if she knows. Maya lowers her hands, straightens her zebra shirt, and sits up, pieces of grass in her hair. She smiles as casually as possible. "Hi, Mom!"

Her mom stands two feet away, at the edge of the garden. No telling how long she's been there.

Brenda isn't usually so imposing—even though she is large, almost a foot taller than her petite daughter, and brawny—but right now she looks like an angry sun-god, arms crossed at her chest, the flyaway curls around her face like golden flames. She's in her EMT uniform: a white shirt, navy pants, black sneakers. Her penciled eyebrows highlight the displeasure on her face, the narrowing of her blue eyes.

"I . . . thought you were at work," Maya says.

"I was. But now I'm home—and this is what I find? A

mess in the kitchen? TV so loud I can hear it from outside? And is that *The Dark Crystal* you're watching?" Her mom knows them both so well.

"Hi, Brenda," Aubrey says in a too-high voice.

"*Hi*, Aubrey."

Aubrey wilts at the tone.

"What did you two take? Hm?" Brenda looks from one to the other, then back again.

Maya feels her trip tanking and tries not to panic. "LSD," she says, knowing it is useless to hide.

Brenda shakes her head. "Get inside, both of you."

The walk through the yard, past the garden, and up three steps to the kitchen is its own ordeal. The ground feels spongy and quicksand-like. "Wait!" her mom says as she and Aubrey track dirt through the kitchen. She hands them each a damp dish towel, glaring at their feet.

They bumble their way to the floor. They'd been watching *The Dark Crystal* when Aubrey had a yen to be in nature, so they'd crawled around the garden awhile before coming undone because she said *chortle*.

Maya wipes the dirt from her toes, her heels, the hollows of her ankles.

"Are you going to tell my stepdad?" Aubrey asks.

Brenda sits down at the table. "I don't know," she says. She sounds tired.

That's when Maya notices the bandage on her mother's hand. "What happened?"

"Just a few stitches," her mom says. "Don't worry about it."

But Maya worries. Her mom's job is scary—the flashing lights, screaming sirens, and screaming people. It scares Maya even when she's not tripping—now she stares at the white bandage.

"Please don't tell Darren," Aubrey says, crying.

Maya cries too. She loves her mom, doesn't want her to be in pain.

"Okay, you two, settle down," Brenda says. She says it kindly, holding up her hand to prove it's okay, and not freaking out the way other parents might, because she can handle this. She sees all kinds of things at work—bad trips, actual overdoses, stab wounds. "How long ago did you take it?" she asks calmly.

Maya and Aubrey share a look. How long ago indeed? Six hours? Seven?

Brenda sighs. "What *time* did you take it?"

"This morning?" Aubrey says. "Like, maybe at eleven?"

Brenda glances at the clock on the microwave. 1:32 p.m. "Looks like we've got a ways to go . . ."

———————

They watch *The Dark Crystal* from the beginning, all three of them, Maya and her mom on the couch, Aubrey draped across the love seat. A fan in the corner circulates a cool breeze through the living room that is also the wind through the jungles of Thra. Maya understands that she's in trouble, that her mom is only waiting for her to come down before delivering whatever stern talk and punishment she has in store, but for now, everything is perfect. Maya is here, but she is also in the movie, feeling the kind of wonder she'd felt watching it as a young child, before there was a difference between reality and magic.

Like how people at church must feel when contemplating Eden—a longing for a time before anyone knew they were naked, when conversations with God were the norm. Maya yearns for that time in her own life, not out of some need to escape reality—reality is fine—but simply because she was born that way. Born to yearn, as some people are, for more magical times. This is her fourth acid trip, so she knows about the sadness of coming down, the sense of God having vacated the garden. And Aubrey takes it even harder than she does.

Aubrey looks glum as Maya's mom drives her home that evening, even though Brenda had agreed not to say anything about the acid. No one says anything as they pull up in front of Aubrey's duplex.

Silver Lake glitters just beyond, obsidian in the dusk. Aubrey lives even closer to the lake. If she's being honest, this is why Maya had wanted to take the acid at her own house rather than at Aubrey's. The truth is that Maya is slightly afraid of the lake. She'd never admit this to anyone because to do so would be to sound like Aunt Lisa.

(Though if she could speak freely, Maya would point to local legends about the lake changing colors at night and steam rising from its surface in winter. She would say that the lake really *is* polluted, and who knows the extent of what PCBs can do to a person?)

"Thanks for the ride," Aubrey says as she gets out of the car.

"This ever happens again, I'm telling your parents."

On the drive home, Maya asks how long she is grounded for.

Her mom doesn't answer for a while. She's changed from her EMT uniform into a T-shirt, cotton shorts, and sandals, but still wears the white bandage on her hand. Now Maya knows that she cut herself on shredded metal while extracting a young man from a car wreck.

Maya expects her mom to be angry, but instead she just seems sad. "I don't want to ground you," she says. "You'll be out of here in less than three months anyway, doing whatever you want. I just wish . . . I wish you could see what I see. On the ambulance, I mean. You'd understand how easily, how *quickly*, everything can go wrong."

"I know, Mom. I'll be careful. It's not like we were driving."

Her mom pulls into the driveway, cuts the engine, and turns to her. "You know there's more to it than that. You could end up like—"

"Let me guess. Aunt Lisa?"

"It's in your genes. You're *susceptible*—why can't you see that? A drug like LSD could trigger something—an episode."

Maya sighs theatrically. Why can't her mom see that a single acid trip is nothing compared to Lisa's heavy meth use and obvious drinking problem? Maya will be attending BU on a full scholarship. She is smart enough to understand two things at once—both that her aunt suffered from delusions and that Silver Lake is, to some extent, toxic. But her mother seems intent on seeing the world in black and white, so all Maya says is, "Okay, I'm sorry. I'll be more careful from now on."

EIGHT

Maya leaned her pounding head on the car window as her mom drove them home from the bus station. They passed St. Joseph's, where her grandparents went to church, and the YMCA where she'd learned how to swim. The streets of downtown Pittsfield were lined with grand historical buildings. Former department stores. A Gilded Age theater. A marble courthouse. When Brenda was a child, teenagers would drive up and down North Street on Thursday nights—they called it cruising. Maya didn't get it. If she saw someone doing that today, she'd assume they were selling drugs.

The car turned onto the street where she grew up. She knew this place by heart, its large houses carved up into apartments, the peeling paint, satellite dishes, patchy lawns. Even the neighbor's Christmas decorations were familiar to her, the giant candy cane and blow-up Santa. The house she grew up in was rickety-looking clapboard, like the others.

The paint was lemon yellow. A blue tarp protected the small garden out front from winter. It was the smallest on the street, but as Brenda liked to say, the house was theirs. She had bought it for the two of them when Maya was eight.

Brenda was less robust these days, and no longer an EMT but a sous chef and baker at a luxury rehab center. She'd switched careers because she was, in her words, too old to work on ambulances. She'd had back sprains, migraines, and twisted ankles. She couldn't bear to see another person die. Her arms were skinnier, her torso wider, and her dark blond curls were turning gray, but Maya liked to think her mom seemed happier. Or at least more relaxed.

Cold slush seeped through the soles of Maya's sneakers as she got out of the car. It was noon on a winter Sunday, the street quiet, the day overcast. The gray in her mom's hair seemed more pronounced in this light. Or maybe Maya had been away for longer than she thought.

She rarely came home these days, and knew this hurt her mom, but the truth was that Maya still harbored resentment about the past. To admit this, though, would be to concede that some part of her still believed that Frank had murdered Aubrey—which Maya could never admit to her mom. Brenda would only panic, think her daughter was going the way of Aunt Lisa, and get on the phone with Dr. Barry.

"Can't wait to see what you think of the room," Brenda said now as she sat on the low bench beside the door to take off her boots. "You'll be the first to sleep in the new bed."

"You got rid of my bed?"

Her mom snorted. "*Your* bed? When's the last time you slept in it?"

The question hung heavy with guilt.

"The new bed's a pillow-top," her mom said.

Sliding out of her sneakers and coat, Maya went to see the "new room," which was her old bedroom converted into an Airbnb rental. Her mom seemed more at ease since leaving her old job, but she'd also taken a pay cut and wouldn't be able to retire for years.

Opening the door, Maya hardly recognized the room that had been hers between eight and eighteen. It was a shrine to Berkshires tourism, the vacationers her mom was hoping to attract. Instead of *Pan's Labyrinth* and Tender Wallpaper posters, the walls held framed Norman Rockwell prints and photographs of Pittsfield in its heyday, when classic cars decked out in chrome rolled down a happening North Street. A lamp on the desk gave off a burnished glow, and the red-and-gold curtains evoked fall foliage.

Maya hoped for her mom's sake that the tourists would come. But Pittsfield wasn't quite the destination that Stockbridge was, or Lenox, or any number of other small towns in the Berkshires. Every few years or so, a magazine would include it on a list of up-and-coming cities or write that it was making a comeback, and Brenda wanted so much for this to be true, for her hometown to be the place it had seemed to her as a child. But as far as Maya could tell, that had yet to happen.

"Well? What do you think?"

"Looks great," Maya said. But there was something unsettling about seeing her old, familiar room filled with unfamiliar furniture. The bed was new, the dresser, the small flat-screen TV. The only thing her mom had kept was the nightstand. "Try the bed," her mom said, pointing to the bare mattress.

Maya sat down and let herself fall back, sinking. "Soft."

"Sheets are in the dryer. I'll go get them."

Staring at the ceiling, Maya recognized the view—this hadn't changed. The water stain above her bed was as familiar as a birthmark. Alone now, she turned onto her side and saw that her mom had peeled off the stickers that Maya had stuck to the nightstand when she was little. Her old sticker collection. Traces of it still clung to the wood. She leaned closer, peered over the edge of the bed, and saw part of a sticker that hadn't quite come off. A band sticker, black with purple lettering. Tender Wallpaper had been Aubrey's favorite band; she and Maya had seen them in concert the night before she died.

This sticker had come with the tickets Maya bought for that concert, and the sight of it brought back the night (dancing with her eyes closed, Aubrey beside her) but also the next day (Aubrey collapsing on the stoop).

Maya heard footsteps.

Her mom knew at once something was wrong—Maya could see it on her face as she walked in with an armload of sheets: the worry of a mother for her child. Maya's instinct was to tell her everything, to lay it all down at her feet, unburden herself of the fear and guilt that weighed on her.

But Maya couldn't risk sounding like Aunt Lisa. Not when she needed to be taken seriously. She did, however, have to explain the tears on her face, so she came clean about her other problem: "I've been taking Klonopin every night for sleep, and last week I ran out. I've hardly slept at all since."

The worry deepened on her mom's face. Before Frank, Maya had talked to her mom about everything. They made up the bed together as she spoke, fitting the sheets onto the mattress and topping them with blankets. There was such comfort in returning to the way things used to be. Before she had habits to hide.

"How much were you taking?"

"Two or three milligrams a night . . . and usually another half during the day."

Maya's mom looked disappointed but not surprised. "Dr. Barry never prescribed you that much, did he?"

Maya shook her head. When her mom walked over, she thought it was to hug her. But it was to check Maya's pulse. "Do you know how dangerous it is to quit cold turkey?"

"That's why I'm here." Not the whole truth, but at least factual.

Her mom peered deeply into her eyes. Checking her pupils.

Maya leaned away. "Pretty sure I'm through the worst of it, though. I just need to ride it out, get some sleep." That was the main thing, really—she hadn't slept for more than a few hours in days, and she really could have used that hug, or any other comforting gesture. But instead Maya felt, as she had in other times of distress, that her mom, in her worry, was treating her like a patient.

She pressed her palm to her daughter's temple. "At least you don't have a fever, but tell me if you start to feel worse."

"I—"

"Or start seeing flashing lights. Or hear anything that's not there."

"Okay, but—"

"Or notice any unusual smells."

"Fine."

Already, Maya regretted saying as much as she had. Her mom would clearly keep an eye on her now, which would make it even harder to do what she had to do, but there seemed to be no walking it back. Now her mom was looking at her with the vigilance of a retired paramedic who had never really made it off the ambulance.

NINE

Maya's grandmother dies the month before Aubrey.

Later, Dr. Barry will point to these two losses, suffered so close together, as evidence that Maya was in a vulnerable state. Hence the psychosis. But later still—years later—Maya will see that it was grief that left her vulnerable to Frank. When she looks back at this time, it will seem obvious: He would have known that she was hurting when they met. He would have sensed it. Even if she hasn't yet.

She doesn't know how to feel at first. She has never even met her grandmother in person. She doesn't know what to say when her mom knocks gently on the door of her bedroom to tell her that Abuela has died.

Maya had just started packing. She's still two months away from moving into the dorms but had been too excited to wait. She started with her books and spent the last hour sorting through the hundreds that she has in order to decide what to take. She only has room for twenty and has just moved *It* by Stephen King over to the leave-at-home pile to make room for *Bridge to Terabithia* by Katherine Paterson, which her mom read aloud to her when she was ten and stuck at home for a week with strep throat. Holding the book brought back the sound of her mother's voice and the story of two children who invent their own world. The memory glowed with such contentment that Maya hadn't been able to part with it.

Her excitement to leave Pittsfield is tempered by sadness and a nagging guilt at leaving her mother behind. She tells herself she'll come home once a month. This is what she's thinking about when her mom gives her the news.

"What?" Maya says, staring up from the piles of books surrounding her on the floor, even though she'd heard the words just fine.

Her grandmother has died of a stroke in her home in Guatemala City. She was a constant, but distant, presence in Maya's life. A voice on the phone several times a year. A photograph. Handwritten birthday cards. Maya's father may be dead, but that's how it's always been. No one she actually knows has ever died.

"Aw, Muffin," her mom says, entering the room as Maya flips back through her memory for the grandmother she has suddenly lost. And what Maya realizes is that she never really knew her. Her grandmother had been as abstract as death itself was up until this moment—an idea, nothing more—but suddenly Abuela's absence seems very real, a hollowness growing in her chest.

Abuela was a connection to Maya's father. The person who knew him best. There are so many questions Maya should have asked.

Her mom sits beside her on the carpet, careful not to disturb the stacks of books. She looks almost apologetic.

"I never wrote back to her last birthday card," Maya says.

Her mom always impressed upon her the importance of getting to know her father's mother, reminding Maya to write back to her, to call her. But Maya was too young to understand, or maybe too selfish, as children are. Too wrapped up in herself. Too self-conscious of her terrible accent to speak Spanish on the phone, forcing her grandmother to make all the effort on the rare occasions that they did speak.

Her mom puts a hand on her shoulder. "Don't worry about that," she says. There are tears in her voice.

"I want to go to the funeral."

Her mom stares at her.

Maya has never been to Guatemala.

Her mom has always said it's too dangerous—and all she has to do is point to what happened to Maya's father: Jairo Ek Basurto was shot dead in the doorway of his parents' house at the age of twenty-two.

The year was 1990, the Guatemalan civil war just beginning to wind down, and the army was killing people who didn't agree with them.

Maya was twelve when she managed to wrangle this information from her mom. It had shocked her. Why would the army kill their own people? Brenda, who'd been in the country on a missionary trip for her parents' church when she met Jairo, had explained as best she could to someone so young.

The land where the Mayans had been living for millennia happened to be perfect for growing large quantities of bananas. Chiquita, back in the '40s, was the largest landowner in the country. It was called the United Fruit Company then, and it had a lot of control over the Guatemalan government.

But in 1944, the Guatemalan people got rid of the government loyal to the fruit company and elected a president who wanted, among other things, to buy back some of the company's land and return it to the ones who'd lived there. Land that was sacred. The dense jungles and misty highlands. Volcanos and cenotes.

This newly elected president, and then his successor, believed that people are worth more than money, more than cheap bananas. The United Fruit Company disagreed. It wanted that land. The fruit company was the forefather of the modern PR campaign, and just as it convinced Americans to buy more bananas, it convinced the president of America that the newly elected Guatemalan president was a communist. This was in the 1950s, as the Cold War snowballed. Maya hadn't known anything about the Cold War at twelve but sensed from her mom's tone that things were about to get dark.

President Eisenhower listened to the fruit company. He sent the CIA down to secretly stir up a small Guatemalan opposition. The US trained them and gave them guns. And in 1954, that opposition, with a lot of help from the US, overthrew the democratically elected president. They installed a military officer in his place, a man happy to let the fruit company grow its bananas.

Things grew very hard for the Mayan people then, especially the peasants, along with anyone who supported them. The students, the teachers, the artists, the writers, the neighbors. All these people made up most of the country, but it was the top few who had all the power. Some people grew so angry that they ran off into the mountains to fight, recruiting starving children to their side. The civil war lasted for thirty-six years, and two hundred thousand people died, many of them tortured, thousands upon thousands *disappeared*—a term that twelve-year-old Maya hadn't understood.

It means the police secretly arrested them, her mom had said, *and they were never seen again*.

Twelve-year-old Maya was, by this point, beginning to regret she had asked.

She'd been bugging her mom for as long as she could remember to explain why her father had died. And how. And where. And when. But once her mom had started telling her, Maya felt her throat tighten.

Her father was a college student studying literature. He was also a writer—but that was another story, one that Maya already knew.

This was the story of his death. Finally. (But at the same time too soon.)

Her father was part of a student organization that went

out to a small village in the highlands. The army had recently carried out a massacre in the village, and Maya's father, along with other students and a few professors, went to march alongside the survivors, demanding an end to the army's presence in the village. Maya's heart had puffed with pride at this, then clenched in fear as her mom explained that someone had photographed him there.

That was all it took in those days.

The world had begun to notice what would someday be called the Silent Holocaust, but in 1990 the army was still getting away with killing people who didn't agree with them.

People like Maya's father.

This was the why of what happened to him.

The how was a bullet to his head.

The when was two months after the protest. Jairo had been photographed that day marching beside a well-known history professor who had recently gone missing—and not just him, but three of his friends too. A baker. A teacher. A priest. Being associated with this particular history professor was enough in those days.

The killer would never be named, much less brought to justice. He could have been in the army, or moonlighting for them, or perhaps a member of Guatemala's notorious death squads. He walked right up to Jairo's door on a Saturday morning.

Jairo's mother was behind the house, rinsing a red-flowered tablecloth in the pila. His father was in the living room, reading the paper on the couch.

Maya's mom was in the kitchen.

Brenda was making herself a cup of instant coffee—one spoonful of Nescafé, one of sugar, and two of powdered milk. She'd been in Guatemala just over a month, was pregnant but didn't know it yet, and this was part of her routine: she liked to take her coffee outside and up the rickety metal stairs to the roof on sunny mornings such as this one.

(But that was another story too.)

She was stirring the instant coffee into a steaming mug of water when she heard the gunshot. She will never forget this.

She stares at her daughter.

"I want to go to the funeral," Maya says again, as if she has forgotten that her mother told her all this when she was twelve.

"You know it's too dangerous." Brenda had promised to take her once it was safe enough, but to this day, it hasn't been.

"I'll be careful," Maya says.

Her mom shakes her head.

"I'll be eighteen in August."

Anger flashes in her mom's eyes.

Maya never met her grandmother, and now she never will. And all that she has of her father are a few pictures and a handful of stories—all stories told by her mom, who only met him a month before he died.

Suddenly Maya is hit by the weight of all that she doesn't know about her own family.

"I'm going," she says. Her own eyes flashing.

TEN

Brenda started work at five in the morning these days, baking breads, pastries, and desserts to accommodate the array of dietary restrictions among the patients at Lakeside Serenity Center. The patients were, in her words, a choosy bunch, and with what they were paying, they felt they deserved a lot of options: macrobiotic, vegan, gluten-free. They had their choice of art and yoga classes, music therapy, and forest bathing. They swam in the pool, relaxed in the sauna, and got acupuncture. The center was a few towns over, nestled into the kind of view that tourists thought of when they thought of the Berkshires. Mountains covered with trees that flamed into red, orange, and gold foliage in fall.

Brenda was up each day at four a.m., and usually in bed by eight—and it was 8:30. Her head tipped forward, but she hauled it back up, fighting to stay awake as she sat with her daughter in the small, tidy living room.

Maya waited at the other end of the couch. As soon as her mom fell asleep, she would take her keys and drive ten minutes to the Blue Moon Diner in the YouTube video. The *Berkshire Eagle* article said that Cristina died on a Sunday, and today was Sunday, a likely night to catch the waitress at work.

The radiator clanged in the corner over the *Simpsons* rerun on TV. Reaching for the remote, Maya turned the volume down, and before long, her mom began to snore softly. Sneaking out of the house, creeping down the dark hall and through the kitchen as an adult, felt ridiculous. Like being a teenager again (the walls between then and now growing thin), a muscle memory of lifting her mom's car keys from her messy, oversized purse and slinking into the night. Outside was cold and starless. A light snow had fallen. Maya brushed off her mom's windshield with the sleeve of her coat and got in.

She couldn't say exactly what she hoped to learn from talking to the waitress who'd been there when Cristina died, but maybe there was more to the video than what the camera had caught, some nuance to the blank expression on Cristina's face, so subtle you'd only see it in person.

Or maybe the waitress had heard something. Maya had to try. Steven Lang still hadn't written back. Maya took Lincoln, driving past more houses like her mom's, an old silk mill, and the public library. The library had been one of her favorite places when she was growing up. She would hang out in the free air-conditioning all summer, reading books or sunning herself on the terrace. But now the old brick building brought on a wave of dread. The library was where she'd met Frank.

She drove across the icy Housatonic and into the parking lot of the Blue Moon Diner. Maya remembered coming here as a child, but it had been a Friendly's then. Then, as now, the parking lot had been mostly empty. Maya took a deep breath as she got out of the car, going over what she planned to say to the waitress.

Entering the diner, she stood face-to-face with a statue of Betty Boop. A neon jukebox played "Dream Lover." The floors were black-and-white checkerboard, the booths red vinyl, but the layout hadn't changed since the place was Friendly's. Maya remembered sharing a sundae with her mom at a table now occupied by a middle-aged man, eating alone while he looked at his phone.

"Sit anywhere you'd like," said a teenage waiter.

Maya looked up and found the security camera, and used it to orient herself, then sat in the same booth where Cristina had sat with Frank.

"Anything to drink?" the waiter asked.

"Water, please." She opened her menu, but as soon as the waiter walked away, her eyes skimmed the room. Less than half of the tables were full. Several diners sat alone at the counter. Maya recognized the décor from the video: the chrome-plated stools, the faux-vintage clock. Nothing seemed out of the ordinary. She was about to get up and walk around when the waiter returned with her water. "What can I get you?"

"Tea, please."

"Anything else?"

Just then, behind the counter, the kitchen doors opened, and the redheaded waitress from the video walked out. She stayed behind the counter, filled a few coffees, apparently working a different section tonight.

"Actually," Maya said, "I think I'll sit at the counter."

The waiter looked annoyed.

Approaching the counter, Maya wondered if this was, in fact, the right person: The waitress in the video had looked to be her own age, while the woman before her was easily in her fifties. Creases framed her heavy-lidded eyes and painted lips—but then, the camera might not have seen those things. And the waitress's hair was right—short and red. Her name-tag read BARB.

She handed Maya a menu. "Know what you'd like?"

"Tea, please. And buffalo wings." Maya was much too addled to eat, but ordering food seemed a step toward the waitress's good side.

"'Cruisin' or 'Come On, Snake, Let's Rattle'?"

"I'm sorry—what?"

"You want your wings mild or hot?"

"Oh. Hot."

The waitress turned to make Maya's tea, poured hot water, while behind her, Maya steeled herself. She dabbed her face with a napkin. Three other people sat at the counter, two elderly men with newspapers and a woman in hospital scrubs.

"Here you are," said the waitress, setting the mug on the counter. "Do you want honey with that? Milk?" Her voice was kind but cautious, as if she'd sensed something off about Maya.

"Actually, I was wondering if I could ask you something. My name's Erica. I'm a friend of Cristina Lewis."

"You saw the video. That thing's all over the place." Barb sounded almost proud of this. She glanced up at the security camera. "Still no idea who posted it online . . . Who'd you say you were again?"

"Erica," Maya said, dropping her voice. Even with all the lies she'd told recently, she felt self-conscious. "Cristina and I went to school together back in Moab. Kindergarten all the way to high school."

From the corner of her eye, Maya saw that everyone at the counter had fallen silent.

"I'm sorry for your loss," Barb said. Then: "They find out what happened to her?" Her voice was bright with curiosity.

"Not that I've heard."

The waitress looked disappointed.

"I was hoping you could tell me what you saw that day?" Maya said. "Or maybe you heard something?"

"Burger, extra rare!" said a voice from the kitchen, and the waitress turned to take a plate from the window.

"Need an order of wings! Hot!" she called back. She served the burger to the woman in scrubs, then turned back to Maya. "I didn't hear a word they said. There was music playing, just like there is now. And what I saw is pretty much what anyone can see on the video."

"Pretty much?"

"There was one thing the camera didn't pick up. I told the cops about it, of course."

Everyone at the counter was listening, and Maya sensed that the waitress didn't mind. "What was it?"

"Cristina's eyes," the waitress said. "The video makes it look like she was staring at Frank. But if you were standing over there, you would have seen that she was actually looking *past* him, at something in the corner."

"What was it?"

"Nothing. Literally. An empty booth." Maya followed the waitress's gaze to the red vinyl booth. "No one was sitting there that day either, but she just kept staring as if she could see something the rest of us couldn't. My cat does the same thing sometimes. Creeps me the hell out."

A cold dread bloomed in Maya's chest. "Did she seem . . . normal?"

"Well, sure, if you call that normal." The waitress leaned closer to Maya as if to tell her a secret, but then spoke loudly enough for the whole counter to hear. "Between you and me, I've always thought this place was haunted. I can sense these things, and I think maybe there *was* something over there that day."

Maya's dread turned to skepticism. "What—like a ghost?"

The waitress nodded.

One of the elderly men leaned over to Maya. "Don't get her started."

The waitress scowled. "That's enough out of you, Doug." She refilled his coffee.

"So you think," Maya said to the waitress, "that Cristina saw some kind of ghost and it . . . killed her?"

"All I'm saying is she definitely saw *something* right before she died. Something only she could see."

"Hot wings!" said the voice from the kitchen.

"You making a podcast or something?" the waitress asked as she set the steaming plate before Maya.

"Not exactly," Maya said, before asking if she could please take her wings to go.

The foam box filled the car with the salty tang of buffalo sauce. The heat blasted on high, but she couldn't seem to get warm.

The talk of ghosts called to mind what Dr. Barry had said about the link between sudden unexplained death and what he called magical thinking. *Some cultures blame evil spirits.* The idea was that the mind has ways of explaining things to itself. Grief can make the imagination extra creative. She understood all this. Dr. Barry would have said the waitress was delusional, and Maya might have had to agree with him.

Seeing this behavior in someone else was sobering. Her body flushed with empathy at the thought of Barb explaining her haunted diner theory to the police, but her mind sided with Dr. Barry on this one. Maybe this was Maya's problem after all. Maybe her mind couldn't see its own illness.

ELEVEN

Four days after her grandmother's death, Maya walks slowly alongside her mom and dozens of other people through the Cementerio General in Guatemala City behind the casket of Emilia Ek Basurto. The cemetery is enormous and mazelike, taking up several city blocks, yet feels overcrowded. High, thick walls line the route of the funeral procession, each wall a grid of row upon row upon row of what look like file cabinets to Maya, but which are actually graves. Each cabinet has a body inside, sealed off by a layer of concrete, bearing, in most cases, a placard naming the person contained therein, and the years of their birth and death.

Flowers in all stages of decay adorn the tombs, their colors bright against the gray concrete and dark green moss that crawls over everything. This is the rainy season, the usual afternoon showers on the way, the air thick, and the procession so slow they could be walking underwater. Sweat dampens the long black dress she wears, plasters it to her back, and she breathes through her mouth, trying not to let on how affected she is by the smells filling her nose. First there are the flowers—lilies, roses, daisies, gladiolus—bursting from the buckets of vendors at the cemetery gates, spilling from graves, fallen petals browning every surface. They fail to mask what Maya can only assume is the smell of death. Like bodies turned inside out.

Vultures swirl overhead. Their numbers swell the deeper the funeral winds into the cemetery, and Brenda explains to her daughter, as calmly as possible, that graves here are rented like apartments. Families must pay regular fees to keep their loved ones interred. And if a payment is missed, the body, as if it were a tenant, is evicted and thrown into a mass pit at the edge of the graveyard.

The walls of tombs give way to a field of crumbling mausoleums. Abuela's plot is deep within the cemetery, beside that of her son. The family mausoleum is about the size of a phone booth, with a rusted metal door and a stone crucifix on top. A vulture perches on the low branch of a nearby tree, preening its creaky black wings. The smell is somehow even worse here at the edge of the cemetery, a chemical smell, burning tires mixed with death and flowers. A smoky haze fills the air.

Maya clutches her mom's hand.

"The city dump," her mom whispers. "It starts just over there at the edge of the cemetery. Thousands of people live in it, picking through the trash for whatever they can sell or eat." Brenda came to Guatemala after college as part of a missionary group even though she didn't believe in God, still doesn't, and disagrees with the premise of missionary work. She'd simply thought that she might do some good with the certificate in respiratory care she had earned from Berkshire Community College. Not to mention that she'd never been outside the US.

Her days were spent volunteering at an orphanage not far from the city dump. Her evenings consisted of getting to know the family who'd volunteered to house her for three months. Brenda hadn't expected to fall in love while she was in Guatemala, but the rest is Maya's favorite story in the world—the story of her mom and dad. This is the story she tries to remember while she is here, as opposed to the story of her father's death.

Brenda has seemed on edge ever since they arrived in Guatemala City, losing things at the airport and laughing nervously at nothing. It can't have been easy, Maya realizes for the first time, for Brenda to build a relationship between her daughter and the Basurtos. All the letters and phone calls and, later, emails that grew less and less frequent over the years. Brenda only knew Jairo and his family for a month before he was killed, and she fled the country immediately afterward. This is the first time she's been back.

She is the one who taught her daughter most of what Maya knows about Guatemala. Brenda hung Mayan tapestries on the walls and played CDs of marimba music while she and Maya baked together. Brenda taught herself to make tamales wrapped in banana leaves and made them every Christmas. She encouraged Maya to learn Spanish in school.

Yet to convince her to go on this trip, Maya had resorted to threats. She threatened—not that it was a bluff—to buy herself a plane ticket with the money she'd made tutoring middle school students, money she'd been saving for college. She said that if she couldn't go to her grandmother's funeral, she would fly to Guatemala—alone—on her eighteenth birthday.

So Brenda caved, and now here they are, clinging to each other among all this death and flowers. Everyone around them dressed in black, veiled in tears. Walking in slow motion. Maya is related to many of the people in this crowd, yet they are strangers to her. But never in her life has she encountered such warmth. She's been here less than twenty-four hours, but her family treats her and her mom as if they've been there all their lives. Brenda's offer to stay at a hotel wasn't even entertained. Instead, Maya's grandfather handed over the bed he'd shared for decades with his wife so that Brenda and Maya could sleep there while he slept on the couch.

"Mija," says a voice directly at her back. "Toma estas flores."

Maya turns to see her father's sister, Carolina, standing behind her. Carolina looks like how Maya will look in a few decades. They're exactly the same height. Carolina's skin is darker, but she shares her niece's high cheekbones and mahogany eyes. Meeting her for the first time, Maya felt a pang of familiarity, as if she'd suddenly caught her own reflection in a mirror she hadn't known was there. Carolina hands her a spray of yellowed roses, gestures for Maya to hold them to her nose to block out the smell.

"Gracias," Maya says.

She buries her face in the flowers and closes her eyes as the pallbearers begin to lower her grandmother's casket from their shoulders. When the priest begins to speak, the vulture spreads its wings with a snapping of air.

A chorus of whispered prayers fills the small living room and dining area of Maya's grandfather's house: "Santa Maria, madre de Dios, ruega por nosotros pecadores, ahora y en la hora de nuestra muerte. Amen . . ." Sisters, brothers, nieces, nephews, cousins, and neighbors crowd onto the couch and love seat, and stand along the walls. They hold rosaries in their hands, rotating them slowly, every bead a prayer.

Sandwiched between her mom and Tía Carolina on the couch, Maya finds herself praying along, the repetition taking hold. Easing her into the language. Carolina serves Nescafé, black beans, tortillas, and fried plantains after the novena, the first of nine nights of prayer following the funeral.

Carolina and her husband, Toño, moved into the extra bedroom last year to help take care of Abuela, who, as it turned out, had been sick for a while.

Maya will always wonder why no one told her this.

Her grandfather Mario Hernández Basurto is a man of few words. He has thick, wavy hair, eyebrows like caterpillars. His wife had been the talkative one, handing him the phone to wish his granddaughter a happy birthday or to congratulate her on a good report card. Emilia's death has left him silent with grief. In this small house, with family, friends, and neighbors streaming through to honor his wife, Mario, in his living room recliner, is never alone yet rarely talks to anyone.

Maya spends most of her five-day trip within these walls, a home of about 1,200 square feet, surrounded by a wall too high to see over. She had thought she would see more of Guatemala, or at least of the city, than she does. Even with the somber occasion, she'd assumed that she and her mom would visit a few landmarks, snap some pictures, try a few restaurants. But instead, the two of them spend their entire trip, aside from the funeral, within the high cinder block wall that surrounds the house on all sides.

It's hard to gauge from these walls if Guatemala City is really so dangerous, but her mom assures her that it is. The civil war ended in 1996, but its bloody spirit lives on in the gangs that took in some of its orphans who had fled to the US. The Reagan administration might have denied them refugee status, but the gangs of LA welcomed these trauma-tized kids with open arms, and it was only when the US began deporting them that MS-13 and other maras, as they're called, took root in Guatemala's war-cracked system and grew into the strangling vines they are today.

Carolina nods her head in agreement. She rarely goes out either, other than to work. She doesn't speak much En-glish but seems to understand perfectly, as do a lot of people here. She lights a cigarette, sitting across from Maya and her mom at the glass-topped patio table, her head just inches beneath the flaming red and yellow bloom of the heliconia plant at her back. The wall is a warm cantaloupe color, studded with decorative tiles and ceramic planters overflowing with ferns and bougainvillea. The night is cool, rinsed clear by the day's rain, and the novena prayers have ended, which means it's time for Carolina's nightly cigarette.

Maya knows this now that she's on her last night here: her aunt smokes exactly one each night and tends to wink at whoever's nearby as she lights it, as if she's just kidding about being a smoker. Carolina, a second grade schoolteacher, doesn't have kids but babies the hell out of her plants, many of whom she has named. Yesterday she introduced Maya to a ficus tree named Ursula and the music of Mano Negra, which is now Maya's favorite band; Carolina may be the coolest adult she's ever met.

And she grew up with Maya's father. Over the last few days, Carolina has told Maya how she'd looked up to her big brother. He'd made her laugh like no one else, and he was clever, always reading something—comics, novels, then later newspapers and poetry. He'd confided to his sister that he dreamed of being a writer one day.

He'd been studying history and literature at the Universidad de San Carlos, with a focus, Carolina says, on the magical realists. Something about the way they wove magic into the lives of ordinary people as if refusing to abide by the colonizers' obsessively realist literary style.

Jairo could have explained it better than I have, Carolina had said in Spanish.

91

But part of the problem was Maya's limited ability to understand. The accent here is different from what she'd learned in school, so she'd needed to ask her aunt to slow down many times over the past few days, to repeat herself. And even then, Maya wasn't always sure she understood.

Carolina's cigarette burns low. Soon she'll go to bed, and there is still so much Maya wants to ask her, so much she wants to say. Running out of time, she settles on a question that she's had for years. "El libro de mi papá . . ." she says. *My father's book*. She knows that her father began to write a book before he died, but her mother didn't know much about it. *It was a mystery* was all Brenda could say.

"¿Qué fue el . . . ?" Maya says—but now she can't remember the Spanish word for title. She searches her brain, and as she does, detects an unusual smell on the patio, an ethereal floral note beneath her aunt's cigarette smoke. At first, she thinks she must be imagining it. "¿Qué era el nombre," she tries again, embarrassed by her bad Spanish, "del libro de mi papá?"

"Ah, el título . . ." Carolina says. She narrows her eyes, tries to remember the title of Jairo's unfinished book. Then she shakes her head in frustration. Explains that she can't recall at the moment—it's been a long while since she thought of her brother's writing. All she remembers is that the title was long, the entire line of a very old poem he had loved.

The smell grows stronger as Carolina says this, heady and sweet.

Maya's sense of smell is stronger than most—she once

detected a gas leak in the kitchen hours before her mom noticed anything amiss—and now she's pretty sure she's not imagining it. There is something otherworldly about this smell blossoming beneath her aunt's smoke, as if it were wafting in from another realm. A paradise. Some timeless place where flowers bloom at night—a place Maya shouldn't be able to smell from here, but she can and it's the exact opposite, she thinks, of the smell at the cemetery. And every bit as real. "Mom?" she says.

"Yeah, Muffin?"

"Do you smell that?"

Maya's question prompts both Brenda and Carolina to sniff the air.

Carolina smushes out her cigarette in an ashtray. A look of wonder comes over her face as the smoke clears and the mesmerizing smell fills her nose. "No puede ser . . ." She rises from the table and walks around the corner of the house. Maya and her mom follow.

There they see that an ordinary-looking cactus stationed in a plain plastic pot has erupted with a single dinner-plate-sized flower. The long white petals yawn into the most dramatic bloom Maya has ever seen, like the gaping eye of some god or a firework frozen in time. It gives off the strongest smell of any flower she's ever come across.

"¿Qué es?" she asks her aunt.

"La Reina de la Noche," Carolina says.

"¿Qué?" Brenda asks.

Carolina explains that each bud of this type of cactus only blooms for one night. This particular plant hadn't flowered in years, and she had thought it was dead. "No lo puedo creer," Carolina says, shaking her head in near disbelief as tears fill her eyes. *The Queen of the Night*, she says in Spanish, *was my mother's favorite flower.*

———————

Maya is folding her black dress back into her suitcase when she hears a light rap on the open door and looks up to see her grandfather.

"Hola!" she says.

"Hi, mija." His voice is small but warm. They've sat in rooms together over the past five days, but their exchanges have been brief.

"Por favor, entra," she says, realizing that he is waiting for her to invite him into his own room.

He's in his late sixties but seems older because of his creaky gait and all-white hair. He opens the wooden cabinet in the corner, takes out a cardboard box the size of a wine crate, and sets it on the bed beside Maya's suitcase. He takes out a photo album. "Look," he says in heavily accented English. "Your grandmother made this." He opens the cover to reveal a photo of Maya when she was a baby, sitting on her mom's lap, then a few more baby pictures, the turning pages revealing Maya growing up before their eyes. There she is at her fifth birthday. There she is jumping on a trampoline with Kayla, her best friend in second grade. Grimacing into a camera for school picture day. Smiling at the top of Mount Greylock. Her mother, it seems, has been sending Abuela photos all of Maya's life.

"Your grandmother loved you," Abuelo says. "And I do too."

"Oh . . ." Maya says, momentarily stunned. Then the words rush from her. "I love you too, Abuelo. Te quiero también. Gracias para—para todo."

He nods. Closes the photo album, pats it with his hand. "I keep this," he says. "But I have something for you."

He reaches back into the cardboard box and takes out a thick manila envelope. He unwinds the thin piece of twine holding it closed. Opens the flap and pulls out a stack of yellowed pages. Maya's eyes go wide. She knows at once what this is. Her father's name is on the title page, spelled out in yellowing typewriter ink. And above his name, the title of the book, the mystery, he'd been writing before he died: *Olvidé que era hijo de reyes.*

TWELVE

Maya wasn't always sure what she believed in, but she knew that she didn't believe in ghosts or evil spirits. She'd gone looking for the redheaded waitress hoping to learn something about Frank but had instead wound up questioning herself. Again. She was exhausted. She stopped at a red light outside a liquor store and debated going inside. She had no appetite for the buffalo wings cooling beside her on the passenger seat but could really go for some gin, just enough to help her sleep tonight.

The light turned green and she continued on, passing back across the Housatonic River. Her head still ached from last night's daiquiri and wine, and her mother would be on to her. There was something eerie about Cristina, in the final moments of her life, appearing to stare at something no one else saw—Maya could understand why Barb's thoughts had turned to the supernatural. But it was also possible that Cristina had been acting that way because she was high.

THE HOUSE IN THE PINES

Maybe Dan was right. An overdose was the most obvious answer, and the most likely.

Cristina could have gotten high right before she and Frank walked into the diner. That would explain how she'd seemed okay walking in, perfectly upright, only for the drugs to hit her when she sat down. Maya could picture this. She knew how easy it was to lose track of how many pills you had taken or what all you'd added to the cocktail. She wondered if this was ultimately what she shared with the dead woman, something other than dark hair and eyes: the tendency to get very high sometimes, as if trying to rise above the world on a bed of clouds.

It made sense that the person who'd painted such cold, uninviting landscapes had wanted to escape her own head sometimes. The more Maya thought about it, the more she related to her, and the more she questioned her own experience. Maybe all Frank was guilty of was choosing women who wanted out of the world sometimes. She snuck in through the kitchen as quietly as she'd left, carrying her chicken wings in one hand.

But her mom was already awake. She sat at the kitchen table doing a sudoku puzzle in her pajamas. Her phone was on the table. Maya's was too—she'd left it here for a reason.

She held up her foam box. "I was craving wings."

"You should have asked for a ride."

"I didn't want to wake you."

"What if you'd had a seizure while driving?"

"It's not that serious, Mom. I have insomnia." Maya felt herself slipping back in time, her voice taking on the drama

97

of a teenager's. This happened every time she came home. She hung her coat from a peg by the door, set her mom's car keys on the table.

"I'm telling you," her mom said. "Benzo withdrawal makes people paranoid. Confused. A lot of the benzo clients at work end up on antipsychotics."

"You see all that baking bread?"

Her mom frowned. "I work in the kitchen. You hear everything. Point is, I don't think you should be driving."

Maya sighed. She didn't feel like eating but felt like she should try. She'd spent more on the wings than she should have and left Barb a big tip. She put the wings on a plate and then in the microwave and waited by the counter for them to heat. She could feel her mom watching her and imagined her in EMT mode, eyes narrowed, checking off symptoms in her head.

But when the microwave dinged, and she turned around, Maya saw that her mom wasn't angry or suspicious. She just wanted her daughter to be okay. This was all she'd ever wanted, which was what had made the years since Aubrey's death so difficult for both of them. The light over the table highlighted all the new wrinkles on Brenda's face.

"What is it, Muffin?"

Maya's eyes burned.

"Is it Dan?"

It was so many things. The room blurred with tears.

Brenda had loved Dan from the moment she met him because it was obvious that he made her daughter happy.

The problem was that Brenda hadn't seen him since, a fact she'd brought up before in a guilt-inducing way.

"I'm worried I really screwed things up," Maya said.

Growing up, she'd talked to her mom about everything, but a lot of her behavior in recent years—the drinking, the drugs—had called for secretiveness. The change was so slow that she hadn't noticed, but now, telling her mom about how she had lied to Dan and vomited in front of his parents, she felt unburdened in a way she hadn't for many years.

Brenda was disappointed but didn't blame her daughter. The Klonopin had been Dr. Barry's idea after all. The uneaten wings grew cool again on Maya's plate as they talked.

"What should I do?" she asked.

Brenda weighed her words with care. She reached for her daughter's hand across the table. Squeezed. "I think you need to tell him."

Maya sighed, knowing she was right. "I'm afraid he'll never trust me again."

"I'm sure he will, even if it takes him awhile."

But her mom didn't know Dan like Maya did. "He's literally the most honest person I've ever met," she said. "I don't know if he'll be able to see past this."

"He will," her mom said.

Maya had dated plenty of guys but never felt close enough to any to fall in love. After Frank, she'd been afraid to let anyone in. She had needed to be drunk or high or both to let down her guard, and those mental states had been their own kind of armor. But then she met Dan, and nothing about him was guarded. He wore his heart on his face and spoke with no filter, and she loved him for it. It had taken her a year to realize how deeply she'd fallen, and it felt less like lightning than like the desire for him to be there when she woke, every morning, forever, even if it meant that he would see her too, lying there, looking back at him. Maybe it was just that Dan was the first person she had ever fallen in love with who made Maya so determined for him to also be the last. "I don't know," she said to her mom. "I really hope so."

The dark was easier on her eyes, so she lay in bed, though she knew she wouldn't sleep. She was covered in blankets, as her mom turned the heat down at night. The new mattress shaped itself to her body. She turned onto her side, propped herself up on an elbow, and checked her phone to see if Dan had texted.

He hadn't.

She reminded herself that he was cramming for finals. *Good luck tomorrow!* she texted him, followed by three hearts.

She waited. In the dark, the room felt like hers again. The furniture was new, but the smell of the house she'd grown up in hadn't changed. A smell like a time machine. Musty, coffee- and dish-soap-scented, a touch of cinnamon, and a few other things she couldn't name. It was so familiar to her that it took only a moment to realize something was off.

She smelled fire.

The tame, cozy kind. Sweetly crackling wood. A pleasant smell in most circumstances, but her mom's house didn't have a fireplace.

Her eyes snapped open. She was still on her side, face turned to the wall about two feet away. But the wall had changed. Now it looked like it was made of logs. She could almost see the whorls in the wood by the flickering light of the fire she felt at her back. She wanted to get up—to run—but she couldn't move. She was paralyzed. She felt a presence in the room. She couldn't see the person, but she felt the weight of their eyes on her neck, the part of it the blankets didn't cover.

Then she heard footsteps getting closer. Creaking their way across the floor, moving as slowly as a funeral procession. Maya felt the bed dip as someone crawled into bed with her. A scream curdled in her lungs. A feathery breath brushed her neck.

THIRTEEN

The day Maya meets Frank, she is rereading a particularly enigmatic passage of her father's incomplete novel on the sunny reading terrace of the public library, where she's come to warm her bare arms and legs after several hours of blissful air-conditioning. She comes here often in the summer when her mom is at work and Aubrey is busy, like today. Maya doesn't have other friends. She has people she's friendly with, people who'd invite her to a party, but few she is likely to keep in touch with now that high school is over.

And anyway, she'd rather be alone, sitting on this wooden bench, poring over these forty-seven pages. She's been back from Guatemala for two weeks and has already, with the aid of a translation dictionary, translated the whole document into English. It helps that the pages are double-spaced and that her father's sentences are clear and straightforward. She now knows what every word means on a literal level.

But on some other level, the language remains coded, as if the story it tells is symbolic of a deeper story just beneath the surface.

It's very much a mystery, just as her mom had said it would be—both in genre and in practice, as all Maya has here is the novel's opening and one scene that seems to skip ahead, as if Jairo had planned to go back later to fill in the intervening chapters. Because of this, she has only the barest sense of what the plot was going to be.

The story opens in an unnamed village so high in the mountains that its inhabitants spend all their time in the clouds. There's hardly any description of the village, as the main character can only see a few feet in front of his face at all times, yet he never bumps into anything. A warm light suffuses the mist. There's a touch of magic to this part of the story. The main character is a young boy named Pixán, who lives with his mother and father, who love him very much, in a small hut with a grass roof and stone hearth.

One day Pixán's mother tells him that a distant relative of theirs has died, a great-aunt, and left him an inheritance. Not money, but something else—a surprise! Pixán is to go down from the mountain and into the city to collect from the great-aunt's cranky husband, who isn't so keen to give the prize up.

Pixán's mother explains that the husband is selfish and wants to keep the inheritance for himself, but the great-aunt had written her will in ink, and Pixán's name is clearly on it.

So his parents give him a backpack, which they claim contains everything he needs, and a compass. He's told to walk west. He seems so young, Maya thinks, to be doing this on his own, but his age is never given, so maybe she's wrong. The clouds part as he walks down the mountain, and it's here that the tone changes. It grows less magical. Guatemala City appears in the distance, rendered in sharply realistic detail.

Pixán is scared—the city is loud and bright. And no sooner does he step onto its hectic streets than he is hit by a car. His head slams against the pavement. For a moment it seems he will die, but he doesn't—he pulls through, only now he has total amnesia. He doesn't think to look for his backpack, having forgotten that he had one, along with the parents who had given it to him. He has forgotten his home. His own name.

A childless couple takes him in and calls him Héctor. And for reasons not entirely clear, this inexperienced young couple pretend to be his real parents. They do it not out of malice but out of some vague sense that it's the right thing to do. Pixán becomes Héctor. Maya's heart aches for his true parents (and she can't help but think about her own mother, how she'll feel when Maya leaves).

The narrative skips ahead here a few decades to a day at the shore of El Lago de Atitlán. No explanation is given for this time jump.

Very little happens in this brief, final scene of the novel, and almost no context is given. Héctor, now a man, sits barefoot in the sand on the shore of a deep, wide lake, gazing out across the water at the towering volcano on the other side. The top of the volcano is wreathed in mist, and something about the sight of it strikes a chord in him. He has a sudden longing to climb it. To pull the clouds around his shoulders. He can't explain why the beauty of this place makes him want to cry, makes him yearn for something he can't name.

"You ever been there?"

Maya snaps back to reality. She's on the library reading terrace, probably sunburned by now. She squints as she looks up from her father's book at the guy who's just interrupted her reading.

She's seen him somewhere before but doesn't know him. He's older than she is, probably at least twenty. Average build and forgettable looks. His skin is pale, his dark hair lightly disheveled, and he's smoking a cigarette in casual defiance of the NO SMOKING sign. The smell of it fills her nose.

"I'm sorry—what?" she says.

"Lake Atitlán." He points with his eyes at the photography book sitting beside her on the bench. She'd checked the book out earlier from the library, a collection of photos of the lake mentioned in her father's book and its surrounding towns and volcanos.

"Have you been?" he asks her again.

She shakes her head, annoyed at being interrupted in her reading.

"You should go," he says. "It's gorgeous."

"Cool," she says flatly. "Thanks." That's when it clicks.

"You work here," she says. She's seen him sitting at a computer behind the reference desk.

"Part-time," he says, "and just for the summer. I tend not to stay anywhere too long."

Maya's not sure what to say to this, so she smiles tightly, then looks back down at her book, hoping he'll get the message.

"Just last year," he says, "I backpacked through Central America. I was in Guatemala for a while. I was at that lake. One of the most beautiful places I've ever seen."

Maya has to agree with him. She's never been, of course, but the lake in the photographs is indeed as beautiful as described by her father in the scene set on its shore. Her eyes drift from the page in her hand to the cover of the book on the bench.

"I went to each one of the little villages that surround it," he says. "Most of the people are Mayan, everyone walking around in the most colorful clothes you've ever seen. The women weave this cloth covered with patterns and symbols that convey information to whoever knows how to read them."

Maya looks up. She already knew this about Mayan weaving, having recently read the library's other book on Guatemala, but here is someone who has been there.

He smiles down at her, the sun shining at his back, and now that he has her attention, she realizes that she likes his smile. It makes her feel like they're in on a joke together. "Anyway," he says. "I'll let you get back to your reading. It was nice talking to you." He turns to leave.

"What else did you see in Guatemala?"

"You really want to know?"

She smiles back at him. She can't tell if he's flirting with her, or if she wants him to be. But he's piqued her interest, and there is something easy about talking to him. She moves the photography book and the marbled notebook containing her translation aside so that he can sit beside her on the bench.

"You've never been there?" he asks.

"No, I have, but . . ." How to explain? "I didn't end up going out much while I was there. I was visiting family."

The librarian seems interested in this, as if he wants to know more, but then seems to sense, and respect, her vague answer. "My best memory of Guatemala," he says, settling back onto the bench, "is the morning I got up before dawn and biked from the hostel I was staying at to an ancient Mayan pyramid. Temple of the Jaguar, it's called. It was still dark out when I got there and the jungle was kind of scary, but I was the only one there, so I knew if I was ever going to climb that pyramid, this was my chance."

"Wow," Maya says. Her voice isn't flat anymore.

"Picture a temple as tall as a twenty-story building," he says, "with a steep staircase going up its side. No one's allowed to climb the staircase—that's how dangerous it is. But I did. I climbed all the way to the top, got there just as the sun began to rise. I felt like a king from up there. I watched the whole jungle wake up. The monkeys, the birds. It was incredible."

"Wow," she says again, both about his story and the extent to which it differs from her own experience of

Guatemala. The thought of all that freedom makes her dizzy in a good way. It also makes her wonder if it was only her mother's fear that kept Maya from seeing more of the country. "Temple of the Jaguar," she says. "I'll be sure to check that out next time."

His gaze drops to the yellowed pages on her lap. "What's that you're reading?"

"Oh, this . . ." She doesn't know why her instinct is to keep it to herself. It's not as if the book is a secret, but for a brief moment she feels as if it is—as if it's a thing she must protect. "My father wrote this," she says.

"Really? Your dad's a writer?" He sounds impressed. "Would I have heard of anything he's written?"

"No, he's, uh—he's dead."

The librarian's kind, expressive eyes fill with compassion. "I'm so sorry to hear that."

She shrugs. She never knows how to respond to that statement. Is she supposed to say it's okay? No problem?

"That's cool that you have some of his work," the librarian says. He smiles warmly at her, and she can't help but notice that he's actually kind of hot. Alluring in a way that sneaks up on you. There are lines around his eyes but something young about his demeanor. His small chin is smooth, his gaze velvety. "Guess I should probably get back to my desk," he says. "My break must be over by now. Hey, it was really nice talking to you."

"You too," she says as he stands up. "My name's Maya, by the way."

"Nice to meet you, Maya. I'm Frank."

FOURTEEN

A ringing phone woke Maya from her dream.

She reached for the phone beside her on the bed, but that wasn't the one that was ringing. She sat up, blinking into darkness. The digital clock read 2:57 a.m. She was drenched in sweat. She took a deep breath as, elsewhere in the house, the ringing went on.

Why wasn't her mom answering her phone?

Maya got out of bed, the dread of her nightmare still clinging to her skin. She walked slowly down the dark hall, stopping outside her mom's closed door. The ringing wasn't coming from in there.

She turned on the living room lights, nearly blinding herself. She turned them back off. The ringing was coming from the kitchen, and it wasn't a sound she was used to— there was something different about this ring, but also familiar.

The old landline. A phone mounted to the wall behind

the kitchen table—Maya had forgotten it was there and couldn't remember the last time she'd used it. She was surprised it still worked. She stepped closer as it continued to ring.

A bad feeling crawled over her. Frank must have been the last person who'd ever called her on her mom's landline. Who even had one of these anymore? She felt like she was still dreaming as she reached for the receiver and held it to her ear.

Silence.

She held her breath. She felt sure that it was him. He could have guessed that she'd seen the video—many thousands of people had. He could be calling her mom's phone to see if Maya was back in town. To see if she was looking for him. She stood frozen as the thoughts flew through her head. Was that breath on the other end? It was hard to hear anything above her own pounding heart, her lungs begging for air.

She was about to hang up when the kitchen flooded with light.

"Maya?" said her mom.

Maya stared at her.

A click on the other end of the phone.

"Who are you talking to?" Brenda asked. She took in her daughter's fearful expression and pale skin, her sweat-darkened shirt. The dial tone blaring from the phone in her hand. "Are you okay?"

"The phone was ringing. Didn't you hear it?"

Her mom's brow knit with worry.

"Whoever it was called like three times in a row. I answered it, but . . . there was no one there."

Brenda shook her head. "I didn't hear anything."

Anger rose in Maya's throat. "What—you think I hallucinated it?"

"No, no, of course not," Brenda said, but it was obvious that she was just trying to de-escalate. She laid the back of her hand on her daughter's forehead. "You're a little warm. How are you feeling?"

Maya felt like screaming. She had the urge to tear the phone off the wall and smash it on the floor. Her mom didn't believe her. Again.

"You must be losing your hearing," Maya said coldly as she slammed the receiver back into its cradle.

She strode past her mom on her way to her room.

"Wait," Brenda said. She followed her daughter a way down the hall. "I'm only trying to help, Muffin. You know that, right?"

Maya almost laughed at that. As if her mom could help her. If that was Frank on the phone, he knew where she was now. After all, why else would she be back in Pittsfield? Hadn't she always wanted to escape?

"I don't need your help," she said to her mom as she closed the door in her face.

FIFTEEN

H ere," Aubrey says, "try this one."

She turns from her bedroom closet to hand Maya a white tank top with tiny silver clasps running up the front.

Maya stands at the mirror in her cutoffs. She pulls the shirt over her head. She knows this is one of Aubrey's favorites.

"Looks good on you," Aubrey says, and the mirror confirms this. The white sets off the summer gold in Maya's skin—although it doesn't fit her the way it fits Aubrey, who has cleavage.

"I don't know," Maya says. "I don't want it to look like I think this is a date."

"Isn't it, though? I mean, don't we want this to be a date?"

Maya grins. "We do."

"So?"

"All we're doing is going for a drive."

"A lot can happen on a drive."

"I don't even know if Frank likes me."

"Of course he does. He picked you up at the library, of all places."

They laugh, although Maya's not sure why it's funny. She feels giddy and nervous: she's supposed to meet Frank in twenty minutes and still isn't sure why. She leaves for BU in three weeks, and all they've shared so far are two conversations at the library: the first when they met, and the second when Maya went back in the hope that he was working.

Hey, do you want to hang out sometime? She had been the one to ask. She's had plenty of crushes in her life, but this might be the strongest, the most sudden. She can't stop thinking of that look he had given her, glittering and sly, like they were in on a joke together. Maybe she's just setting herself up to be hurt, but she had felt compelled to see him again. And she felt comfortable asking him out, which is a first for her. She's made out with boys—three, to be exact—but never had a boyfriend.

"Mascara?" Aubrey says. She approaches, mascara wand in hand, and Maya closes her eyes. She feels the bristles dragging through her lashes and smells the Jolly Rancher on Aubrey's breath, and beneath the candy, the smell of a cigarette snuck out back. Maya opens her eyes again, and there they are, side by side in the mirror: Maya-and-Aubrey—their two names had blurred together since ninth grade. A clique of two. Hard to say what high school would have been like if they hadn't sat beside each other in honors English.

Aubrey's green eyes are stark against the cherry-black

dye of her hair, and her outfit, as usual, is more stylish than Maya's. A man's vest over a bralette and black bicycle shorts. Beside her, Maya wears the borrowed shirt with its silver clasps and her own fraying cutoffs. And behind them, the familiar mess of Aubrey's room. Piles of clothes on the floor, notebooks, novels, orange soda cans, and CD cases. Polaroid pictures on the walls, more than half of which Maya is in, and strings of Christmas lights. Maya knows this room as well as her own. She knows it's not just with Frank that she is running out of time. She believes she and Aubrey will always be friends, but they will never get this time back.

The digital clock by Aubrey's bed reads 6:48.

"I better go," Maya says.

"Have fun. Don't forget about next Friday."

"Next Friday?"

Aubrey frowns.

"Oh, right . . . Tender Wallpaper. Duh."

Aubrey's favorite band. Maya likes them too, but not as much; she likes music that makes her want to dance. She knows the steps to every new dance as soon as it comes out, even if she only dances in her room.

"I seriously can't wait," she says as she heads out the door.

———

At seven, she waits in front of the library for Frank to get off work. It's as muggy and bright as it was all day, but that's not why her palms are sweating. When the doors swing open, she does her best to appear casual, but it's not him.

She waits. Strange now to think of how often she must have walked past him without noticing him. When she'd asked how long he'd been working there, he had said six weeks. How many times had she strolled obliviously by?

Maya had told Aubrey he was hot, but he isn't really. It's something else, some other quality he possesses. A magnetism. Frank exits the library a few minutes past seven, smiling warmly, but his hug feels platonic. A quick, one-armed clasp.

"Hey, sorry I'm late."

"No worries."

His car is a boxy sedan with cracked leather seats, and it's not actually his, he says—the car belongs to his dad. As he steers them out of the parking lot, Frank explains to Maya that, although he is from Pittsfield, he hasn't lived here for years. His parents had divorced when he was twelve, and his mom took him to live in Hood River, Oregon, which was where Frank had been prior to this summer. The reason he came back, he tells her—the only reason he'd taken a part-time job at the library—was that his father was now dying.

"Oh," Maya says, "I . . ." She imagines how it must feel to have a father and to lose him. She reaches for Frank's hand, then stops herself. "I'm so sorry to hear that."

He gives her a sad smile, then changes the subject. He drives them along Onota Lake, its shimmering blue surface flashing through the trees. Maya wonders if he plans to stop here and park, but then the car keeps going, the lake receding in her side mirror. The cool wind tousling their hair. Frank asks her what her favorite book is, and she tells him that she has more than one. She says *Like Water for Chocolate* is the best book she's read all year, *A Wrinkle in Time* was her favorite as a child, and as far as she's concerned, nothing compares to the Greek myths. Frank's attention on her is delicious, total absorption, like she's the most interesting person in the world.

"What about your father's book?"

"My father's book?" She can't explain why the question takes her aback, but it does, and in that moment Maya realizes she has no idea where they are. She had been so caught up in the conversation that she hadn't noticed them turning onto an empty narrow road through the woods. A flash of disorientation, then a fear too quick to articulate, a fear of strangers, of night, of forest. Very soon it will be dark out.

"Where are we going?" she asks.

"You ever been to Balance Rock?"

Now that he's said it, she recognizes the place—she has been here, but not in years. Once on a field trip in second grade, and other times to hike the trails with her mom. As the small, familiar parking lot comes into view, and Frank pulls a bag of weed from the glove compartment, Maya's fear melts away as quickly as it had taken shape. She hopes Frank hadn't heard it in her voice.

They're just here to get high. She watches him roll a joint, his quick fingers reminding her of the magicians Aubrey likes to watch.

They smoke in the parking lot, at the edge of the trees, Maya on the lookout for people while Frank doesn't seem to care. He smokes as leisurely as he had at the library, his brazenness casual and confident, and yet to her, he is so conscientious, careful to blow his smoke upward so that it won't waft into her face. She falls quiet as they inhale, and so does he, but the silence isn't awkward; it fills with the singing of cicadas and the rustling of wind through leaves. A much more comfortable silence than might be expected between two people who hardly know each other. "So," Frank says. "Should we check out the rock?"

Maya giggles as the high rolls in on her, tugging up the corners of her lips. "Have you never seen it?"

"I have. Still think it's amazing, though."

She feels delightfully floaty as they make their way down the short path from the parking lot to Balance Rock. It's eerie how the van-sized boulder balances so precariously on a much smaller stone. The sculptural quality suggests a human touch—some ancient, Stonehenge-like altar—but the arrangement is natural, a boulder left behind by a retreating glacier in the last ice age. Hiking trails wind through the surrounding woods, but for now Maya and Frank have the place to themselves. She feels like sitting, so she finds herself a spot on a smooth, wide stone and Frank sits beside her.

"So," he says. "What's your story?"

The question feels leading—in a good way—and makes her regret what she has to tell him: "I'm moving to Boston in a few weeks."

He looks disappointed. "I figured you were in college," he says.

"This will be my first year. What about you?"

"I was about to start at the University of Portland when I found out my dad was sick."

"Wow," Maya says, shaking her head. "That was good of you to stay."

"I knew I'd regret it if I didn't."

This time she doesn't stop herself from laying a hand on his arm.

Frank turns to look at her, his gaze soft and open. He's going to kiss her, she's sure of it. All the blood rushes to her face and the moment swells with terror and excitement—but then, just as she leans in to meet him halfway, Frank says: "Anyway, I like it here. I met you here, didn't I?"

Maya freezes. She smiles through her mortification.

"I like working at the library," he continues. "It's nice to be around all those books."

"I can imagine," she says weakly.

"And there's something else, something I've been working on." His eyes twinkle. "You're one of the first people I've told."

Maya feels a little more confident. His excitement about whatever he's going to tell her is contagious.

"I'm building a cabin," he says.

"A cabin? Where?"

"In the woods behind my dad's house. Out by the state park."

He tells her that he has always wanted to be an architect. Even as a child he had drawn houses with colored pencils and imagined living inside of them, houses with fire poles instead of stairs and indoor Slip 'n Slide corridors.

THE HOUSE IN THE PINES

Maya smiles.

He tells her that as he got older, he loved to read about famous architects like Buckminster Fuller. Like Maya, Frank has spent a lot of time reading, he says. *It's amazing how alike we are*, she thinks. She notices that they are sitting the same way, with their legs outstretched on the rock, their right ankles crossed over the left. When she notices this, Maya changes her position, embarrassed, as if she had copied him, even though she didn't. Not on purpose anyway. She's really feeling the weed now and has lost track of what Frank is saying—something about his dad.

There's no telling, he says, how much time his dad has left—could be a week, a month, or a year—so Frank has decided to stick around. Rather than go away to study architecture, he'll stay here, take care of his dad, and build his own cabin. He says he's already started. He's laid the foundation, poured the concrete. Because what better way to learn to build homes than to build one with your own hands?

"Wow," Maya says, stoned.

She does her best to follow along as Frank tells her about the cabin, but her short-term memory isn't working, and she keeps forgetting what he just said. Even so, she gets the gist, his words conjuring images, vivid, if disconnected: a small cabin in a clearing in the woods. The curved glass of its skylight. A stone fireplace. He even shows her the key to the place, holding it up in the light of the moon, which has risen as they've sat talking. The key to his cabin looks heavier than the others on the ring, and there's a sharpness to the cut of its teeth. Maybe it's just that she's high, but Maya can see the place through Frank's lovingly detailed telling, the deep honey color of its pine floors, the forested view through its generous windows. She can hear the stream that runs out back.

———————

Maya wishes she had a mint as she enters her house. She waits for Frank, who's just dropped her off, to drive away before she goes inside. She doesn't want her mom asking questions. She opens the door quietly.

The living room is empty and dark. Closing the door behind her, Maya slides out of her flip-flops and tiptoes down the hall. She's almost to her room when she notices how quiet the house is.

"Mom?"

In the kitchen, she finds a note from her mother, scrawled in her big, messy hand.

Call me when you get in.

Maya flips open her cell phone. She hasn't checked it in hours. Four missed calls from her mom.

"Where are you?" her mom says as soon as she picks up. Her voice is low and restrained, and Maya can hear the other EMTs sitting close by, huddled together in the back of an ambulance.

"Home," Maya says.

"You knew I had a shift tonight. I was hoping to see you before I left."

Maya remembers her mother mentioning this, but doesn't

see what the problem is. "But your shift isn't until eleven, right?"

Her mom is about to say something when ambulance chatter erupts in the background. "Shit," Brenda says. "We'll talk about this later, okay?"

"But—"

On her mom's end, a siren starts to wail.

"Love you," her mom says. "Don't stay up too late."

"Love you too."

She hangs up, and Maya registers the time on her phone. 12:02. It doesn't make sense. She met Frank at seven. Did she really just spend five hours with Frank at Balance Rock?

SIXTEEN

Maya walked headlong into the icy wind sweeping down North Street. Her face was numb beneath layers of makeup. She hadn't fallen back asleep after the phone call, whoever it was from, and now it was ten a.m., but she still wasn't tired. She felt, if anything, too awake, like she had to keep moving. She was sleep-deprived and wired yet somehow more clearheaded than she'd felt in years, and her mom's suggestion that she'd imagined last night's ringing only deepened Maya's certainty that someone—Frank—had called.

Passing St. Joseph's, she entered the downtown area and found it decked out for the holidays. Wreaths hung in the windows of shops and restaurants, and the giant Christmas tree was up at Park Square, covered in lights. The street was mostly empty, the cold wind blowing. She pulled up the collar of her coat.

She hadn't told anyone about the hours she lost that

THE HOUSE IN THE PINES

night at Balance Rock. Not at first. At the time, she had chalked it up to the weed; Frank had said it was his father's special stash. Between that and the deep connection she'd felt, it seemed reasonable enough to Maya that she'd simply lost track of time, and wasn't that just how all the love songs said it would be? Like losing yourself completely? It's not like she had ever been in love before. Two of the three boys she'd made out with were friends of guys who were after Aubrey. Guys who happened to be there.

Now she wished that she could reach back through the years and shake herself. Why had she trusted Frank so completely? And what had he done to her? She'd blacked out plenty of times in the past several years, usually on alcohol, sometimes on Klonopin, but never on weed. She would have thought that Frank had laced the joint with something, but that wouldn't have explained the second night she lost time around him.

Or the third.

By the time she told an adult about this, Aubrey was dead, and the missing hours at Balance Rock were just one more thing Maya couldn't prove. Neither could she explain why—if Frank really had done something to her—she hadn't gone immediately to the police. Or why she had continued to see him afterward.

Part of her would prefer never to know what went on during those hours.

But if Frank knew she'd seen the video, she couldn't afford to stay in the dark.

As she neared the museum, Maya spotted what appeared

to be an elderly woman with stooped posture, frizzy gray hair, and an oversized coat making her way along the sidewalk. Only when she was a few feet away did Maya realize that this was Aubrey's mom.

Elaine West wasn't old—she was several years younger than Brenda—but her daughter's death had aged her. She and Maya had seen each other only once since the funeral, in the frozen food aisle at Big Y, and the sight of Maya had seemed to pain Elaine.

Or maybe it was Maya who had made things awkward. The guilt she felt, her secret certainty that Aubrey would still be alive if Maya hadn't brought Frank into their lives.

The encounter, an exchange of no more than two minutes, had felt interminable.

Maya braced herself as Elaine looked up and met her eyes, and for a moment, it seemed they would greet each other. But they didn't. Each looked down at her feet as they passed each other on the sidewalk, and neither said anything.

What was there to say?

The Berkshire Museum was housed in a faded brick building with a stone walkway and a statue of a dinosaur out front. Maya hadn't been here since middle school. She was here to see Steven Lang, who had yet to write back.

The lobby looked smaller, its marble floors less expansive. "Welcome," said a man at the counter who wasn't Steven Lang. This man was slim with a head full of dreadlocks pulled into a knot on top of his head.

"Hi," she said. "Is Steven working today?"

"Security guard Steven?"

Maya nodded.

"Is he expecting you?"

"I was just hoping to talk to him for a minute."

The man looked at her with suspicion, or maybe she was just feeling paranoid. "Yes, he's here. Walked by not too long ago. I think he's down in the aquarium."

"Oh. So, can I . . ."

"You need a ticket."

She thought of her job as she handed over her credit card and reminded herself to call out sick again. She couldn't afford to mess things up with work. She took her ticket and walked down a wide flight of stairs to the aquarium. This had been her favorite part of the museum when she was little. A cavernous room with dozens of glass tanks built into deep blue walls. Maya walked from one end to the other. Orange clown fish peered out through the purple fingers of anemones. Baroque-looking seahorses bobbed alongside her as she passed. If Steven had been here, he must have moved on. He was probably the only guard at the museum.

Upstairs she found the annual exhibit of Christmas trees decorated by local schools and businesses. Maya walked through all three rooms of the exhibit, an indoor forest of bauble-laden pines. Hand-sewn garlands and painted ornaments, mostly the work of children.

She found Steven resting against the wall in the room of taxidermied birds, but when he saw her, he quickly stood up straight. He was heavier than in his profile picture, but she recognized the round, cherubic face and bald head. His eyes were sad, puffy from recent crying or too little sleep, but his uniform was crisply ironed.

"Hi," she said, walking toward him.

"Hi?" He seemed shy, not thrilled about being approached. "Are you looking for the restroom?"

"No." She gave him her friendliest smile. "I was looking for you. My name's Maya. I messaged you yesterday, not sure if you saw it . . ."

Steven's face flushed.

"I was hoping to ask you a few questions."

"Do you realize you're the fifth person who's contacted me about that video? Apparently, I'm the only one of Cristina's friends anyone can find online."

Maya sagged. Of course random people had theories about Cristina's death. She thought of the waitress.

"You're the only one who's tracked me down in person, though."

"I'm so sorry." Maya looked down at her feet. "I can see why that would be upsetting."

He waited for her to leave.

She didn't. "I lost a friend once too," she said. "What happened to her was a lot like what happened to Cristina. That's why I'm here. I just want to understand."

Steven sighed. "Look," he said, "I get that everyone

deals with grief in their own way. Maybe you need to find someone to blame. But I want to remember Cristina as she was while she was alive. I'll leave her death up to the police and the coroner, not to amateur sleuths who happened to see the video online."

Maya opened her mouth, then closed it again. It was no small thing to accuse a man of murder. "I think," she said, "that Frank had something to do with what happened to her. To both of them."

"Such as?"

"To be honest, I'm not sure."

He nodded slowly. "Right. I didn't like Frank either. But Cristina was an adult. So was I. I saw the path she was following him down and didn't do anything about it." His eyes flashed with emotion. "Am I guilty too?"

Just then, a woman walked in with two young children. Steven adopted a professional pose while Maya studied a barn owl. Its ghostly white face stared back at her. She waited as the woman and her children perused the exhibit.

Maya caught Steven looking at her by his refection in a glass case and wondered what he saw. She had taken a shower, washed her hair, and assembled herself a mask of her mother's concealer, but that wouldn't have covered up the spun-out look in her eyes. The desperation and possible paranoia. "American tree sparrow," said the smaller child. She pronounced the words slowly, as if learning how to read. "Raven." When the woman and her kids drifted into the next room, Steven drifted after them. Away from Maya.

She followed. She walked alongside him past a wall of sparkling quartz specimens in the Rocks and Minerals Gallery.

"You look like her," he said.

"Frank has a type."

Steven nodded, piecing it together.

"We dated when I was seventeen."

He stopped walking. Maya had him cornered beside a meteorite. He crossed his wide arms over his chest and peered down at her. He was twice her size but seemed fragile, unable to maintain eye contact.

"You didn't like him either," Maya said. "Why?"

"Because he was bad for her. I think part of what drew him to Cristina was that she was unattached. Her parents hadn't talked to her since she left the church, and her only friends were a bunch of meth-heads back in Utah. And me."

"You were close."

His lips trembled. He let his arms fall to his sides. "Things were great before Frank came along. When Cristina started working here, she had just finished her residency at MASS MoCA. That was a huge deal for her. She was completely self-taught. She'd been clean for two years."

"I've seen her work online," Maya said. "She was talented."

"She could've been famous. When I met her, she was living out of this little studio she rented. Painting every day. Then she met Frank and he was her new drug. She was obsessed. Started canceling on me all the time."

Maya's stomach tightened. He could have been talking about her seven years ago. "Did you ever see them together?"

"They always hung out alone, which I'm sure was his idea. I think he felt threatened by me. Wanted her all to himself. I only saw him the few times he picked Cristina up from work, and always from a distance. He never got out of his car."

"Did she seem . . . different to you?"

Steven looked around the room as if for a museum patron who might need his help, but he and Maya were the only ones in the silent mineral gallery. She felt a twinge of guilt at making him so uncomfortable, but when he spoke again, the words tumbled from him as if they'd been pent up. They sounded like a confession. "Yes, she changed," he said. "I saw it happen and it killed me, but I didn't do anything. I was so afraid of pushing her away that by the time I confronted her . . ." He took a deep breath. "Two weeks ago, there was this day that she didn't come to work. Didn't call in or anything, and it was so unlike her—Cristina loved that she got to work at a museum. I drove by her studio that night, and her car was there, but she was gone, and I knew she had to be with Frank. She didn't come back the next day, or the day after that, but then on Monday, I got to work and there she was. Like she never left. And she never said anything about all the frantic voicemails I had left."

"Where had she been?"

He shook his head. "All she would say was that she and Frank had gone away for the weekend. She kept her job, so she must have had a better excuse for the boss. I still have no idea where she went, but wherever it was, she got herself a tattoo while she was there. Right here on the inside of her arm . . ." He ran his finger down the soft skin between his inner elbow and his wrist.

"What of?"

"A key."

Maya's blood ran cold. "A key?"

"Like a car key or something," he said. "But with sharp edges. I don't know what it meant, but I wish I'd asked. I should've asked more questions . . ." His voice was heavy. "Instead I got mad. I accused her of being back on drugs. When she denied it, I called her a liar."

"Do you think she was on drugs?"

"Cristina had a close call two years ago, and it permanently damaged her heart. It's what kept her clean—she knew that if she started using again, it would kill her. She never would have started again if it wasn't for him." Steven's hands clenched at his sides, a vein throbbed in his neck, and Maya glimpsed how deeply he'd cared about Cristina. "That's what I think happened," he said. "I blame Frank for getting her back on meth, putting too much strain on her heart."

Maya weighed this theory against her own and understood that his appeared to make more sense.

"I knew she was in trouble," he said. Tears welled in his big brown eyes. "Cristina knew it too. I think she knew that she was going to die."

Voices approached from a few rooms down, and Steven talked faster, as if he needed to get the words out. "The day before she died, she came over and said that she was sorry for the way she'd been acting. She gave me her newest painting. It was beautiful, different from her usual work. I asked her why she was giving it to me, and she said she was getting rid of some stuff. Cleaning out her place. I got the worst feeling when I heard that."

The voices were almost in the room with them now, but Steven went on, needing to come clean. "She knew what would happen if she started using again. She knew, and I'm sure Frank did too."

An elderly couple entered the mineral room. "And so did I," Steven said, his voice cracking. "I could've stopped her from dying, but I didn't. So yes, I blame him, and I blame her for falling for him, but most of all I blame myself."

SEVENTEEN

F rank never tells Maya where he's taking her, and she likes this about him. She prefers surprise to knowing what comes next. Today he's driven them in his dad's car onto Thomas Island, which is actually a peninsula dipping down into Onota Lake. Most of the two dozen houses on the peninsula line up along its western shore, each with its own grassy beach and floating dock, many with boats tied to them. The houses have decks. Two-car garages. As they drive, Maya realizes she's never been here, despite living less than three miles away.

She leans back, savoring the breeze off the lake as they cruise Shore Drive, "Sweet Jane" dripping from the speakers. She has her feet on the dash, and the sun through the window feels like bathwater. The air is alive. She doesn't know where they're going, and it doesn't matter. Today is the day he will kiss her. She's sure of it. And if he doesn't, she will kiss him.

They reach the end of the peninsula, then loop back up as if to leave, but instead of driving them back across the land bridge, Frank turns down a narrow, wooded road marked by a DEAD END sign. A weeping willow trails its leaves over the car as he drives them to the eastern shore of the peninsula. This side is thick with trees. The few houses are large and expensive-looking, set back from the road behind manicured lawns. Frank pulls into an unpaved driveway that disappears into the trees. He slows to a stop.

"What are we doing here?"

His smile is mysterious. "You'll see."

He gets out of the car, and she follows. They continue on foot along the wooded drive until they come to a house larger than the others with white colonnades and a wraparound porch. Maya glances at Frank as they cut across the wide lawn, headed for a stand of trees between the house and the lake.

"Whose place is this?" she asks.

"Belongs to a friend of my dad's."

He leads them down a footpath, then onto a dock.

Maya's swum at Onota Lake for as long as she can remember but has never seen it from here. It could be an ocean. The water at her feet mirrors the sky, blue upon blue, clouds floating like lily pads.

Frank lifts the hatch of a large storage box near the end of the dock. Inside are life vests, bodyboards, and a few foam noodles. He reaches inside, runs his fingers along the rim of the box until he finds what he's looking for. A key. He jingles it on its plastic key chain as he walks over to the

classic wood-paneled motorboat lolling by the dock. The
boards beneath her shift as Frank steps across several feet of
water into the boat.

Maya tenses.

He turns. Offers her his hand.

"Your dad's friend said you could use it?"

"Anytime I want."

She relaxes, steps closer to the edge. Takes his hand. His
touch is a thrill. He helps her over the gap onto the swaying
boat, and for a moment—too short—they hold on to each
other for balance. His smell is musky, sun-kissed, his neck
inches from her lips. She flushes all over as he turns away to
untie them from the dock. She sinks down onto the red
leather seat.

He sits beside her, turns the key in the ignition, then
gives her the sexiest smile she's ever seen. He presses the
throttle. The engine growls. They begin moving as Frank
steers them onto open water. She remembers the life jackets,
but now it's too late to say anything—the boat's picking up
speed. She feels the spray on her skin, the wind in her hair.

"You ever driven one of these?" he asks, shouting to be
heard above the motor.

"No!" she shouts back.

Frank eases off the throttle. The boat slows, the engine
quiet. Maya sees people in the distance, wading at one of
the public beaches she would have attended herself on any
other day.

"Switch seats with me," he says.

She shakes her head. "I've never driven a boat."

"You can drive a car, right?"

"Yeah, but—"

"Then you can do this."

The boat, gliding slowly now, rocks onto its side as Frank moves to take her seat. Maya moves to the driver's side mostly just to even out their weight, but then she sits behind the big, gleaming wheel. The lake stretches out ahead of her like open road.

"The throttle's your gas pedal. Push it forward to go."

She pushes it too far, and they lurch ahead, kicking up waves. She shrieks. Releases the throttle. The boat rocks forward, then back, a real-world version of the swinging ship ride at a fair. She grips the edge, panicked.

She hears Frank laugh. She turns to him, heart in her throat, as the boat settles. He laughs but not in a cruel way, his voice wide with delight. Maya draws a shaky breath. Her fear gives way to exhilaration, and before she knows it, she's laughing too. Not because anything's funny but because she's okay and intoxicated off danger.

He moves closer, takes her hand, and this time she's sure he'll kiss her. She swallows, looks at his lips, leans in closer. She closes her eyes, but instead of kissing her, he lifts her hand and places it back on the throttle.

"You just have to be gentle," he says. He keeps his hand on hers, easing them forward. They begin to coast. Her pulse pounds. She keeps her eyes on the water. They're in the middle of the lake now. He lets go of her and settles back into his seat.

"So," he says. "When do you leave for Boston?"

The question is a splash of cold water. "The week after next. I've been trying not to think about it."

Frank is quiet beside her. They're nearing the far side of the oblong lake, the shore embroidered by forest. Leaves float across the water. She'd been so sure he was into her too. Could she have been wrong? Or is this because she's leaving?

"Got any plans tonight?" Frank asks.

"Going over to Aubrey's," Maya says. "But tomorrow—"

"Hey, Gary!" someone yells.

Maya and Frank turn to see a woman in a kayak two dozen yards behind them. Her features come into view as she glides closer: Silver hair and wiry arms. Good posture. Her smile falls as she sees they're not Gary.

Frank waves at the woman. "Ready to switch back?" he asks Maya.

She doesn't have time to react before he's on his feet, gesturing for her to slide over. The boat sways as they switch positions. He pushes the throttle, eases it up to speed. Maya glances over her shoulder at the woman, getting smaller as they leave her behind. The woman stares after them, her oars still.

"What was that about?"

He shrugs. "Must be a friend of Gary's." He slows as he turns, heading them back toward the dock. The boat hugs the shore, giving the kayaker a wide berth.

Maya looks at Frank. He seems calm, relaxed even, head tipped back like he's enjoying the spray and the sun. But suddenly it seems possible to her that he's taken the boat without permission. She flashes back to when they met, the cigarette he smoked in full view of the NO SMOKING sign at his job, like he didn't care what happened, or what anyone thought. And she can't help but wonder what that feels like, that kind of freedom. The confidence. He hasn't hurt anyone, so if it's true—if they're joyriding in the fancy boat of someone he doesn't know—she decides she's okay with it.

They skip across the water, faster than before, and she brims with excitement spiked with fear. What if they get caught? She's nervous as they pull up at the dock. Frank hops out, agile and quick but not in a hurry. He smiles as he helps her out, but the heat from before is gone. She thinks back over the past half hour, tries to see what she did wrong. He ties the boat to the dock and returns the key to its place in the unlocked storage box.

"Can I ask you something?" she asks as they arrive back at the car, parked in the trees as if hidden. She asks carefully, not wanting to offend him. "Is Gary the guy who owns the boat?"

"He is."

"Did he really say you could borrow it?"

"Ha!" Frank says. "You can't be serious." They get in the car. "Gary and my dad have known each other since the '80s," he says. "My dad helped him out once." There's a weight to the words, something he's not saying.

Maya lets it go. She's inclined to believe him, not for any reason she can point to, but instinctively.

"Speaking of my dad. I need to get back to him."

"Of course," she says.

He's quiet as he drives her home. His mood has shifted.

He stares ahead, eyes dark, and she thinks it must be about his father. Frank rarely talks about his father—she still doesn't know what's wrong with him or how long he has left—and she assumes this is because the subject is too painful. She wants to ask Frank if he's okay, but there's a hardness to him now, a tuck to his chin, a tense jaw. The silence stretches out around them and she starts to worry she's upset him.

"I had a really good time today," she says.

"Yeah, me too. Hey, why don't you throw on a CD?"

Maya feels stung. She's only known him for two weeks, but it feels like so much longer, and she's never seen him act this way. She picks up the CD case on the floor. "Any requests?"

He shrugs. "Surprise me."

She unzips the black case, begins flipping through the plastic sleeves. She sees *The Downward Spiral*, by Nine Inch Nails, and *There Is Nothing Left to Lose*, by the Foo Fighters, two bands she hasn't heard in a long time. Green Day and Rage Against the Machine; apparently Frank likes music from ten years ago. She stops when she sees a home-made mix CD. Her stomach clenches as she reads the words sharpied in black across its shiny front: *Songs for when we can't be together. Love you forever, Ruby.*

Who the hell is Ruby?

Maya pretends she didn't see the message. She flips the page and chooses the next album she sees, *Mama Said*, by Lenny Kravitz. Frank turns it up, and a few minutes later they're in front of her house. She dawdles on her way out of the car. "Thanks for the boat ride," she says. "That was really fun . . ." *Do you have a girlfriend, by the way?* Maya can't bring herself to ask. "Hey, what are you doing tomorrow?"

"Hoping to get some work done on the cabin."

"Cool," she says, like she doesn't care. "See you around, I guess."

"See you. Have a good time with your friend tonight."

He doesn't drive away immediately, and for a moment, she thinks he might call her back, having changed his mind about tomorrow, but the hope fades as she keeps walking and Frank says nothing. He's just being a gentleman, it seems, waiting for her to get inside the house. The door opens, and her mom pokes her head outside, greets her daughter with a smile. "There you are," she says, glancing over Maya's shoulder just in time to see Frank's taillights as he drives away.

EIGHTEEN

Maya paced back and forth in the kitchen. Her body ached from all the walking she'd done earlier, but her feet moved as if trying to outrun her thoughts, every neuron and nerve ending on the fritz. The kettle shrieked. She made chamomile tea when what she really wanted was the pint of gin she'd bought at the package store on her way home from the museum—but she'd told herself she wouldn't drink before five p.m. The metal spoon clattered noisily in her mug as she stirred in honey.

She'd all but forgotten the strange key Frank had showed her, the key to his cabin, but hearing about Cristina's tattoo had sparked Maya's memory of Balance Rock, and though she couldn't be certain, she sensed that this wasn't the only time she had seen the key.

She heard a text message come in on her phone. Maya spilled hot tea on her fingers as she rushed to her room to answer it. *Please be Dan, please be Dan.* He still hadn't responded to her text from last night, but she'd been trying not to worry.

It was her mom: *Chili tonight?*

Brenda was clearly trying to make amends—chili was Maya's favorite—but it wouldn't make up for last night.

Sure, Maya wrote back. She wasn't expecting an apology, but neither did she intend to offer one. She knew that she was right. The key. The cabin. The late-night calls on the landline. They all pointed to the same truth that lay just beyond the dark spots in her own memory.

The problem with Steven's theory about Cristina's damaged heart was that it didn't explain what happened to Aubrey. Steven had never met Frank. He didn't understand. What Maya needed was to talk to someone who knew him in the way she and Cristina had.

She thought of Ruby.

All Maya knew about Ruby was that she'd once professed her love for Frank in Sharpie on a mix CD. Maya had been jealous at the time, but never found out who Ruby was, and four days later Aubrey was dead. Maya had forgotten all about Ruby then, but now she remembered the mix CD—*Songs for when we can't be together*—and wondered if Ruby had loved Frank enough to know his secret.

The battery on Maya's phone was low, so she knelt to plug it in, and as she did, she caught her reflection in the window. She hadn't realized she was grinding her teeth. Her lips were pale, eye sockets like caves, and the backyard bled through her reflection in such a way that the lawn lay across her chest while the trees beyond ran through her head.

NINETEEN

The thought of Frank with someone else takes her hunger away.

She doesn't taste the basil from the garden she helped her mom plant when she was little, or the lemonade. She doesn't feel the breeze through the open kitchen door or hear the familiar wind chimes on the stoop because all throughout dinner, Maya thinks of Ruby. She's thought of little else for the past few hours, ever since she saw the mix CD. She thinks she knows now why Frank didn't kiss her.

"Sheila asked if there's anything you need for your dorm," her mom says. Sheila is a friend of hers who lives down the street.

"Not that I can think of."

"Really? Do you want one of those shower things? A caddy?"

Maya shakes her head.

Her mom frowns. "I thought you'd be more excited about this. Living in the dorms, taking writing workshops. Isn't this what you've always wanted?"

"Yeah . . ." Maya says. She takes a bite of her spaghetti and pesto.

Her mom peers at her from across the table. "I was thinking," she says, "that it would be nice to have Frank over for dinner. I'd like to meet him."

"I don't know . . ." Maya swirls and unswirls her spaghetti.

"Is everything all right?"

"Not really."

Her mom waits.

"I think he might have a girlfriend back in Hood River."

"A girlfriend?"

"Either that or . . . he's just not into me."

"So you're . . . just friends?"

Maya nods, and her mom's confusion gives way to relief. She doesn't like the idea of her daughter spending all that time with a stranger but sees how stricken Maya looks. "Aw, Muffin," she says. "Being friends is better anyway. Friendships never have to end."

Maya sighs.

"Just think—less than two weeks until you're at BU. You worked so hard for this."

Her mom is trying to help, Maya knows, but she doesn't want to think about the move. She's been looking forward to it for so long, dreaming of her future at college, but lately she's begun to dread it.

"You're going to meet so many new people," her mom says. "You'll forget all about him."

So when do I get to meet this mystery man? Aubrey had asked Maya on the phone the night before Frank took her boating. She and Aubrey were supposed to hang out that night, but Maya had canceled, which was unusual for her. She's usually the dependable one—but Frank had surprised her with movie tickets, and she couldn't turn him down.

So when did Aubrey get to meet him? The question gave Maya pause. Her impression is Frank prefers to spend time with her alone, though he's never actually said this. It was only then, with Aubrey waiting for her to say something, that Maya recognized her own reluctance to introduce the two of them. She hated to admit, even to herself, that it was because when Aubrey walks into a room, heads turn her way like flowers to the sun, and Maya realized that maybe she was the one—not Frank—who preferred spending time one-on-one.

Hello? Aubrey had said.

Now Maya tells herself she can't be late tonight. She hasn't been a good friend lately. She feels bad about this, but not as bad as she feels about Ruby. It will be good to talk to Aubrey: Aubrey's good at figuring people out. If anyone can interpret his mixed signs—the gifts, the romantic yet weirdly platonic outings, the mix CD—it's her.

At eight, Maya's mom leaves for an overnight shift. Her schedule is complicated, cycling through days of concentrated work followed by days of rest. She usually winds up with one overnight shift a week, and on those nights, Maya sleeps at Aubrey's house. She does this not because she's afraid to be alone—she isn't—or because it puts her mom at ease—though it does—but because she loves lounging with Aubrey in her room, talking and listening to music or watching movies, smoking pot when they have it, sneaking beers from her stepdad. As Maya packs up her toothbrush, an overnight shirt, and clean underwear, it occurs to her that tonight could be the last time she does this before moving to Boston.

She told Aubrey she'd be at her house at nine, but her mom left a little early, so Maya decides to bike over at eight. She straps on her helmet and is about to leave the house when a knock comes at the door. It's after dark, so she stands on her tiptoes, peers through the peephole. A smile washes through her. A jolt of electricity. It's him.

Frank smiles back as if he can see her, looking right into the fish-eye lens.

She opens the door beaming.

"Had to pick up some cough drops for my dad, so I was in the area . . ." He glances at the bike helmet she forgot she was wearing. "Were you headed out?"

"I was on my way to Aubrey's—"

"That's right! Totally forgot—"

"I don't have to leave for, like, forty minutes. Want to come in?" She opens the door wider.

"I don't want to make you late."

"It's fine."

He glances down at the CVS bag in his hand. "Sure," he says.

This is the first time he's been inside her house. She leads him to the couch, noticing only after he's walked across the carpet that there is dirt on his boots. She'll have to clean it up before her mom comes home, but Maya doesn't fault him for this—she should have told him about the no-shoes-in-the-house rule. He wears the same white T-shirt and dark jeans he wore earlier today, and when he sits beside her, she smells sun and earth and the kind of sweat that comes from hard work. He must have been working on his cabin.

He drapes an arm over the back of the couch so that he almost, but not quite, has his arm around her, and she wants to lean back into it, but the thought of Ruby stops her.

"So," he says casually, "what's up?" Whatever low mood he slipped into earlier has vanished. He smiles.

"Not much . . ." Maya says, but she doesn't look at him.

His eyebrows tent at her tone.

She weighs asking him about the mix CD. Decides against it.

"Hey," he says softly. "You all right?"

She should just tell him how she feels. The blood rushes to her face.

He takes her hands, turns her gently toward him. Looks into her eyes. "Talk to me," he says.

"I really like hanging out with you, Frank. I like . . . *you*. Like maybe more than a friend."

"God, it's good to hear you say that."

"Really?"

He looks like he might laugh, but his eyes are warm. "Don't tell me you didn't know."

"Know what?"

"I mean . . . I spend all this time with you because there's no one else I'd rather be with."

Her eyes go wide, and her heart. She melts. She could do a cartwheel. "I feel the same way."

He smiles, but the smile is sad, and Maya prepares to plummet back to earth. "I just wish you weren't leaving," he says. "I have to keep reminding myself, telling myself I shouldn't get too close to you, that I'll only get hurt. But then, every time we're together, I just—"

She kisses him.

He's surprised at first, lips parted mid-speech, but then he kisses her back. A long, deep kiss that answers, once and for all, how he feels about her. She doesn't want to get hurt either, but why should either of them have to? She'd gladly bus back here every weekend. She wraps her arms around his neck.

Then she remembers Aubrey.

Maya pulls away but stays close, their foreheads touching. "Wish I didn't have to go," she says.

He pouts. "Maybe you could see Aubrey another night?"

She shakes her head.

"Why not?"

"She's my best friend. I've been kind of ignoring her lately."

"I bet she'd understand."

Maya's flattered by his persistence, then by the glimmer of resentment she sees. "I'm really sorry," she says. "I can't."

"I understand. Guess you should probably get going, then."

She glances at the clock; she still has ten minutes.

"There's actually something I want to tell you," he says.

She can't tell from his tone if the news is good or bad, but there's a weight to the words that evokes the same blend of glee and fear she'd felt on the boat.

"I finished my cabin," he says.

She blinks at him. "That's awesome."

"Nothing in it yet, of course, and like I said, nothing fancy, but I worked on it a little each day and now it's done."

"Wow, already?"

A smile spreads across his face. He nods.

"I'd love to see it."

"Would you?" He looks at her thoughtfully.

"Of course! I didn't realize you were so close to being done." Maya wonders when he'd had the time, between caring for his father and spending time with her.

"I'd like that," he says. "You'd be the first to see it."

"I'd be honored."

"How's tomorrow?"

"Tomorrow's great."

"You'll probably want to wear sneakers. Only way to get there is down this abandoned road I found at the edge of my dad's property when I was little."

"Wow, sounds cool."

"Yeah, well . . . wasn't so cool at the time." He sighs like a much older person.

Maya wants to know more but asks only with her eyes,

and Frank looks at her as if trying to decide if he should tell her. Then he does. While he talks, he plays absently with something in his hand. The key to his cabin—Maya recognizes the serrated edges. The key seems to bring him comfort. She's struck by his vulnerability as he opens up to her about something that happened when he was ten.

He says he was in the woods behind his parents' house. He'd go back there whenever they were fighting, and they fought a lot in those days. Those woods went on for miles. One day he wandered onto an abandoned road. It was getting late, but he was curious and decided to follow it. The road was overgrown, disappearing for yards at a time beneath dead leaves and ferns and moss. Eventually it disappeared so completely that Frank couldn't follow it a step farther—yet when he turned around, it wasn't behind him either. He was lost. He was only ten, it was getting dark, and all around him, an endless sea of trees, like that dream where you're underwater and can't tell which way is up.

He doesn't know how much time passed before he shouted and cried himself out. He only knows that it was dark, and he was clinging to patches of moonlight between branches when he finally fell quiet enough to hear the stream. The soothing, lifesaving gurgle of it—what a miracle it seemed when the sound led him not only to the stream but back to the road, which he followed expectantly.

He saw an old bridge and a clearing on the other side of the bridge and decided to cross over, thinking he might find something there. A cabin. Help. He entered the clearing but found only the barest remains of a home: a low concrete foundation being reclaimed by forest. Frank sat down on it, pulled his knees to his chest. He prayed that his parents would find him. But they didn't. He waited all night, shivering with cold and with fear.

Then, sometime near dawn, he closed his eyes and imagined that there really were walls around him, and a ceiling above. A cozy fire. Something hot on the stove. He imagined it until he smelled the cooked meat and burning wood. He must have fallen asleep then, because he dreamed that the place was real, and for the first time in months, he felt safe. Safer than he'd ever felt at home. And in the morning, he wasn't afraid anymore. He'd survived a night alone in the forest and dreamed up a home for himself. The home he promised himself he would build someday, there in the clearing on the other side of the bridge.

———————

Knowing the story behind the cabin, knowing what it means to him, makes Maya want to see it even more. She says it would be an honor to be the first to see it. She feels for the child lost in the woods, clinging to the comfort of an imaginary home, as well as for the deep, caring man beside her, afraid of getting hurt. She admires him for turning his dream into a reality and for doing it without going to college.

"Left or right?" he asks.

The question catches her off guard. She looks out the car window at the dark street rolling past. She hadn't been paying attention, and now they're on Grove Street, passing Stoddard Ave. "Left," she says. They're almost to Aubrey's house, a destination so familiar that Maya is embarrassed to realize that she's allowed Frank to drive several blocks past her street. Now they'll have to turn around, but he doesn't seem to mind. He drives as if he has nowhere else to be.

Maya does, though. She forgot to keep an eye on the time. The clock on Frank's dash flashes 12:00, so she reaches for her backpack to check the time on her phone, only to realize that she's forgotten it. Not just her phone, but the whole backpack containing her pajamas and toothbrush. She can't believe how absentminded she's been. She tries to recall if she locked the door, but now that she thinks of it, she can't remember leaving the house or getting into Frank's car. "Do you know what time it is?" she asks.

Frank shakes his head. "Sorry."

"Turn here. Fourth house on the right."

Most of the windows on the street are dark. Maya has a sinking feeling. She knows, as Frank drops her off in front of Aubrey's duplex, that the polite thing would be for her to introduce them. But she's pretty sure she's late. She'll have to apologize, and if Frank's there, it'll be awkward. "I'm glad you stopped by tonight," she says.

He leans across the console to kiss her. Just a peck, but it brings back the heat of his breath. It sends a shiver through her center.

TWENTY

The last time Maya had tried to find Ruby—before Dr. Barry convinced her to stop looking—all she'd come up with were a couple of MySpace pages. But now Maya found over a dozen Rubys on social media who called Hood River, Oregon, home. She ruled out the very old and very young and was left with seven women named Ruby, any of whom could have made the mix CD for Frank.

They were almost all Hispanic, and two looked like his type: high cheekbones, straight black hair, dark eyes. Like Maya. Or maybe she was imagining it. Her sleep was broken and her dreams felt close. She messaged the seven Rubys, asking them to please contact her if they knew Frank Bellamy.

She waited.

Just two more hours until she could crack open the gin. She felt as if a strobe light was pulsing inside her skull, catching all her thoughts in strange shapes. The key with its jagged teeth. A young Frank lost in the woods, searching for help, for a door to knock on.

She heard her mom get home from work but didn't go to greet her.

Her eyes ached from staring at her phone. "Ruby" and "Hood River" had turned up plenty of Google results: pet videos, a real estate agent, the winner of a spelling bee, an article from 1901 about a girl who'd been thrown from a buggy. Maya couldn't narrow her search down. All she had was a first name and the town where Frank had lived with his mother after his mother divorced his father.

When she came across the obituary of an eighty-year-old woman, a dark thought crossed Maya's mind, and she added "death" to her query. This yielded more obituaries and several articles. Hood River's population was under eight thousand, so it wasn't long before she found an article about a woman named Ruby Garza who'd died in a fire ten years ago. She'd been nineteen, a first-year at Columbia Gorge Community College who had recently moved into an apartment close to downtown. Ruby fell asleep without blowing out a candle beside her bed, and never woke. She was alone. Her hair was black, her eyes brown, and her face still child-like in the grainy black-and-white photo. She died less than two months before Maya met Frank at the library. Right around the time he left Hood River and moved to Pittsfield.

TWENTY-ONE

Aubrey answers the door in the oversized Tweety Bird shirt that she wears to bed, but she doesn't look like she's been sleeping.

"Hey, sorry about this."

Aubrey watches Frank drive away, catching only a glimpse of his face. "No worries," she says. But her voice is frosty, her gaze cool. "Guess he didn't want to meet me?"

"Oh, I—" Maybe she should have introduced them after all. "Just didn't seem like a good time."

Aubrey leads her inside. The lights are off, the living room dark aside from the blue glow of the *Law & Order* rerun on TV. They walk quietly past Aubrey's stepdad, asleep in his recliner, a beer in the cup holder. Maya is surprised he's asleep; that Aubrey's ten-year-old brother, Eric, isn't sprawled on the floor playing his Game Boy; that Aubrey's mom can't be heard talking on the phone or doing an exercise video in the basement. This house is usually much louder than Maya's. She feels terrible for being late.

Nothing from Aubrey as they enter her room. A Tender Wallpaper song wafts from the headphones on the bed; Maya recognizes the slow drums. A can of orange soda on the nightstand. A freshly smoked cigarette hangs in the air, but the whole house smells like cigarettes, so no one will know. Christmas lights frame the open window. Maya's mouth hangs open when she sees the time on the alarm clock. 11:42 p.m. She's three hours late. "Wow, I'm really sorry," she says. "I was about to bike over here when Frank showed up at my house. He was just going to stay a few minutes, but then we started talking, and . . ."

Aubrey peers at her. "What are you on?"

"What? Nothing."

Aubrey narrows her eyes. She sits on her bed, stops the CD on her Discman. "So what happened?"

Maya sits beside her, cross-legged. A soft wind blows in the window, cool with night. Her uneasiness recedes as she tells Aubrey about their kiss and the talk that led up to it. Maya's wanted this for what feels like so long—but Aubrey seems unimpressed. Uninterested even. "So that's why you're late?" she asks. "Because you were making out with Frank?"

"No, we talked too. He told me more about his cabin."

A smirk flicks across Aubrey's face. "The one he's building in his dad's backyard?"

"Not in the backyard," Maya says with a sliver of resentment. "His dad has property out by the state forest. The cabin's in the woods, and Frank finished it. He's taking me to see it tomorrow at one."

"He's taking you to a cabin in the woods. What is this, a horror movie?"

"You wouldn't say that if you knew him."

"Really?"

"Look, I said I was sorry. And I am. I should've been here at nine."

Aubrey softens, but questions swim in her eyes. Maya wonders if Aubrey is jealous. She's never thought this before, but her suspicion grows when Aubrey seems to lose interest in the topic of Frank and suggests they watch a movie, an '80s slasher film where a man in a mask hunts teenagers.

They watch it on an old TV-VCR combo that Aubrey bought at a garage sale. The movie is from a garage sale too, bought with the money she made as a bagger at Big Y. The movie is gory and terrible. Usually they'd be making jokes through the whole thing, but tonight, after a few quips from Maya, they just watch, and with every murder, Aubrey's choice feels more passive-aggressive. She's so quiet when it's over that Maya thinks she's asleep, so she turns off the TV and lies beside Aubrey in bed. The day was hot, but the night air is cold, so she gets beneath the blanket. Closes her eyes.

"What happens when you go away to college?" Aubrey asks.

"Huh?"

"With you and Frank. What happens when you leave?"

"I don't know," Maya says. "Maybe I'll defer." Only as

the words leave her mouth does she realize she's considering it, but now that she's said it, she knows it's true.

"Are you kidding me?"

"Plenty of people take a gap year," Maya says, surprised she hadn't thought of it before. What does it matter if she starts at BU next year instead of next week?

"What the hell is wrong with you?" Aubrey asks.

Maya doesn't know how to answer. Nothing is wrong with her. And who is Aubrey to criticize her for staying? Aubrey will be here too, still working at Big Y while attending Berkshire Community College. She had said it wasn't worth taking out loans to go anywhere else, that community college was fine, more than anyone else in her family had done.

"Thought you'd be happy," Maya says, "to know I might stay in town."

"Wow," Aubrey says sarcastically. Then a pause when it seems she might say more, but in the end, all she says is: "Good night."

Maya is brushing her hair in the mirror after trying on several shirts and settling on a blue-and-white-striped tank top when the knock comes at the door. It's not quite one, and her mom's sleeping off last night's shift, so Maya hurries to the door before Frank knocks again and wakes her up. He's a few minutes early. She's already smiling as she opens the door. But it isn't Frank.

It's Aubrey. She looks amazing. And she's wearing that

dress, the one she wore the night she made out with the drummer of the Screaming Mimis. Maya had watched him eyeing her all night as she danced near the stage, the dress slipping now and then from her shoulders, hugging her swinging hips. Aubrey too had known the drummer was watching her. That was the point. The dress is red, blood red.

"Hey," Aubrey says.

How dare she?

Now all the guilt Maya had felt, all her sympathy, sizzles away like drops of water on a skillet. She steps outside, closes the door behind her so she doesn't have to whisper. "You knew he'd be here at one."

Aubrey smiles and shrugs like this is no big deal. "You said you wanted to introduce us, so here I am."

"Look, we have plans, okay? You can't just—"

"Don't worry, I'm not staying. My mom's having one of her Avon parties, so I had to get out of the house. Thought I'd come here. Meet Frank."

Maya shakes her head. She's about to ask Aubrey to leave when Frank pulls into the driveaway. Gets out of the car. He smiles as he approaches.

"Hey," Aubrey says, extending her hand. "I'm—"

"Aubrey." He clasps her hand warmly.

"You must be Frank." Her voice is light, but she holds his eyes as if trying to read him. "I've heard a lot about you," she says.

"Same here. All good things." He seems comfortable, and Maya wonders if she was wrong in assuming he preferred to spend time with her alone.

She almost dies as his eyes dart down the front of Aubrey's body. "Well," Maya says a little too forcefully, "nice seeing you, Aubrey. But as I was saying, Frank and I have plans today . . ."

Aubrey looks to him, waits to be invited.

To Maya's immense relief, he stays out of the conversation. He's not quite smiling, not quite amused, but close. And she wonders how this looks to him, the obvious tension in the air. Maya's tone. For a moment, she's sure he's deduced the whole situation.

"Okay, well . . . see you around, I guess," Aubrey says to Maya, and she sounds almost sad, but Maya has no sympathy for her. They have never hurt each other in this way. Not like this, with what feels like cruelty.

"It was nice to meet you, Frank," Aubrey says. "And congrats."

He freezes. "Congrats?"

"On the cabin. Maya said you finished it."

The hint of amusement vanishes from his face. He glares at Maya. "You told her about my cabin."

"I—I told her you built it. Was I not supposed to?"

Frank glowers. He could be a stranger.

"Sorry I brought it up," Aubrey says. "I'll . . . go now."

"It's fine," he says as she walks away. "Really. I'm glad you know about it, Aubrey." A smile sparks in his eyes and spreads across his face, brightening him as quickly as he'd darkened. "Maybe you'd like to see it too."

No! Maya wants to shout.

"It'll have to be another day, though," he says. "I actually need to get back to my dad. He had a rough morning. That's what I came here to tell you, Maya. Today doesn't work anymore, I'm sorry."

She doesn't believe him. He was going to take her to his cabin, she was going to tell him her thoughts about deferring, but Aubrey ruined everything.

"I'm sorry," she says.

"For what?" He hugs her goodbye, but the hug is wooden, bloodless. Even as his face pretends nothing's changed. "Good to meet you," he says to Aubrey. His gaze drops again to her body, and Maya feels a gut punch. "Did you walk here?" Frank asks.

Aubrey nods.

"Want a ride?"

Aubrey glances at Maya, then at Frank. She thinks about it. "Sure," she says.

Maya doesn't breathe as she watches him open the car door for her. Aubrey gets in. She avoids eye contact with Maya through the windshield.

TWENTY-TWO

Maya had been drinking since five p.m., the tea in her mug replaced with orange juice and the cheap gin she'd bought on her way home from the museum. Four hours later, the pint was nearly empty, and she felt calmer, but not drunk, as she should have. Any other time she would have been sloppy by now, but it was as if her body wouldn't allow it, as if her every cell intended to stay vigilant.

The smell of chili seeped through the walls. Roasted cumin and garlic, sizzling beef. This was one of Brenda's best dishes, but Maya hadn't had any. She understood that she was being cruel, but her mom had questioned her sanity again.

It wouldn't have bothered her so much if she wasn't tempted to succumb to her mom's fears. If she just agreed that she was crazy, Maya would be given the kind of meds that would make her sleep for twelve hours straight. She added more gin to her mug. She was sitting in the dark, cross-legged on top of the bed with her phone in one hand. Hours of searching for information on Ruby Garza hadn't turned up anything new. And even if it had—if Maya could link a third dead woman to Frank—she still wouldn't know *how* he did it.

And in the meantime, Dan hadn't texted back.

He had been tagged on Instagram by someone with the handle nina_borealis. He was sitting in a booth at Silhouette Lounge, drinking what was probably a rum and Coke across from his law school friend Sean and Sean's girlfriend, Ellie. The three sat close together, presumably with Nina, who'd taken the picture. A quick search had revealed Nina to be a pretty Filipina architect who enjoyed traveling.

Maya had never been insecure in her relationship with Dan, but he'd never ignored her texts before. Was Nina single? Flirtatious?

Maya reminded herself that she had no reason to mistrust Dan—while he had every reason to mistrust her. He must have known she was hiding something, must have sensed it, and this was probably why he hadn't texted back. Dan cared about the truth. Being secretive was so much worse than if she'd told him about the Klonopin, which he wouldn't have judged her for anyway. Half the people they knew were on medication for anxiety, depression, or something else. As the night dragged on and he didn't text back, the possibility of losing him began to feel real.

The thought made her chest cave in. She'd been in such a bad place when they met, drifting through her days, forgetting most nights, and it was Dan who'd cut through that fog. He was her Orpheus who never looked back, helping her return to the land of the living. He made it a place she wanted to be. He was the kind of person who refused to buy jarred tomato sauce because homemade was so much better, and he enjoyed making it. They'd cooked together almost every night since Maya moved in, and now there was nowhere she'd rather be than at his side, chopping herbs and listening to music and tasting everything more than she needed to because it was all so good.

If only she could rewind to a week before she saw the video. They'd put on a reggaeton playlist and had a dance party in the kitchen while a pot of minestrone simmered on the stove. Dan loved dancing almost as much as she did.

Now she pictured herself cooking alone.

None of the apartments she'd had since moving out of her mom's house had felt like home because Maya hadn't tried to make them feel that way. But living with Dan was different. She wished he was beside her in bed but was glad he couldn't see her drinking gin alone in the dark.

A text came in. This time it was from Steven.

She'd asked him if he had a picture of Cristina's final painting, the one he'd said was different from her other work. Maybe the painting would offer some glimpse into the mind of the woman who had chosen to have Frank's key tattooed on her arm.

Steven had agreed to take a picture of it when he got home and text it to her. Now here it was, and the painting was indeed different from the work on Cristina's website.

Bonneville Salt Flats had been striking for its alien beauty, the vast emptiness of land and sky, its cold, crystalline light.

The new painting was warm. It was of the main room in Frank's cabin. An open floor plan with the kitchen on one side and the living room on the other, with its overstuffed couch, shaggy rug, and tall stone fireplace. Everything was painted in photorealistic detail except for the fire. There was something about its glow, a heightened quality to the light. Shot through with orange, pink, and gold, more beautiful than natural light. More beautiful, Maya thought, than the light in Cristina's salt flats painting—but opposite in its effect. This painting was full of what her earlier work lacked. Contentment. Well-being. The feeling of warmth on your face. This must be how she'd felt there.

Like the misty village in Maya's father's book, Pixán's true home, the cabin in Cristina's painting seemed both real and magic.

Dr. Barry would have labeled her thoughts *apophenia*—the false belief that unrelated things are somehow connected. The delusion behind many a conspiracy theory, he'd explained.

If you look closely enough at anything, patterns will emerge.

But Dr. Barry had always talked more than he listened. What did he know? The painting reminded her of the story because her father and Cristina were describing the same place: the perfect home.

Maya laid her phone facedown on the bed. The painting disturbed her. She cradled her head in her hands. There was a reason she hadn't seen her father's book in years. A reason she rarely thought of it and had never mentioned it to Dan, but she'd never articulated that reason to herself. She had instead taken pills and drunk too much to forget. The only way to live with what happened, she had found, was to act as though it hadn't—but this took work. She had to studiously avoid anything that might remind her of Aubrey's death.

And that included her father's book. It hadn't been a conscious decision but one of many underlying beliefs that steered her behavior. The book was too upsetting. Maya had left it behind when she went away for college, tucked it away in its manila envelope on her bookshelf. But now that years had passed since she thought of it, and many days since she took her last Klonopin, it was plain that her father's story reminded her too much of the lie she'd been telling herself.

She had realized this about a year after Aubrey died. Maya had been home for a few days, heavily medicated and trying to move on with her life, when she decided to take the book down from the shelf. A panicky feeling had risen her chest the moment she began to read her own handwritten translation. She had felt like she was choking. And something told her that if she kept going, if she revisited this story with its buried meaning, it would unlock truths she couldn't bear to know.

So she had returned it to the shelf.

But Cristina's painting had reminded her. Like her father's book, she felt sure, it held the key to Frank's secret.

And the key went to a door inside her head. The harder

she searched for Frank, the more people she questioned, the more obvious it was that Maya was never going to find the answer outside of herself. It was locked within her, hidden in those hours she had lost. Dr. Barry would have said that she was teetering on the edge of psychosis, but Maya felt for the first time since she saw the video that she was getting somewhere. She rose from her bed and went to the bookshelf, reached for the old manila envelope—but grasped only air.

She remembered this wasn't her room anymore. She must have forgotten in the dark. She turned on the lights and realized she had no idea where the book was now. She searched the closet, the desk, the empty drawers of her old nightstand. She had taken off her clothes earlier because they were sweaty, but now she pulled them back on, shimmying into her damp leggings and long-sleeved shirt. She checked every shelf in the living room. She knew her mom wouldn't have gotten rid of her father's book.

Unless—what if she'd accidentally donated it to Goodwill?

Her mom had asked her to come home to take what she wanted before her old room became an Airbnb rental. But Maya hadn't come. She'd put it off for weeks, then months, before Brenda announced that she was taking everything to Goodwill, and Maya, still so merrily medicated at the time, hadn't cared. "No," she whispered now. "No, no, no . . ." She remembered her grandfather's face as he handed her the book. The precious ink. Her father's words. She walked back and forth a few times, running her hands through her hair.

Then she thought of the basement. Maybe her mom had been bluffing about Goodwill; maybe all she'd wanted was for her daughter to come home. Maya hurried downstairs, walking lightly so she wouldn't wake her mom.

The basement had scared her as a child. It was colder than the rest of the house, and musty. A long room that got darker the farther back you went. First there were the washer and dryer and a dresser that served as a folding table. Then a shelf lined with kitchen gadgets and the remains of DIY projects. A jar of marbles. Cans of paint, an ice cream machine. Beyond that, boxes of books, but not the one she was looking for. She went deeper. Waded through clothes in bins. *Please be here, please be here.* Crawling now, she opened a crate and found a tea set furred by dust. Another crate held the games she'd played. Sorry! Battleship. Clue. It was all here—her mom had saved everything. A wave of gratitude swelled in Maya's chest. She found her father's book in a box with other stories she had loved, the ones on her old shelf.

She took it upstairs and began to read.

TWENTY-THREE

I forgot I was the son of kings.

This was the title of her father's book. Maya had written it in English on the first page of the marbled notebook that held her translation. The notebook had been tucked into the manila envelope along with his forty-seven pages.

She was glad to have her translation, as she didn't have it in her to wade through the Spanish right now. Translating it had been a major endeavor for her at seventeen, difficult at first, but then it had gotten easier as she got the hang of it, or maybe she was just so immersed in the story unfolding in her hands that hours had passed like minutes. She'd worked on it at the library every day for almost two weeks and had been working on the very last page the day she met Frank.

She'd worked meticulously, searching for clues as to where the plot was headed. This had been the greatest mystery of her life then—and it was a mystery to her still. Holding the notebook in her hands brought back the old questions. Does Héctor remember that he's really Pixán? Does Pixán collect his inheritance? Does he ever make it home again? Is he reunited with his parents?

I forgot I was the son of kings.

Something clicked as she ran her eyes over the title.

The title!

Maybe she had needed to step away from the book for seven years in order to see the most obvious clue, the one typed on its very first page. She had been so focused on the story when she was younger, on the incomplete plot and what it meant, that she had forgotten about the poetry of its title. Her aunt had said it was a line from a very old poem Jairo had loved. Why hadn't Maya thought of this sooner? Her father had loved poetry—surely whatever poem he'd quoted would provide some clue as to what his novel was *about*. What it meant. What it was he'd been trying to say.

Her bed had become a nest, blankets, pillows, and pages heaped all around. She rifled through it for the phone and found it wedged between the headboard and mattress. She typed the title, in quotes, into her search bar.

The poem popped right up—it had its own Wikipedia page. And it wasn't exactly a poem, as it turned out, at least not as Maya understood it, but a hymn. "The Hymn of the Pearl." Carolina hadn't been kidding when she said it was old. It was ancient, its author unknown. According to Wikipedia, the hymn appeared in the apocryphal Acts of Thomas, which Maya understood to have something to do with the Bible.

The Acts of Thomas, she read, was from the third century—but apparently the hymn was even older. It appeared *within* the Acts, sung by Thomas, presumably the main character, while he was doing time in prison. The hymn told a story that had been around for at least a couple hundred years before the Acts was written, a story within a story. No one knew where it came from, though it bore traces of ancient folktales.

Maya wondered where her father had come across this very old hymn, and what, if anything, it had to do with the novel he'd begun to write. She scrolled down to "Extracts from the text" and read:

> When I was a little child,
> and dwelling in my kingdom of my father's house,
> and in the riches and luxuries of my teachers,
> I was living at ease.
> [Then] from our home in the East,
> after they had made preparations,
> my parents sent me forth.
> [. . .]
> Then they made with me an agreement,
> and they inscribed it in my heart so that it would
> not be forgotten:
> "If [you would go] down into Egypt
> and bring [back] the one pearl,
> which is in the middle of the sea
> surrounded by the hissing serpent,
> then you will put on your glorious garment

and your toga which rests (is laid) over it.
And with your brother, our second in command,
you will be heir in our kingdom."
[. . .]
I went straight to the serpent,
around its lodging I settled
until it was going to slumber and sleep,
that I might snatch my pearl from it.
Then I became single and alone,
to my fellow-lodgers I became a stranger.
[. . .]
But in some way or another,
they perceived that I was not of their country.
So they mingled their deceit with me,
and they made me eat their food.
I forgot I was a son of kings,
and I served their king.
And I forgot the pearl,
on account of which my parents had sent me.
Because of the burden of their exhortations,
I fell into a deep sleep.

Maya set down her phone. She picked up the notebook and read over the words so carefully translated into English in her own oversized handwriting from seven years ago. Her mouth hung open as she reread the story she had never really forgotten and saw the parallels: Pixán was clearly the "little child" of the hymn. And the "pearl" was the inheritance his parents had sent him to collect, while the "hissing serpent" was the difficult husband who didn't want to give it up. And just like that, Maya understood what her father had been doing. It wasn't so different from what Thomas, or whoever it was who wrote his Acts, had been doing when they embedded the very old hymn into *their* book.

But where Thomas had made it clear that a hymn was being recited, her father had chosen to hide it in the plot. He'd carried the old story on like an heirloom, bringing it into the present by slowing it down and coloring it in with moments from the life of a boy growing up in Guatemala City. He'd woven it in like a secret. Stretched the hymn out so that, had he lived to finish it, his novel would have been one long prayer. A surprised laugh rose in Maya's chest. She clasped a hand over her mouth, tears welling in her eyes. She'd solved the mystery, or at least one of them (though she sensed that were she to look closer, even this mystery would prove to be a symbol for one that ran even deeper, a truth coursing just beneath the surface). She pulled up the complete "Hymn of the Pearl" on her phone and read it beginning to end. And as she read, the contours of her father's story revealed themselves. And she finally understood how it ended.

TWENTY-FOUR

Maya doesn't want to talk to Aubrey but needs to know exactly what happened yesterday when Frank drove her home. A five-minute drive. Enough time for them to talk, to laugh, to flirt. Maya has never mistrusted Aubrey before, but now she's seen Frank's eyes traveling her body. That stupid fucking dress. It was only a glance, less than a second, but that look Frank gave Aubrey has expanded to fill hours of Maya's life.

She has not thought of much else since. Not while having dinner last night with her mom, or watching TV, or trying to sleep. Two weeks ago, she wouldn't have believed that she could be this upset over some guy she'd failed to notice at the library.

She wouldn't have thought anyone could come between her and Aubrey. Who do they have if not each other? Maya at least has her mom, but Aubrey hasn't gotten along with her mother in years and can't stand to be in the same room as her stepdad. She has boys who would take her out, who would probably do whatever she wanted, but only one best friend. Only one person who knows her through and through. It doesn't make sense that she would push Maya away.

And yet, the more she thinks about it—hasn't Aubrey been building up to this for weeks now? Maya thinks back to the coolness she observed. The anger Aubrey barely suppressed after she arrived at her house three hours late. The scarf she was knitting for someone she refused to name. The fact that she knitted at all. Until now, Maya had been sure she knew everything about her best friend. But obviously she was wrong.

Aubrey hasn't called her back, and it's been a full day now, which could mean any number of things, every one of which Maya has considered. Aubrey could be busy, she could be mad, or she somehow hasn't seen the call.

Or she could be avoiding Maya—because maybe something *did* happen on the drive. The thought is so foreign, so paranoid, that it could belong to someone else. Yet it snowballs: What if Aubrey and Frank decided to hang out after he dropped her off? What if Aubrey invited him inside?

It doesn't help that Maya hasn't been able to get in touch with Frank. She called the number he gave her a while back, but no one answered—which isn't surprising. He said the number is to the landline at his dad's house, where his dad is living out his last days. Frank told her they usually left the ringer off. And he doesn't have a cell.

He is, as it turns out, pretty hard to reach. Maya is only

THE HOUSE IN THE PINES

realizing this now, as she has never had to seek him out before. Frank has always come to her, calling her from the library or from his dad's house to make plans or simply showing up at her door. But now she hasn't seen him since he drove away with Aubrey, and it doesn't make sense—it was just the night before last that they kissed, that they told each other how they felt. Aubrey has ruined everything.

Maya is on her way to the library, walking down First Street, passing another church. She'll arrive just as Frank gets off work. She knows that showing up at his job may seem desperate, but how else is she supposed to reach him? She still doesn't understand why he was so upset that she had told Aubrey about the cabin. But whatever his reason, Maya wants to make things right. Clear the air.

She has, after all, already requested the deferral paperwork from BU. Her mom doesn't know this, of course, and Maya won't tell her until it's gone through.

She walks quickly. The sun is low, but the humidity holds the day's heat, and sweat dampens the back of her neck. She knows that she is probably blowing things out of proportion—Frank has probably just been busy, and Aubrey is probably being an inconsiderate jerk. Surely there is nothing to worry about, and yet Maya can't stop dwelling on the image of them driving away together in his car.

This must be why she thinks she sees them now, sitting together at a table in the window of the Dunkin' Donuts on the way to the library. It must be that she's been obsessing about them all day and has projected their faces onto two strangers. Her steps slow.

Could that really be the two of them talking over ice-blended coffees? Maya can only see the girl's back, but she recognizes the dark hair, the pale shoulders.

It's definitely Aubrey. And Frank.

He smiles the same smile that did Maya in, warm but sly and so strangely intimate.

Maya's heart thuds in her throat as she walks to the entrance. She knew it; she was right. If Frank sees her as she reaches for the glass doors of Dunkin' Donuts, he doesn't react.

Aubrey doesn't see her until she's a few feet away. Her lips part. Her eyes go wide.

Only then does Frank seem to register what's happening. Like Aubrey, he looks surprised, but he doesn't look guilty. "Hey!" he says.

Aubrey's face is pale.

Frank slides out of the plastic booth to greet Maya. He smiles, goes in for a hug. But Maya won't let him.

She steps back, ducking his touch—and this surprises him. He looks hurt. He tries to meet her eyes, but she glares past him at her supposed best friend.

"I just went to pick up a book," Aubrey says. "He recommended it to me yesterday—told me I should come pick it up." She holds up the book, a hardcover with a daguerreotype of what looks like a magician on its front. The magician wears a long black tailcoat.

"That's right," Frank says. "I told her about a book I thought she'd like, and I lent it to her. I work at a library. It's what I do. And because I was leaving, we walked over here for a coffee."

"Whatever," Maya says. "I don't care." But the words come out bitter, and Aubrey looks away.

Dunkin' Donuts is quiet, the only other customers a nurse picking up a large order and an old man dozing at a table by the door.

Frank sighs. "Sorry if I upset you, Maya. I was trying to do something nice for your friend."

"I'm not upset," she says. But her voice is a little too loud, her posture too stiff. Aubrey looks down at the table. No one talks, and Maya wonders if she's overreacted.

Is she being unreasonable?

When Frank speaks again, he sounds tired. Disappointed. "You know I hardly know anyone in town," he says to Maya. "I spend all my time with you or my dad. A man who's dying and a girl who's moving away. Would you prefer I don't make friends?" He gestures to Aubrey, who continues to look like she wants to disappear.

"Of course not," Maya says. Could she really be the bad guy here? "But . . . my best friend?"

"We both like magic," he says. "Illusions, mentalism, that kind of thing. It's nice to have someone to talk about it with." His eyes flit to Aubrey for confirmation, but she keeps her eyes on the floor.

Maya feels like she should apologize. But she doesn't and she won't.

"Anyway," Frank says. "I need to pick up my dad at his

support group. See you around, Maya." Then, to Aubrey: "Hope you like the book."

He takes his coffee with him, leaving a watery ring on the table.

Maya's face burns as he walks away.

As soon as he's gone, she turns to Aubrey. "You did this on purpose."

Aubrey shakes her head. There's a wince to her demeanor. "I know how it looks," she says, "but there's nothing going on between me and Frank."

"Whose idea was it to come here?"

"His. Definitely his."

Maya flinches but tries not to let it show.

"He started asking me about myself as soon as I got in his car yesterday," Aubrey says. "And the second I said I was into magic, he said there was this book I should read." Her eyes flick down to the book, its binding dangerously close to the puddle from Frank's cup. "He said I should pick it up from the library at seven."

"Yeah, well—doesn't mean you had to show up."

"I was curious. I thought I was just picking up a book. I know how Frank made it sound just now—like I *just so happened* to drop by as he was leaving work. But he's bullshitting you, Maya. He set it all up. The library book was just an excuse to see me again."

Maya clenches her jaw.

She can see that Aubrey doesn't like telling her this. She's not saying it to be hurtful, and that look on her face—the one Maya had mistaken for remorse—is actually pity. Au-

THE HOUSE IN THE PINES

brey feels sorry for her. And this is so much worse. They've had disagreements over the years, but until now, neither has truly wounded the other. "Oh, please," Maya spits. "You showed up at my house all"—how to say this?—"*dressed up* when you knew he would be there."

Aubrey doesn't try to defend herself. "I wanted to know what his deal was," she says. "You've been acting weird since you met him, and now I can see why. *He's* weird, Maya. He's controlling. And if I had to guess, I'd say he was the one who suggested you defer at BU?"

Maya doesn't answer. Why should she? She's pretty sure deferral was her own idea anyway. She wonders if Aubrey is enjoying this, if it delights her to point out how easily she captured Frank's interest.

"Listen," Aubrey says. "I'm not the bad guy here. I'm not trying to steal your boyfriend."

"Why not? Isn't Frank better than whatever lame townie you're going to end up with?"

Aubrey stands, picks up the book, looks down at her frozen Dunkaccino. The cup is almost full, but the drink is melted. She stares at it a moment, then shakes her head and throws it away. On her way out the door, she says to Maya, "You don't get it, do you?"

TWENTY-FIVE

Dawn sprang in like lions through the windows. Brenda had left for work at 4:30 a.m., so there was no one to wake, and Maya strode freely up and down the hall outside her old room in a T-shirt and purple sweatpants she had found in the basement. Moving helped her think. She understood her father's story now, but not what it meant in terms of Frank. Was it that Maya, like Pixán, had forgotten something important?

Or was it something else? Something more obvious?

Looking back on herself at seventeen was almost painful. She'd sat alone day after day at the library, so absorbed in the mystery of her father's book—translating it, taking notes, flipping carefully through its brittle pages—that she hadn't noticed the creepy part-time librarian who must have been watching her from behind the reference desk.

As she read the book, he had read her. It must have been easy. Anyone could see that she held those pages close. Of course Frank had used them to get to know her. He would also, as a library employee, have had access to her lending history and seen that she was interested in Guatemala. The Frank she knew could have easily made up the story about sneaking up a Mayan pyramid at dawn. She doubted very much now that this had happened, or that he had ever been to Guatemala, period. He must have figured it would impress her to say he had, and he'd been right.

But he hadn't stopped there. When he'd learned the book was written by her dead father, Frank's interest grew. Now she wondered if this was part of why he'd chosen her. Like Cristina, estranged from her parents, Maya had a hole in her life—and Frank had seen it as an opportunity.

He wanted to take up space in her life, to be the most important person to her—and he wanted it immediately. If she wasn't available when he wanted her to be—if she had plans with Aubrey, say—then he was going to make her late, punish her somehow.

The first time he asked Maya to tell him about her father was on a hot, lazy day as they sat in the grass on the town common, sipping on cherry slushies.

What do you want to know? she'd asked.

His story.

And he would have known that stories were all she had.

The one she told him was her favorite, one her mom had told her when she was young. Brenda had often told it to her before bed, and like so many stories told this way, parent to child, it had taken on the quality of a fairy tale over the years, polished smooth over countless tellings. Some details faded while others grew exaggerated, but the heart of it had stayed the same.

The story went that Maya's mom knew almost nothing about Guatemala before she went there, and this was part of what drew her to it. She was twenty-two years old and had never stepped foot outside the US. All three of her brothers had moved to other states, leaving only her there to care for her parents, still grieving the death of their elder daughter, as they aged. Part of Brenda had always known she'd never truly leave Pittsfield, which was maybe why another, less dutiful part of her had been desperate to get away. And Guatemala seemed to her about as far from Pittsfield as she could get.

The trip had been organized by a group affiliated with the church she'd opted out of as soon as opting out had been an option. It wasn't that she wasn't spiritual; she just didn't buy what the church was selling. She went to Guatemala not to preach the message of Christ but to see what she could learn. How she could let the experience change her. She went, in other words, to do the exact opposite of missionary work, which was typical of Brenda. She was oppositional. Always had been, in her quiet way.

Brenda was supposed to have stayed for a month. She was placed with a host family in Guatemala City, a middle-aged couple with two children: a daughter who'd moved away and a son, a college student, who lived at home.

The middle-aged couple were Maya's grandparents.

The son was Jairo.

Brenda felt shy around him from the start. He was shy around her too, which meant they hardly spoke for the first week she was there, even though they were often in the living room together. They learned each other slowly this way, in stolen glances and broken Spanish and silences that grew more and more comfortable. It soon became obvious that they had feelings for each other, but it seemed that nothing would ever come of it. They came from different worlds. And they were never alone.

Then one night Brenda woke to hear a strange sound outside her window. A rapid pecking punctuated by moments of silence, like a woodpecker, but there was something unnatural about it, as if it were mechanical. It was just loud enough to wake her but not so loud that it kept her up. Although she was curious about it, she soon drifted back to sleep.

She forgot about it until the next night, when it happened again. This time Brenda got out of bed and went to the window. She put her head out—there weren't any screens—and listened. The sound was coming from the roof. She looked up but couldn't see anything, so she got back in bed and fell asleep listening to the sound. She dreamed of a mechanical bird with copper feathers and gears for a heart, dreamed of it pecking at a branch, trying to tell her something in its strange, staccato code. Hinges creaked as it lifted its wings and flew away.

In the morning, she tried to explain the sound to her host family, but her Spanish was poor, and no one could help her. On the third night, as soon as she heard the pecking, Brenda got out of bed, tiptoed outside, and climbed up the rusty stairs that led to the roof.

The air was different on the roof, freer and more open than it was down below, where a cinder block wall surrounded the house on all sides. Brenda was scared as she looked around, having no idea what she would find, but her fear melted away because she saw that it was him.

Jairo. He sat at the edge of the roof, facing away from her, with his legs dangling over the side. He was holding something in his lap. The source of the sound. As Brenda got closer, she saw that it wasn't a mechanical bird but an old typewriter making all that noise. His fingers flew across the keys.

Jairo waited until everyone slept, then brought his typewriter to the roof, where the sound wouldn't wake anyone. Or so he had thought.

He apologized to Brenda for waking her, but she didn't mind. She stayed, and they talked until the stars faded and the sun rose, and after that, she took to joining him several nights a week up there. This was how they fell in love. On the roof of a house in Guatemala City, looking out over a wall topped with barbed wire. They talked about all kinds of things, and everyone complimented Brenda on how much her Spanish had improved.

No one knew about them yet, but they planned to tell his family soon. They wanted to be together and would have gotten engaged if Jairo hadn't been killed three weeks after Brenda found him writing on the roof.

Brenda didn't know that she was pregnant when she packed up her belongings and bid her host family a teary goodbye. It wasn't until three weeks later, when she found herself vomiting every morning, that she knew.

She had always wanted children, but this wasn't what she'd pictured. She knew it would be hard to raise a child on her own, not to mention that it would be years before her Catholic parents forgave her, but there was never any question that she would have the child. The story ended with what her mom called the happiest day of her life. The day Maya was born.

I can see why that book is so important to you, Frank had said.

He had seemed like such a good listener, but now Maya understood that he just knew the value of a person's stories. The ones that tell us about who we are and where we're from. Our personal creation myths, the ones we blow out candles for every year. Maya might as well have handed Frank a key to her head and her heart the day she told him the story of her dead father.

She saw this in the clear light of morning as she paused in her pacing to drink water at the kitchen sink. She told herself she needed to stay focused. She had hoped that reading the book would jostle something loose, some memory—and it had, but it was faint. She set down her glass, closed her eyes, and pressed her palms into the sockets. She could summon the smell of a cozy fire and the sound of a stream, but when she tried to recall what it was that she actually *saw* that night—what it was that happened after she went looking for the cabin—the only image her brain coughed up was that of Frank's key.

TWENTY-SIX

You don't get it, do you?

Aubrey's words simmer in Maya's head as she walks home. She's so distracted that she steps in front of a car as it pulls out of a gas station. The driver honks. The air smells like gasoline. Her plan had been to smooth things over with Frank, but instead the opposite had happened. He was upset with her when he left Dunkin' Donuts—but he was the one who'd made a point of seeing Aubrey again.

Why?

Her mom looks up as Maya walks in the front door. She's on the couch, feet on the coffee table, painting her toenails yellow. A nature documentary plays on TV. "What is it?" she asks.

"Nothing." Maya doesn't want to hear again about how Frank won't matter once she gets to BU. She goes to her room.

Her mom knocks gently on the door. "Hey." She peeks her head in. "Is this about Frank?"

Maya starts to cry. She's never been good at keeping things inside. She tells her mom that she caught Aubrey with Frank at Dunkin' Donuts.

"This is Aubrey you're talking about," her mom says. "Since when do the two of you fight over some guy?"

The words burn because Maya knows they're true.

"You've known him—what? Two weeks?"

"So?" Maya asks even as she sees her mom's point. "So what?"

"Do you think you might be a little too into him? When's the last time you looked at your father's book?"

Maya can't argue, so she doesn't, and her mom gives up and goes back to the living room and her nature documentary.

It's a good thing she doesn't know, Maya thinks, about her potential deferral at BU, as she would hate for her mom to share her awful uncertainty about the future. She has never been one of those teenagers who can't wait to get away from her family. Maybe it's because hers feels so small: her mom is often at odds with her parents, who continue to find reasons to be disappointed in her even now that they've forgiven her for having Maya. It's always been her and her mom against the world. These last few nights living at home would have been emotional under any circumstance, but instead of trying to cherish this time that she spends preparing and eating dinner with her mom, Maya thinks only of Frank. She hardly tastes the fresh basil in the eggplant stir-fry, or the coconut milk in the rice.

Instead she replays the smile she caught Frank giving

Aubrey, like he was her getaway driver in some romantic heist. Maya used to think that smile was just for her; now she doesn't know what to think. Frank had been so vulnerable with her the night before last, telling her painful things about his childhood, and had seemed so sincere when he confessed his feelings for her. *I spend all this time with you because there's no one else I'd rather be with.* She'd memorized the words as soon as they left his mouth. But had he meant them?

You don't get it, do you? Aubrey had said, and she was right. Maya doesn't have a clue. But after dwelling on it all throughout dinner with her mom in the garden at sunset, Maya decides she needs an answer. Because if Frank thinks he can kiss her and discard her for her (prettier) friend, he's going to have to tell her to her face. Maya won't leave town without knowing. If the library were going to be open tomorrow, she'd wait until then, but since it will be closed, she'll just have to go over to Frank's house and ask him.

She knows generally where that is (at the edge of the forest) and can probably find the exact address in the phone book. The only problem is getting there. It's too far to bike. She'll have to borrow her mom's car—but will her mom lend it to her knowing her plans?

"Did you feel that?" her mom asks.

"Feel what?"

A raindrop on her cheek. Maya looks up at the sky. It's lightly cloudy. "Should we go in?"

They wait. No more drops. They have brought out a

folding table and a pitcher of limeade and cups. "I think we're fine," says her mom.

Maya has an idea. "Hey, could I drop you off at work tonight and borrow the car?"

Her mom looks over at her.

"You know," Maya says, "since it seems like it could rain. I was thinking I might go over to Aubrey's tonight."

"Sure," her mom says, unsuspecting.

Another raindrop lands on Maya's shoulder. She feels her face getting hot.

The weather holds as Maya drives out past Onota Lake, where the houses grow farther apart and the trees closer together. There are hardly any lights along these narrow roads. She found Frank's father's address in the phone book, then matched it to the phone number Frank had given her— the phone number to the landline no one answers.

She almost misses the turn onto Cascade Street. Running along the edge of the state forest, it looks more like a paved trail than a street. Trees grow thick along both sides. Maya feels nervous. Frank has never told her what is wrong with his dad. He's used words like *malignant* and *terminal* but never named the illness, and she has never pressed him on it. Because who is she to make him talk about something painful?

Now she wishes that she knew more about what she was walking into. Here on this dark, wooded road, she feels less fired up than she did back home. She thinks back to the troubles Frank alluded to, the fights that had driven him into the forest as a child. There is so much Maya doesn't know about him, so much he's glossed over.

She is thinking about turning around when the mailbox appears on her right. She can see the number on it; the house itself is invisible from the road, set back at the end of a long driveway. Anyone who would choose to live out here must value their privacy—showing up like this could be seen as an intrusion.

And yet she has come all this way. And Frank has always felt free to drop in on *her*.

She tells herself she'll knock quietly so as not to wake Frank's father if he happens to be asleep. If no one answers, she'll turn around and drive home.

The house is bigger and more impressive than she expected. She had taken Frank's worn-out clothes and part-time library job as evidence that he, and by extension his father, weren't well-off. But now she sees that they live in a stately colonial with tall windows and a steeply gabled roof. Frank's car is parked out front, and all the downstairs lights are on.

Maya parks at the edge of the driveway and tucks her flip phone into her back pocket before getting out of the car. Now that she's here, she can't believe she's doing this. Even though they are fighting, she wishes Aubrey were with her.

Tall grasses brush her calves as she walks across the lawn. No one's mowed here in a long time. She hears crickets. The wind in the leaves. The moon is full but mostly hidden, and the air has a heavy feel. She takes a deep breath before knocking.

The footsteps are immediate. They hurry to the door, then pause. *Please be Frank, please be Frank.*

Frank's dad, an older, squatter, paler version of Frank, opens the door. Gray hair and a pronounced gut, but the same small chin. The same thin lips. His eyes narrow as he tries, and fails, to place her. "Who are you?"

"Hi, I'm Maya. I was wondering if—"

"Why are you here?" He speaks quietly but with urgency.

"I'm looking for Frank."

Bewilderment from his dad. "Frank? You're here for Frank?"

"Yes, but . . . if this is a bad time . . ." She can't tell what's wrong with him. He's edgy and strange but doesn't look sick.

"He's not here. I'll tell him you stopped by."

But Frank's car, she thinks. It's right there in the driveway. "Can I ask where he went?"

He waves his hand dismissively toward the woods. "Oh, somewhere out back."

Somewhere out back? "He's at his cabin?"

This question seems to catch him off guard. Then his surprise gives way to a smile that is chillingly like his son's but without the warmth, and it's like the difference between laughing with someone and laughing at them. "Yeah," he says. "I suppose that's where he is."

"How do I get there?" She tries to sound confident, but Frank's dad makes her nervous.

"To the cabin? You'd have to walk there, and it's dark out."

"I know," she says. But even mostly covered, the full moon is bright and there's a small flashlight on her mom's key chain.

"The road starts just back there," he says, a strange mirth to his voice that she doesn't like. He points around the side of the house. "Follow it until you come to a stream, then cross over. You'll find my son on the other side. It's not far, but you really should have a light. Do you?"

She holds up the key chain light.

"That won't be enough. Wait here."

While he's gone, she peers through the partly open door into the cluttered foyer. A small writing desk crouches at the base of wide, dark stairs, its top littered with unopened mail. Stacks of newspapers and what look like magazines or trade journals line the wall. She has a bad feeling. She knows she should leave but feels compelled by something darker than curiosity, some other impulse she doesn't try to name.

A light blinks on—a strong white beam—directly in her eyes. It blinds her, and she stumbles back, hands flying up to cover her face.

"Sorry," Frank's father says, standing right in front of her now. "Just making sure it works."

The light clicks off, but its afterimage is all she can see. He presses the heavy flashlight into her hand. She's disoriented as he follows her back outside and points her to the abandoned road out back. An old logging road, reclaimed by forest but still holding its shape. The smell of rain is in the air, rich, earthy. No one's driven on this road in a long time, its old asphalt carpeted in dead leaves and growing things. Saplings, ferns, moss. She's grateful for the flashlight as the trees thicken around her. She runs the light ahead of her as she walks. A rabbit darts across her path and she flinches. There are other dangers out here beside getting lost, and yet it's like she is helpless to turn around.

She tries to anticipate how Frank will react to her showing up unannounced. Why is he so secretive about the place?

You don't get it, do you?

Maya walks faster. She hears the stream before she sees it, a light trickle just ahead, and it reminds her of Frank's story about how it was that sound that led him back to the road when he was lost. The sound of its water as he described it to her was so clear that she feels something like recognition as she begins moving toward the bridge.

A cloud covers the moon. The flashlight flickers in her hand.

The door closes at her back.

"Wow," she says.

Frank has just let her inside and although she had known what to expect, nothing could have prepared her for this. The amount of work and love he must have put into the place. The level of skill. It's hard to believe this is the first cabin Frank has built. Tilting her head back, she looks up and recalls how he had used the term *cathedral ceiling*, and she hadn't known what he meant, but now she understands how a ceiling can make a place feel holy. The height, the soaring beams, everything made of pine and rose gold by the fire. Between its light and the many votive candles glittering on windowsills and countertops and the moonlight streaming through the windows, Maya can see everything, and it is beautiful.

"What do you think?"

"It's . . ." She turns to him. "Amazing." She doesn't mean to speak so slow. Moments ago, she'd been rushing here through the woods, all upset about Frank and Aubrey having coffee. (But then what? And why can't she remember crossing the bridge? Or knocking on the door, or Frank letting her inside? It's as if she has skipped the last few minutes like a track on a CD.) That hardly seems to matter now, though. All Maya knows is that being here, she feels better. Safe. She is ready to let go of all that other stuff.

She's just so happy to be here with him.

"Here," he says, offering her his hand. "Let me show you around."

Her hand is strangely hard to lift, so he catches it for her. He threads their fingers together. Her steps are unsure as he walks her around the airy, open floor plan. She feels heavy. Pleasantly drowsy. It must be the fire.

The stone fireplace is built into the wall. The gray stones go all the way up to the ceiling, smooth and round, ranging from the size of her fist to as large as a cantaloupe. Maya and Frank pause, basking in the warmth. She closes her eyes, feels the heat on her face. She smells the burning wood.

He leads her up a wooden ladder in the center of the

room. The ladder is made of the same honey-colored pine as the walls. The rungs are solid in her hands, polished to a shine, but like in the rest of the cabin, the natural unevenness of the wood has been preserved. The rungs are like branches.

The loft is like a tree house she might have wished for as a child. The ceiling slopes down to meet the floor on either side of an oversized bed covered with pillows and blankets. The perfect place to lie and look up at the stars through the round, curved skylight in the roof. Frank has lit candles here too, and she sees flowers arranged in a glass jar on the wooden table by the bed. He must have known that she was coming.

When she feels his hand on her shoulder, she thinks that he will lead her to the bed. And that she will go. But instead he guides her gently back down the ladder, telling her that he has something on the stove.

He's making them dinner, and when he pulls the lid off his pot, a fragrant wave of steam tumbles out. The smell of cooked meat and aromatics, earthy vegetables and comforting spices. Sage. Garlic. Her mouth waters, even though she already ate dinner. Frank sets two bowls on the table. It's a stew, but she can't tell what kind. Some kind of meat and vegetables.

"Do you remember," he says before picking up his spoon, "when I told you that I had never shown this place to anyone?"

She nods. She wants to start eating but thinks the polite thing would be to wait.

"Well, it's true," he says. He gazes at her from across the table, candlelight gleaming in his eyes. "You're the only one who's ever been here."

"Oh . . . I'm . . . honored."

"I don't invite just anyone," he continues. "This cabin . . . it means a lot to me. It's the one place my dad can't find me."

She flashes back to his father. His anxious eyes. His health. She can't explain why she has such a bad feeling about him.

Frank leans forward. He rests his forearms on the table. "I put everything I had into this place. I thought I had everything I needed. But you know what? It felt empty, lonely. I needed to bring someone else here, but not just anyone would be able to find it. But you, Maya. As soon as I saw you, I knew that I'd bring you here someday."

"Why . . ." she asks. Her hand rests on the spoon, but she doesn't pick it up.

"Why?" he says. "Because of the way I watched you read your father's book, day after day. It was like nothing else existed. I don't think you even knew where you were."

Maya tilts her head.

"And, of course," he adds, "I chose you because . . . well, look at you, Maya. You're beautiful."

This makes her redden. She has been called cute before, even pretty a few times, but only her mom has ever told her she's beautiful.

Frank looks like he's about to say something else—something big, like *I love you*. He looks vulnerable. Full of hope.

"I think you should stay," he says.

She blinks at him. "What?"

"Stay."

He smiles and leans back in his chair, relaxed. He picks up his spoon and begins to eat.

"Are you . . . asking me to move in?"

"Mm-hmm," he says around a mouthful of stew. "I'm asking you to think about it. Think how easy it would be. No need to pay rent or deal with some random roommate. Nothing to worry about. No trying to make it in the big, crowded city, trying to find a job. Here . . ." He opens his arms to her, welcoming. "You'd have all this."

"Frank, I . . ."

Something's definitely off here. She practically flew here tonight in a fit of jealousy, yet now she is thinking about moving in with him.

The fragrant steam rising from her bowl tickles her nose, distracting and enticing, and she thinks about how she *had*, after all, been thinking about deferring at BU. Her mom wouldn't like her living with Frank, but soon Maya will be eighteen and can do whatever she wants. And maybe this is what she wants. To be with Frank. To live in this beautiful cabin he's built.

Her mouth waters. Her stomach growls.

"You don't have to decide right now," he says. "Let's just enjoy dinner. You haven't even tried it yet."

Maya dips her spoon into her bowl but doesn't bring it to her mouth.

There's something about the sight of him across the

table, his face shrouded in steam. A half-formed image of people walking through clouds. Faces emerging from mist. Where was it that she'd seen this? In a movie?

"Maya?"

She stares at him, unable to explain her growing unease. The image, remembering where it's from, feels urgent, like a gas stove accidentally left on in the kitchen. A thing she must articulate, must attend to before something bad happens.

"What are you thinking about?"

"Something's . . . wrong."

"Oh, sweetie . . ." He smiles lovingly at her. "Nothing's wrong."

She closes her eyes, unease blooming into dread.

Caras en la niebla. The words come to her in Spanish, though she doesn't know why. *La niebla*—she only recently learned the word for mist, having come across it while translating her father's book.

Her father's book! The village in the clouds. This is what she's reminded of here—Pixán's true home, the place he yearns for. She opens her eyes to find Frank staring at her. A wave of dizziness.

"Listen to me," he says. "Whatever's wrong, we'll figure it out together. Nothing to worry about."

But the story feels like a warning. Like Pixán, Maya has forgotten something. Her heart beats faster as she thinks back to the last moment she can recall before arriving here: The sound of water as she approached the bridge. The flickering flashlight in her hand. "Why . . ." she says, face growing crowded. "Why can't I remember?"

Frank sets down his spoon. He stands, walks slowly around the table, never breaking eye contact, his face calm.

Maya begins to shiver.

He kneels at her side, eye level, as if he intends to propose.

Her shivers grow deeper. The cold is in her bones.

"Relax," he says. "You're having a panic attack."

He takes her left hand, which she has curled into a fist, and pries it open, finger by finger. He presses something small and hard into her palm. She knows what it is before she sees it. She feels its metal teeth.

———————

The rain strikes her face, her arms, her chest. She draws a sharp breath. The drops are like a bucket of ice water sloshed unexpectedly on her head. She clutches her elbows, unsteady on her feet.

Frank is there to catch her. He walks beside her, arm around her shoulders, his father's flashlight in the other hand. He shines it on the ground just ahead of Maya so she won't trip over anything as they make their way back down the abandoned road. The forest is dark. "What—what's happening?" she asks, but her voice is lost beneath the drumming of rain on leaves, branches, and earth. The rain soaks her clothes, running in rivulets from the frayed hem of her shorts.

Her hands feel raw, and when she looks at them, she sees dirt. There's dirt on her palms and knees. She stops walking, shrugs out from under the weight of Frank's arm. Turns to face him.

He looks worried. "What is it?" His voice is measured, but his jaw is tight, as if he's more upset than he's letting on. He doesn't try to shield himself from the rain plastering his hair to his scalp.

"What the hell is going on?" she asks.

He looks confused.

She can't stop shivering.

He opens his arms to her, offering warmth, but she flinches away from his touch, and he looks hurt. But this time she's sure of it. This time there's dirt on her hands and knees, and the fact that she doesn't know how it got there chills her more than the cold rain.

"What did you do to me?"

The question takes him aback. He raises his hands as if to show her they're empty, that he doesn't mean her harm. "You said you wanted to leave," he says. "Asked me to walk you back to your car, so that's what I'm doing."

Bewildered, she looks back over her shoulder, as if the way they'd come might hold a clue to the last few minutes, but all she sees is the overgrown road disappearing into dark woods. "Why can't I remember?" she asks. The wind picks up, sharpening the rain. She shouldn't be here. Aubrey was right—Frank is weird—and for the first time, she senses he could be dangerous.

She turns and continues walking in the direction they've been going, hoping that it is, in fact, the way back to her car.

"Wait, Maya." But the note of pleading in his voice makes her walk faster. He follows her, lighting her path even as she tries to get away from him. She breaks into a run as soon as she sees the dark outline of his father's house, the rain pounding, her sneakers kicking up mud. She's soaked and out of breath as she crosses the wild lawn to the street where her car is parked and unlocks her door with trembling hands. She turns back, expecting to see Frank, but now he's gone, and the only sound is rain and her own heaving breath and heart.

TWENTY-SEVEN

Thanks for this, Maya texted Steven at nine a.m., which felt like the earliest she could reasonably text someone she didn't know very well.

It's beautiful, she added, referring to Cristina's painting as well as to the warm home it portrayed. Maya had forgotten. These days, when she thought of Frank's cabin, she thought only of the time she had lost, dirt on her knees and hands, and fear as she ran through the woods to her car.

What she'd forgotten was the wonder of entering Frank's cabin for the first time, but Cristina's painting reminded her, the loving details of the fireplace, the natural wooden beams. Somehow, though she often dreamed of it, Maya hardly remembered (while awake) how the place looked and all the thoughts that had flown through her head as she first took it in. Now the table in the painting brought back the memory of sitting across from Frank over bowls of some soup he'd made. That tantalizing smell, her sudden hunger—it was as if the place had cast a spell.

But Maya never tried the soup, did she?

Then—as now—her father's story leapt to mind.

This time it came to her in the form of the hymn. *So they mingled their deceit with me . . . and they made me eat their food . . . I forgot I was the son of kings.*

And as it had then, the story felt like a warning. What was it she'd forgotten? The last thing she remembered of that night—just before finding herself in the rain—was thinking of Pixán's true home and the beginning of a realization that never came because Frank put a stop to it.

Her phone pinged, disrupting her train of thought.

It was Steven; he'd responded to her text with a thumbs-up.

Wondering if you might be around to talk about this later? she wrote back. *Maybe I could buy you a drink?*

She waited.

She still hadn't slept. She walked around the neighborhood on aching legs, hoping to exhaust herself, and her body was certainly tired enough, but her mind and heart galloped on. The streets were cold and quiet. The snow in the gutters had melted and frozen again into a jagged slush the same gray as the sky.

Dan hadn't written back, and now it had been two days. Maya would have been worried if his social media accounts weren't public, or rather she'd have been a different kind of worried. She told herself that at least she knew he was okay and tried to leave it at that. Because she couldn't let herself think about his silence and what it meant. Not now. Back home, she shivered on the floor of the shower, cloaked in steam, but she couldn't warm up. She told herself this had to be the worst of it. Her withdrawal could only get better from here. She crawled into bed afterward and passed out for forty-five minutes, only to jolt up at the sound of her phone.

Sure, Steven had texted back.

Maya disentangled herself from the sheets wrapped around her torso and typed, *Great! What time?*

I get off work at five. How's Patrick's? Patrick's was the pub around the corner from the museum.

Sure! Maya texted back. *Thank you!*

She ventured out of the dim Airbnb room to find her mom putting up a Christmas tree in the living room.

"There you are!" Brenda said, smiling. "Just in time to help with decorations."

Maya scowled.

Her mom flinched. They had always decorated the tree together when Maya was young. A crate of ornaments sat on the floor, silver tinsel spilling through the slats. Brenda was doing all she could to make amends with her daughter. Other than apologize, it seemed.

Maya was still mad but unwilling to argue further. Her mom wasn't the only person who could pretend like nothing was wrong. "I have plans," she said. "I'm getting together with Erica O'Rourke."

"Erica from the school newspaper? Didn't realize you were still in touch."

Maya wasn't. She hadn't kept in touch with anyone from

high school beyond the occasional email, but Erica was someone she had been friendly with and who still lived in town. A plausible lie. "We're going for coffee. Catching up."

Her mom peered at her over teal reading glasses.

Maya had washed her hair and clothes and put on makeup. She felt almost refreshed after her nap.

"Why don't I drive you?"

"No," Maya said a little too quickly. If her mom had any idea what she was up to, she'd get on the phone with Dr. Barry.

Brenda narrowed her eyes.

"I could use the walk is all. We're meeting at that new café on North Street—it's less than a mile." She didn't wait for her mom to try to stop her. "I'll only be a few hours," she said as she slipped out the door.

Patrick's was an Irish pub that had been around as long as Maya could remember. Blessedly dark inside, with exposed brick walls and a long row of beers on tap. It smelled like onion rings. Maya was a few minutes early, so she ordered an extra-dry martini, even though she was still hungover from last night's gin. Alcohol was the one thing she knew would loosen the vise that withdrawal had clamped around her head. She took her martini to a small table in the corner and drank most of it in a few gulps that burned the whole way down, then faded to a pleasant warmth. The bar was quiet, most of the booths empty. Classic rock played on the speakers. She raised a hand as Steven walked through the door.

He got himself a beer and came over. He seemed less guarded than when they'd met, but still reserved, or maybe just shy. He was at least a decade older than Cristina and was wheezing from his walk from the museum, but he wore a Fitbit and a nice wool coat over his security guard uniform. He respectfully removed his hat, a tan beanie, upon entering, revealing his polished-looking head. Maya had sensed by the strength of his reaction to her earlier questions that he been in love with Cristina, and wondered how she had felt about him.

"Hey, thanks for meeting me," she said.

"No problem, happy to talk about Cristina's work. I want more people to see it." He set his phone on the table and pulled up a picture. "I brought another one to show you." The painting was of a cold and severely shaded landscape that might have been the salt flats again, but flooded this time, pewter water mirroring an inhospitable sky. "This one's my favorite," Steven said. "You really have to see it in person, but even here you can see how striking it is."

"Beautiful. She really was talented."

"I'm trying to get ahold of all her work, but it's been hard since I'm not family. Her paintings belong in a museum."

"I agree," Maya said carefully. "Especially her last one. Interesting how different that one is."

"Isn't it?"

Maya nodded thoughtfully and sipped her drink. "Did she ever tell you about Frank's cabin?"

Steven deflated a little as he gathered what Maya was

here to talk about, and she wondered why he'd come. Was it to talk about Cristina's work—to keep it alive in the world—or might he have thought Maya was asking him on a date? She was, after all, his type, it seemed. "Sure," he said, "she mentioned it."

Maya waited.

He sipped his beer, a sour look on his face.

She felt for him and would have dropped the questions if it weren't her life that was in danger. "Cristina must have really liked it there," she said leadingly. "To have painted it that way . . ."

Steven sighed, resigned. "You could say that," he said. "The cabin was one of the first things she told me about him. I remember it impressed her, and to be honest it impressed me too. I mean, who else our age owns a home? Not to mention builds their own? But then the more I heard about him, the less impressed I was. Honestly, the guy's a loser."

"Why?" she said, hiding her agreement.

Steven's mouth puckered with distaste. He sipped his beer. "Well, for one thing, he didn't have a job. Cristina didn't know how he made his money, but apparently he had clients of some sort."

"Clients?"

"Yeah, but don't ask me what he did for them. My guess is he was actually living off an inheritance. His dad was some big professor at Williams who died several years ago."

Maya wasn't surprised to hear that his father had passed away—though it reminded her that she'd never learned what was wrong with him.

"Not to mention," Steven added, "that Frank basically hangs out at a bar every night. The Whistling Pig. Cristina would go with him sometimes. I never knew her to hang out at bars before Frank."

Maya filed this away for later. She looked down into her drink, where a shiny olive sat pickling in her last sip of martini. "Did she ever mention anything . . . strange that happened at the cabin?"

Steven looked annoyed. "Not that I can think of. Why?"

"Another round?" said the waitress.

"Yes, please," Maya said, at the same time that Steven said, "No, thanks." He wasn't even halfway through his beer. She saw him watching her through the bottom of her martini glass as she tossed back the last briny sip.

"I ask because Frank brought me there too," she said. "Only once, but he did something to me there. I blacked out."

"*What?*"

"As I was arriving and as I was leaving," Maya said. She'd never seen the bridge or the outside of the cabin. "I had dirt on my hands and knees afterward, and I still don't know why."

"Jesus, that's . . . I don't know what to say. I'm sorry to hear it." He sounded like he meant it. "What do you think he did to you?"

"That's what I'm trying to find out."

The waitress returned with Maya's martini, and she took a fortifying sip before continuing. "Frank was secretive about his cabin. I never knew why. He said I was the only person he'd ever brought there, and now he's brought Cristina there too. And I can't help but think that whatever he did to me . . . he probably did to her too."

This clearly upset Steven. His whole hairless head flushed red.

Maya leaned in closer. "Whatever's he's hiding," she said, "it's there at his cabin. Which is why I need to go there—it's the only way. But I'm scared. I don't want to go alone."

"You're asking me to go with you." He sounded both taken aback and not at all surprised that she'd ask this of him.

She nodded.

He was quiet for a long time. The bar had begun to fill, and someone had turned up the music. Finally, appearing to arrive at some conclusion, he pulled up Cristina's painting of the cabin on his phone. "Look," he said, "I don't doubt that Frank hurt you. I had a bad feeling about him from the start. But I just don't think Cristina would have painted *this* if he . . . did something to her. Like you said, she seemed to really like it there."

Maya's eyes filled with tears, but she managed to keep them from falling.

"I know she did," Steven said, his tone growing soft, "because she gave me something else before she died. She gave me a few things, actually—like I told you, she said she was getting rid of some stuff. She'd remembered that my old coffee maker was broken, so she gave me hers." Now he was the one verging on tears.

Maya bowed her head. "She sounds kind."

"I didn't make coffee in it until the next morning," he said. "And when I did, when I went to fill it with water, I found a note she'd left me inside the little tank." His mouth trembled. "I'm not going to tell you everything the letter said. But I will say that she apologized for the way she'd been acting. She thanked me for being her friend. And she said she was going to live with Frank in his cabin."

Maya's blood froze.

"Might not make sense to you or me, but she loved the guy." Steven sounded resentful. He took a small sip of his beer, then set the rest at the edge of the table as if he was done.

Maya reached for her own drink but found it empty.

"I came here," Steven said, "because you said you wanted to talk about Cristina's painting. Her art. But I don't think it's good for me to speculate about what might have gone on between her and Frank. Nothing I can do about it anyway."

"I understand," Maya said as she reached for her purse. "I'm sorry." She dropped her wallet on the floor.

"Are you all right?" He sounded tired, as if he'd only asked because he felt obligated.

"Fine."

"Did you drive here?"

She shook her head. The waitress returned with the bill. "I got this," Maya said.

"Sure you don't want a ride?"

"No, thanks. I could use the walk."

"Be careful," he said.

"It's not far," she assured him.

"If you go to Frank's cabin, I mean. I know you didn't ask for my opinion, but if I were you, I'd stay away from that place."

TWENTY-EIGHT

Maya wakes refreshed, birds singing in her window. The clock reads 10:42, much later than she usually sleeps. She yawns, turns over, content to sleep a little longer, because why not, it's summer, but then she spots the wet clothes crumpled on her bedroom floor and remembers last night.

She bolts up. She had planned to tell her mom about the time she lost in the woods with Frank. She gets out of bed, hurries down the hall. The house is quiet, her mom in her room with the door closed.

Just as she's about to knock, Maya thinks of the overnight shift she worked. Her mom could really use the sleep, and now that she's paused here a moment, Maya asks herself what it is she will say.

She's less sure of herself today, and last night is already feeling like a blur, a vague impression, almost as if Frank drugged her, but then—how could he have? It's not like she ever tried his soup, or anything else at the cabin. Never drank or smoked anything. So she'd spaced out a few minutes here and there—is that really so unusual for her? She has been known, after all, to gaze out of windows rather than listening to her teachers at times and has missed many a bus stop due to daydreaming. She's been this way since long before she met Frank.

Could someone like her really blame him for lost time?

She returns to her room. Maybe she'll tell her mom later.

Maya began packing for college weeks ago, then stopped after she met Frank. How strange to consider this now—that she actually thought about deferring. After all the work she poured into earning a full ride at BU.

What the hell was she thinking?

She resumes packing to distract herself from her uneasiness, and it works. Her thoughts turn to her soon-to-be dorm. Warren Towers is home to over 1,800 undergraduates, and in three days, she will be one of them, surrounded by people her age from all over the country and the world. Her new roommate is named Gina, she's from San Francisco, and Maya can't wait to meet her.

Each of them will have, on her half of the room, a narrow bed, a desk, a dresser, a shelf, and a slim closet. Not a lot of space, but Maya has plans for her side. She'll hang her Salvador Dalí poster, the one of elephants on legs like stilts, and her cork bulletin board covered with photos, most of them of Aubrey and her. Maya will only have room for her favorites of everything at the dorms: CDs, clothes, decorations, and books, including, of course, the one her father wrote.

Her father's book sits on her desk. She hasn't looked at it much since meeting Frank. As she picks it up, she flashes back to last night, steam rising from their bowls at the table. Her father's book is the last thing she remembers thinking of before she found herself walking in the rain with Frank.

It used to be that these pages made her think of her father, but now they bring back the smell of Frank's cabin—his soup, the fire, the cold night air—so she leaves them behind. Tells herself she won't have time to read the book anyway once classes start.

Moving on to her closet, she takes out a chunky sweater that will be good for fall, and her thoughts turn to fall in Boston. Cool days and crisp, glittering nights. Foliage in the city. Halloween parties. It's like all the excitement she should have been feeling for the past few weeks is finally upon her, and now she can't wait. Strange, she thinks, how she has thought of only Frank pretty much since the day they met, yet today it's like all her outsized feelings for him—the longing, the jealousy—were a house of cards that suddenly collapsed.

Aubrey was right. She'd mistrusted him from the start. Which is probably—Maya suddenly realizes—why she wore the red dress: to bring to the surface what she had sensed in Frank before she even met him. That he was bad for her best friend. Maya can't explain, much less excuse, the way she's been acting these past few days, but she can apologize.

They've argued over small things before, like what DVD to rent at the video store, but never anything like this.

She'll apologize before the Tender Wallpaper concert tonight. She has her ticket tacked to the corkboard on her wall, and the band sticker that came with it stuck to her nightstand. Around noon, she goes to the kitchen for cereal and a glass of orange juice. The phone in the kitchen blinks red with missed calls—the ringer's on silent, as it usually is after her mom works a night shift.

She gets a bad feeling even before she sees who the seventeen calls are from.

As she goes to check, the receiver lights up with yet another call.

It's him.

She recognizes his father's landline on the caller ID and sets the receiver down as if it were alive. She doesn't want to answer but knows that if she doesn't, he'll keep trying until someone picks up—and Maya doesn't want that person to be her mom.

"Hey," she says.

"Hey, Maya . . ." He's always been so confident, so cool, but now he sounds raw and anxious. "How are you?"

"Fine."

She should've thought more about what she was going to say. How she would tell him.

"You seemed pretty upset last night. I was worried."

She considers explaining why she was upset, but doesn't, because what good would it do? Frank's a liar. She just needs to make him stop.

"Maya?"

"I'm here." She takes the cordless phone to the porch, so she won't wake her mom.

"What are you up to today?"

"I'm actually pretty busy . . ." she says as gently as she can. "I have a lot to do before I go . . . Listen, I don't think we should see each other again." This feels like the easiest way out—quick and to the point. And it's true she wants to spend what little time she has left with the people she's going to miss the most: her mom and Aubrey. Maya's only sorry she didn't realize this sooner.

Frank is quiet a long time. "Okay," he says. "Cool. No problem."

She exhales.

"Oh, so the other reason I was calling," he adds, "and I hope this isn't weird, but I was wondering if you could hook me up with Aubrey's number?"

A knee-jerk flash of envy is unavoidable—it was only yesterday that this question would have punched a hole right through Maya—but today it is hard not to laugh at Frank's pitiful attempt to make her jealous. "Sure," she says with purposeful, pleasant indifference. "I don't see why not. Do you have a pen?"

"Mm-hmm." A yes through clenched teeth.

"Four-one-three . . ." she begins. But then it occurs to her that Aubrey probably wouldn't want Frank to call her.

"Hello?"

"You know," Maya says, "I should probably ask before giving out her number."

Frank lets out a dark, sarcastic laugh. "How is it," he asks, "that you can be jealous of Aubrey at the same time that you so obviously look down on her?"

"I have no idea what you're talking about," she says angrily. "Listen, Frank, I have to—"

"You know what I'm talking about. You don't want me to call her, do you?"

Maya grips the phone tighter. "I honestly don't care what you do, Frank."

"You don't want me to call her, but at the same time, you don't want to call her either. I've seen the way you treat her, it's like she doesn't matter. Like she's some townie and you're not. Like you're smarter, you're going places, and she's a loser for staying here."

"What?! But I—"

"And now you're doing the same thing to me. Blowing me off because I'm not good enough, just like I've seen you blow off your best friend and your own mother whenever you had something better to do."

Her eyes sting with tears.

"I mean, is there *anyone* you're loyal to?"

"Fuck you, Frank. Don't ever call me again." She hangs up.

But Frank does call again. And again and again.

Eventually she has to tell her mom, who has taken the day off work and is relieved to hear the relationship is over. "We'll just leave the ringer off," her mom says. "I'm sure he'll get the message. Let's get out of the house, go do something."

Maya feels her departure in the air as they hike up Bousquet Mountain that afternoon. She remembers when she was little, and her mom had to carry her part of the way. Now they walk straight up the slope without stopping, in and out of the chairlift's frozen shadow. Her mom yodels when they reach the top, as usual, something that usually embarrasses Maya, but today it makes her smile, and when she looks out over the hemlock and white pine sea and sees her hometown in the distance, it's more beautiful to her than the Alps. She can't explain the tenderness she feels today, not just toward her mom but toward Pittsfield as well. To be from here is to know the Housatonic River, to have walked alongside it, maybe crossed it on the way to school each day, but been unable to swim in it because General Electric had contaminated the river with PCBs. It's to have grown up either *before* GE left—back in the days of holiday window displays at England Brothers, the popcorn wagon on Park Square, and cruising North Street on Thursday nights—or to have grown up after. Maya has wanted to leave Pittsfield for so long, but now, even before she has left, she feels as though she is seeing it through the eyes of someone who's already gone.

———

Summer is fading, the light tinted orange, and for the first time in a while, it isn't too hot out as Maya parks on the street in front of Aubrey's duplex. It's late enough that most of the birds have gone quiet, but a single mockingbird sings in the hemlock out front.

THE HOUSE IN THE PINES

Aubrey is knitting again on her porch, bare feet kicked up on the wooden railing. She wears cutoff shorts and a D.A.R.E. shirt, not dressed yet for the concert, but then again Maya is early.

"Hey," she says. The porch creaks as she crosses it and sits in the other plastic patio chair.

"Hey," Aubrey says. She puts down her knitting. She's still working on the scarf she began the day they went to Wahconah Falls, the day Maya learned that Aubrey knitted. Now the scarf is almost finished, and its pattern is apparent. Stripes of lime green and viridian.

"Pretty colors," Maya says.

"Glad you like them." Aubrey relaxes into a genuine smile. "This is for you. A going-away present."

And, once again, Maya thinks she might cry. She has carried Frank's words with her all day, each one a heavy stone she takes as punishment, because the truth is she has been jealous of Aubrey's beauty, and although she hadn't realized it, not until Frank pointed it out, a small part of Maya had looked down on her choice to stay in Pittsfield. "Wow," she breathes. "Thank you. I'm sorry I've been such an asshole these past two weeks."

Aubrey is quiet. "I don't know about asshole, but yeah, you've been kind of a jerk." Her tone is light. She swigs from a can of orange soda on the plastic table, then offers some to Maya, who accepts it gratefully.

I mean, is there anyone *you're loyal to?*

"But," Aubrey says, "it's not like I've been the world's best friend either."

It's true, Maya thinks—but then, a bigger part of her understood from the start that this is just Aubrey's way. She hasn't had other long-term friends. And isn't it easier to say goodbye to someone you can't wait to get away from?

"So, yeah," Aubrey says. "Me too. Sorry."

Their apologies hang between them. Maya doesn't even consider bringing up the red dress.

Aubrey snorts out a laugh. "We're such jerks."

Maya laughs too, and the laughter builds until there isn't any awkwardness left.

Aubrey's little brother, Eric, wanders home as the sun sets, clutching a set of cards. "Hey," he says, dawdling on the porch. He looks up to his teenage sister and knows he could be shooed away at any second. "Guess what?" he says. "I got my Charizard back!"

"No way!" Aubrey says. "Way to go, dude."

Eric beams and shows them a Pokémon card, a little orange monster on its front. Maya's known him since he was six, blue eyes wide with curiosity at whatever his cool big sister and her friend were up to. Maya used to think he was annoying, but now she has an urge to hug him. "Nice!" she says about the card.

"There's mac 'n' cheese on the stove," Aubrey says.

"What are you guys doing?" he asks.

"Just talking, Smalls. Go inside and eat."

He looks disappointed but does as she says.

Maya's about to tell her about Frank when Aubrey says, "I decided to apply to LSU. Not this year, obviously, but next."

"What? Oh my god!"

"I know!"

"Why LSU?"

Aubrey thinks Louisiana is cool, all the bayous and Spanish moss and Mardi Gras in New Orleans. She wants to catch beads at a rowdy parade. The other reason is that she has a scheme to pay in-state tuition. "My mom has a cousin, Justina," she says, "who lives in Lafayette, and as of today, I get all my mail at her house. Next month I'll visit so I can register to vote there and sign up for a library card. I've also been checking Craigslist for a onetime temp job I can do while I'm there, stuffing envelopes or something, so I can establish a work history."

"You think that'll work?"

Aubrey looks hopeful. "Maybe?"

"I bet you'll get in."

"They have a high acceptance rate. Seventy-five percent or something. Still have to figure out what I want to study."

"That's okay, a lot of people don't know going in."

"You do."

Maya shrugs. She would, of course, be an English major so she could study the magical realists as her father had and go on to become the renowned writer he should have been. "You write poetry," she says. "Maybe you could do creative writing too?"

"I was thinking more along the lines of psychology. I've always been interested in why people do what they do. Then there's philosophy . . . I honestly don't know anything about that, but I *want* to, you know? Feels like something I'd like."

"Definitely," Maya says. "You're *so* philosophical."

Aubrey smiles, happier than she's looked all summer. "And," she adds offhandedly, "just in case I don't get into LSU, I'll also apply to UMass Amherst, UMass Lowell, and, um . . . BU."

Maya rushes in to prop up her best friend's pride—Aubrey would hate anyone, even Maya, to think that she was following them. "Good idea—but I'm totally sure you'll end up at LSU. And it'll be amazing and I'll come visit you and—"

"We'll go to New Orleans!"

"Yes!"

They beam at each other. The sky is getting dark.

"You know," Aubrey says, "I don't think I'd do this if not for you."

"Oh, I don't know . . ."

"No, really. College always seemed like something other people do. Never thought I wanted to go, but then when you got in, and you went to see the dorms and started talking about classes you were going to take . . . it made me so jealous I didn't know what do. And it made me realize that—duh—I *do* want to go to college. And why the hell shouldn't I?"

Fireflies blink in the yard, a restless constellation that Maya and Aubrey watch for a while before going inside to get ready. When Aubrey asks about Frank, Maya considers telling her everything—about his beautiful yet eerie cabin in the woods and the time she lost there—but with every hour that passes, the more improbable that all seems. The fuzzier her conviction. Not to mention that tonight is supposed to be fun, and she doesn't want to make this about Frank too. Doesn't want to revisit what he said to her on the phone. "You were right" is all she tells Aubrey for now. "Long story, but yes—Frank is definitely weird."

Tender Wallpaper is a trio of sisters who harmonize as only sisters can to the accompaniment of synthesizers and percussion. They and their music are moody and theatrical, appearing onstage draped in sequins and underwater lighting. Their sound is vaguely underwater too, siren-like, a shipwrecked warble to the piano. Maya and Aubrey have seen them in concert once before, and last time the band capitalized upon their sisterhood by dressing as the Three Fates. A giant spool of platinum thread figured into the choreography: one sister unspooled the thread, another measured it, and the third snipped it with a large pair of scissors.

But tonight Maya can't discern the theme. She and Aubrey have pushed their way up to the front of the medium-sized venue and are standing near the stage, swaying along to the music. The sisters wear long, slinky gowns and capes, one dressed entirely in green, one in red, one in blue.

"Who are they supposed to be?" Maya asks Aubrey between songs.

Aubrey smiles. "Really? You can't figure it out?"

A new song begins as Maya puzzles over the concert's theme, but she can't think of any other famous trios that the sisters might be dressed as and she starts to wonder if Aubrey is messing with her. It would be a very Aubrey thing to do.

Toward the end of the show, the sisters begin fluttering their fingers over the audience as if casting spells, and the lights go crazy, beams of green, red, and blue overlapping into darker hues as the voices build into what sounds less like harmony than the single voice of some enormous, divine, not-quite-human creature.

"Just tell me," Maya says when the song is over.

Aubrey cups her hands over her friend's ear and says, "Flora, Fauna, and Merryweather."

Of course! The fairy godmothers in *Sleeping Beauty*. Maya hasn't seen the movie since she was a child, but now it comes back to her, the colorful spells unfurling from magic wands. A magic cake. A magic dress. Of course Aubrey remembered this. She loves fairy tales and magic. And sad songs. The last song of the night is her favorite, and when it comes on, she closes her eyes and disappears into the music.

TWENTY-NINE

Maya waited once more for her mom to fall asleep before taking her keys and driving her car to Frank's cabin. Nighttime wasn't ideal, but Brenda never would have let Maya borrow the car, not in her current state, all feverish, fidgety, and seized by an urgency she refused to explain. She just hoped Frank was at his usual bar tonight rather than at his cabin. Her plan was to go there, look around, peer in through the windows if it seemed no one was home. If nothing else, she imagined just being there would bring her closer to the truth, seeing as how the painting, a single image, had triggered memories she thought she had lost.

She drove faster as she left downtown, with its traffic lights and other cars. Two hours had passed since her second martini at Patrick's Pub—she'd made sure of this before driving, and had even forced down a bowl of leftover chili while assuring her mom, between bites, that it was just as delicious as it had always been. She just wasn't hungry.

Seven years ago, Maya had almost missed her turn onto Cascade Street, but this time her phone made it easy, stating the directions from the passenger seat—for now, anyway, while she still had service. The trees crowded in. The state forest, so green in summer, was skeletal this time of year, and Maya had no problem spotting the mailbox as she approached it on her left. She seemed to remember more than she knew.

She parked at the end of the long, winding drive and walked the rest of the way to what once was Frank's father's house. Someone else must have bought it by now, although she supposed it was possible, if Frank had, in fact, collected a large inheritance, that he'd kept it. Her heart sped up as she approached the house and saw a light on in one of the upstairs windows. It wasn't as nice as she remembered, or maybe it had gone downhill in the last seven years. The porch sagged, the paint peeled, and two of its shutters were missing.

She slowed her steps and walked lightly, as if whoever was inside might hear her sneakers crunching over snow. In summer, she might have stayed low as she crossed the wide yard, hidden in the tall grass, but if anyone were to look out the window right now, they'd see her starkly against a white sheet. The moon brought out its arctic blue. An ancient poplar loomed at the entrance to the abandoned road, its rounded mass of huddled gray limbs reminding her of a brain.

She passed beneath its lobes, twigs branching like arteries overhead as she entered the forest. This time she had a flashlight, one she'd borrowed from her mom, but Maya found that she didn't need it. The snow glittered, and if it was cold, she couldn't tell. Adrenaline kept her warm. She thought of all the effort she'd put into repressing her memories of the last time she was here, all the pills she'd taken, only for the truth to go on simmering beneath that fake comfort that never quite fit. She should have been terrified right now, and she was, but there was also relief in feeling that she was finally getting to the root of Frank's secret— and she sensed that she was close, that she could almost reach out and brush it with her fingers.

This time she didn't hear the stream as she neared the bridge—it must have frozen—but it didn't matter. The road, though clearly abandoned, was easy enough to follow. A straightforward path through the woods.

Although now that she was on it again, there was something so *off* about this road—about the very idea of it. Suddenly she couldn't believe she hadn't thought of it sooner. How could she have been so dense at seventeen?

It was obvious—both then and now—that no one had driven on this road in years.

You'd have to walk there, Frank's father had said.

And all at once she understood the cruelty of his smile. He really had been laughing at her. There's no way Frank could have carried the supplies needed to build a cabin—the lumber, the stove, two sinks, every one of those chimney stones—all this way on foot.

But then Maya hadn't been so dense back then, had she?

She *had* figured this out before—she remembered this now. It all came back to her the moment she saw the bridge.

THIRTY

Maya stops dead in her tracks as it comes into view, a bridge that not so much as a bicycle could safely cross. The flashlight from Frank's dad flickers in her hand. A cool wind slithers thought the leaves, scattering the last of the day's heat as she stands piecing it together.

A chill claws up her spine.

The bridge before her isn't just abandoned—it's crumbling. Lost to history, a bridge of rusted bones, turrets exposed like a giant's rib cage. Large chunks of concrete have fallen away, leaving only a sliver of passable road in the middle.

She's about to turn back, rattled to the core, when she notices a light on the other side of the stream. She squints. The light is larger, steadier, and more diffuse than a flashlight. She takes a few steps closer, and now she's sure of it. There is someone over there, across the broken bridge. She assumes it must be Frank, though she can't see him.

Every instinct tells her to leave, but she doesn't. That same curiosity that feels almost like a compulsion has gotten stronger with every step, as if she has been drawn here tonight by some invisible string. Plus, if Frank crossed it, the bridge must be safe enough. She's extremely careful as she makes her way across, walking as if on a tightrope when she gets to the middle portion, where the edges of the road have fallen away on either side.

The bridge here is only about three feet wide, the water below fast and black. It looks deep. She's trembling as she arrives on the other side and passes through a last stand of trees into a clearing. She's figured it out now, the reason Frank's so weird about his cabin, yet what she sees takes her breath away all the same.

There is no cabin. Only the weathered concrete remains of a foundation, a wide, cracked rectangle in the middle of the clearing. This is where she finds Frank, reclined on top of a plush red sleeping bag several feet in front of where a fireplace seems to have been. He's set up a battery-powered lamp in the spot, the orange glow she saw from the other side of the bridge a crude replica of the cozy fires that might have burned here once, back in whatever era this house actually stood.

He squints in the glare of her flashlight as she approaches but doesn't look surprised to see her. He smiles weakly, apologetically even, not moving from his comfortable-looking position as she takes in his surroundings. The portable lamp and sleeping bag, a jug of water, his backpack, and a half-peeled orange.

He wears a flannel shirt and jeans, but no shoes. His shoes sit several yards away at the edge of the foundation, as if he had left them at the front door, like he hadn't wanted to dirty the floors, and the thought of him playing make-believe out here, acting as if the house is real, is so absurd and sad and strange that a startled laugh rises in her throat, and she covers her mouth as if to hold it inside.

"Hey," he says. He sounds sheepish, or tired, or both.

"Frank . . ."

"I know . . . I'm so sorry, Maya."

But she's too bewildered to be angry. "Why would you lie about something like this?"

He lets out a long sigh. "I guess there's really no excuse, is there?"

Maybe not, but she still wants an answer. She stares down at him, waiting, the flashlight at her side beaming down at the cracked foundation.

"The truth," he says, "is that I'm just some guy who lives at home and takes care of his dad. I don't even have my own car, and my job is embarrassing. And you . . . well, you obviously could do better."

Another shocked laugh bubbles up. "Are you saying you made up the cabin . . . to impress me?"

He hangs his head.

"You've got to be kidding."

"I'm sorry," he says again.

But it's like Dorothy pulling back the curtain to reveal a man pretending to be a wizard. "You really . . . *really* didn't need to do that," she says. "I was totally into you."

She hadn't meant to use the past tense, but they both register it. The wind picks up, churning through leaves, and when he speaks again, Frank's voice is so low that Maya has to step closer to hear him. Now she stands at the edge of his sleeping bag, looking down into his sorrowful eyes.

"It's just that you're going away to *BU*," he says. "I didn't want you to think of me as some townie with nothing going on. I'm twenty years old and live at home with my dad."

"I never thought of you that way," she says.

But now she doesn't know what to think. She rushed here tonight on fumes of jealousy and infatuation, needing to know why he was with Aubrey, but seeing him now—barefoot and alone in the woods—the spell has been broken. He might have lied about the cabin to impress her, but that doesn't explain why he's here now. It doesn't explain the sleeping bag, the shoes left by an imaginary door.

"Are you okay? How long have you been out here?"

"Not long," he mutters, looking away.

"And why . . ."

He takes a deep, shaky breath. "Because I feel safe here."

"Safe? From what?"

"From my dad."

Maya thinks back to Frank's reference to troubles at home when he was young. "Did he do something?"

Frank exhales sharply. It could be a sigh of grief, or a scoff—he's looking down now, so it's impossible to know. "He's done a lot of things. To me . . . to my mom . . . and total strangers. It's the reason my mom took me away from him when I was twelve. He's dangerous."

Maya glances back over her shoulder as if his father might have followed her here. She knows now, as she should have before, that Frank might be lying. But then, his father *had* made her nervous. "Why are you staying with him, then?" she asks. "If he's dangerous, you should go to the police."

Frank shakes his head. "They wouldn't understand. My dad's never laid a finger on anyone. He hurts people in other ways. He's manipulative. Controlling. He used to be a psychology professor, but then he got into some trouble and lost his job, his psychology license, everything. He was ruined. He took it out on me and my mom."

"I'm sorry to hear that, Frank . . ." But now she senses him gliding past the situation at hand, the strangeness of it, and she tries to reel him back. She won't get sucked into another of his stories. "I still don't get what you're doing out here," she says.

Frank pulls his knees to his chest, folding in on himself. He speaks so quietly that she doesn't hear and must move closer so that she is standing right over him. He looks small from here. Helpless.

"What did you say?" she asks. Her voice is gentle.

"I said it was real to me. Back when I was ten, that night I was lost. I thought I was going to die alone in the woods, and I know it sounds crazy, but the cabin . . . it saved me. I needed it to be here for me. And it was.

"I pictured it so clearly, down to the littlest detail, and when I closed my eyes, it was like I was there. Like I was home. A safer, more loving home than the one I had left. A place without my dad. I came back a lot after that, days and nights when I had to escape. This is where I would come, the truest home I ever knew. I would sit here, just like I am tonight, and picture the door of my cabin. I really had to see it before I could go inside. The color of the pine, the brass knob. I had to feel the doorknob in my hand, but if I could do that, then I could turn it, and everything would be waiting for me on the other side. Home. Something good on the stove, a fire in the fireplace. The big, cozy couch."

Maya nods. She can easily picture what he's describing—she has before, and she allows herself to now.

There is sorrow in knowing it's not real, but what's even sadder is understanding how he had made it seem that way. The reason the cabin seemed real to her was that Frank has spent hours and hours building it in his head. Here in this clearing. Alone. He knows every floorboard and cabinet as if he had hammered it into place himself; he knows all the whorls in the pine. He knows it so well that when he speaks of the place, as he speaks of it now, it comes to life. The warmth of the fire. The smell of it. She doesn't know why he's telling her this now that she knows it's not real. Yet it relaxes her to hear it. She understands. She doesn't fault him for anything he's done. Everyone needs somewhere to return to.

She has lost track of what he was saying, and now he falls silent.

She hears what sounds like a door slam shut at her back. A sound that makes no sense out here and yet is unmistakable—a creak of hinges followed by the low clap of a door landing in its frame—directly behind her. Something tells her not to turn around, but she does anyway. She has to know. She turns slowly back to see Frank standing behind her.

Just inside the front door—the wind must have blown it shut.

Her mouth hangs open as she takes in his handiwork. He was too modest about the cabin. It's perfect. Fingers interlaced with her own, he gives her the grand tour, and Maya can't stop smiling. Then comes the tantalizingly fragrant soup that she never tastes because the sudden reminder of her father's book threatens to shatter the illusion.

And Frank doesn't want to let her go. Frank thinks she should move in with him.

He tells her to relax, eat her soup, and when she doesn't, he sets his spoon loudly on the table. Gets down on one knee like he's about to ask for her hand in marriage, but there's rage boiling in his eyes, and instead of a ring, he puts something slightly larger in her hand. She feels its metal teeth against her palm and looks down to see the key to the cabin. And for the briefest of moments, she's confused.

Why would Maya need a key to a cabin she's already inside?

But as soon as she thinks it, the thought slips away, and what happens over the following few minutes will lie buried beneath the lowest cellar floor of her head for seven years.

———————

She relaxes.

Her breath slows.

And her heart. It feels so good to be here. She sinks deeper, slouching in her seat at the table.

"Good," Frank says. "Good." He gets up off his knee and smiles down on her. "You're feeling better now," he says. "Calmer."

She feels better now. Calmer.

"Maybe you'd like to sit by the fire?" The way he says it, it doesn't sound like a question. "Get comfortable," he says. "Relax your tired legs."

Maya would like nothing more than to sit before the fire, get comfortable, and relax her tired legs.

"You feel safe here," he says.

Her body gives a sluggish jerk as something cold and wet strikes the back of her neck. She frowns.

"You feel safe here," he says again.

A second cold drop hits her knee. The bracing liquid trails down her bare calf, and Maya focuses on it. The tingling sensation moving toward her ankle. Then another drop and another—her shoulder, forehead, wrist—leading her back to herself. The rain cuts through Frank's voice just enough for her to understand that she needs to run.

He stands. "Come with me."

She doesn't intend to obey, but (oh god) that is what she does. She rises from her place at the table as if her legs and feet belong to someone else. She can't stop them from following as he leads her closer to the fire, orange light flickering on his face. She smells the sweetly burning wood.

Look into the light, she thinks she hears him say, or maybe it's the stream, the watery hush of it lulling her closer and deeper until the fire is all she can see. And taste. And feel. And it feels like coming in from the cold, like suddenly catching everything she's ever chased. Confidence. Approval. Love. The light feels like contentment, like the sun on her face, and smells like melting snow. It sings like bells. *You're safe now*, says the stream. *You're home.* And that's just how it feels, like coming home. But she knows. Even as she craves the fire's warmth, the flames shimmering red, orange, blue, and gold, a part of her knows that *home* isn't the right word for this place.

Like in the story. Like Pixán, taken in by imposters, gazing up into the mist, Maya knows her true home is elsewhere.

"You . . ." she whispers, although her intent is to shout it.

A raindrop on her cheek!

Every part of her wants to dissolve into the light. But she tears her gaze away to glare at Frank. "You tricked me."

"Relax," he says. But he doesn't sound so confident now.

She shakes her head, anger rising, threatening to break through whatever spell he's cast. "What did you do to me?"

"Listen to me, Maya, you need to calm down—"

"I *know*," she says.

And just like that, the roughly hewn logs that make up the wall at his back begin to look even more rustic. They start to look like trees. Weeds sprout up between the floorboards, and it isn't the roof she sees above her now but the endless abyss of the night sky, and it's like looking down to find yourself suddenly at the edge of the Grand Canyon. A great, swirling terror. Overwhelming vastness.

"*Maya,*" he pleads.

She looks at his face. He'd been talking to her, has been all along, while she was busy looking at the sky, or the wall, or the fire, or the soup.

But Maya doesn't have to listen. She knows this now. Frank begs her with his eyes not to say it, but this only sweetens the words on her tongue. "There is no cabin," she says, and as if on cue, what's left of it dissolves and the ceiling returns to sky and the floor to earth.

A loss of orientation as she tries to run. Her legs won't work, or she has forgotten how to use them. With what's left of her strength, she tries to lurch ahead, but the lower half of her body feels bound in an awkward position.

The problem reveals itself as soon as she looks down. The problem is Maya isn't actually standing in front of the fireplace but sitting in the dark, in the rain. No wonder she can't take off running—her legs are crossed.

She and Frank are sitting on his sleeping bag in the feeble glow of his battery-powered lamp, getting soaked. All her limbs are asleep, and she's clumsy as she pushes herself to her feet, the sleeping bag slick beneath her hands.

"Maya, wait—"

A head rush darkens her vision, but she pushes through it, nearly tripping on the uneaten orange Frank had been peeling when she arrived. She steps off the foundation onto wet earth, breaking into a run. Clouds cover the moon now. She's forgotten the flashlight and can only see a few feet ahead of her as she plunges through the trees outside the clearing.

She doesn't see the edges of the bridge as she runs out onto it.

"Stop!"

She ignores him. The road is gravelly and wet. Alarm bells clang in her chest, and something tells her to slow down as she nears the middle of the bridge, but she ignores her intuition in her desire to get away from him. She hears his footsteps close behind over the sound of rushing water.

"Look out!" he shouts.

The flashlight flares on at her back, revealing the crumbled section of bridge just ahead—the sheer drop she was about to race over.

Maya shrieks, pinwheels her arms. She staggers back from the edge directly into Frank's embrace. "Shh . . ." he whispers, holding her close. "You're okay now, just relax. There's nothing to be afraid of."

But Maya won't believe him twice. She squirms her way out of his arms and is about to dash across the narrow length of collapsed bridge when he turns off his father's light.

The darkness is complete.

The wind picks up, and the rain. What started as fitful showers earlier has swelled to a deluge, the kind of rain you'd have to shout to be heard over. Without the flashlight, the edges of the road disappear into darkness, and if she were to walk across that narrow stretch right now, every step would either bring her closer to safety, to the car, her mom, her home, or down into an angry river, no longer the placid stream it had seemed to her before.

So she lowers herself to the ground and feels her way

across. She runs her palms along the edges, broken concrete rough beneath her hands and knees. She knows how easily she could fall and she's never been a good swimmer, not that it would matter if she landed headfirst on a boulder.

She moves carefully but quickly as he's still behind her—she can tell he's speaking but does her best not to hear, listening only to the rain pelting the bridge and the river, turning the dirt beneath her to mud. Eventually the strip of road she's on widens again. She's on her feet in an instant, unable to see much, but all she has to do is stay on this road and it will lead her back to her car.

She breaks into a run and he follows—she hears his heavy steps—not slowing even as the road plunges back into the forest.

But then she hears the jingling keys at her back.

Her heart drops. Her feet slow and Frank moves closer until she can feel the heat of his body pressing in. "You forgot these," he says into her ear.

She doesn't turn. She thinks she could outrun him—but that won't matter, will it, if Frank has her car keys.

"Give them to me." She speaks forcefully, but the rain makes her sound small.

"Of course," he says, mildly indignant.

She holds out her hand for the bulky key chain, weighted down with her mom's many keys—house, car, work locker, garden shed—and mini-flashlight, but this isn't what Frank drops into her waiting palm.

The only key he gives her is his own.

THIRTY-ONE

Maya's tears melted holes in the moon-blue snow as she walked back from the abandoned bridge to her mom's car. She thought of the last time she had passed this way, Frank's arm around her shoulders while she tried to figure out what they were doing in the rain. She remembered looking back, unable to see the bridge or summon any memory of it or how she'd crossed it, the leafy road branching into darkness.

Frank had tried to make her think she was the one acting strangely, that he was just walking her to her car as requested, but she ran from him as soon as she had her bearings, sure that he'd done something to her, planning to tell her mom when she got home.

But then—tell her mom what exactly?

Brenda had been working that night, and Maya, soaked to the core, drained and fuzzy-headed after her time at the cabin, decided to sleep on the situation and do her best to explain in the morning. But the self-doubt was there when she woke, like a seed he'd planted, growing in her overnight, a vagueness to her understanding of what had happened.

Now Maya cried for the version of herself so willing to question her own experience. Of course Frank did something to her! He had convinced her of a place that didn't exist and somehow made her believe that she'd been there. He'd fucked with her head. The tears returned the feeling to her face, though the rest of her stayed numb, snow melting through her shoes as she crept back across the blank lawn of the house that had belonged to Frank's dad. It seemed obvious now who lived here these days.

Because where else would Frank sleep? How could he find shelter beneath a roof existing only in his head? The light in the window was no longer on, and as she got into her car, she pictured him sleeping in his childhood room at his father's house, defenseless, alone, as vulnerable in this moment as she was at seventeen.

She imagined standing over him with a knife.

———

Maya chased the word for what Frank had done to her the way that a dog chased its tail, in dizzying circles, the answer so near yet still that maddening last inch away. She held the steering wheel with both hands and tapped her brakes at every bend. She had to be careful on these roads this time of year, exhausted as she was.

The flood of memories had left her spent, ready to collapse, and yet she knew that when she did lie down, she wouldn't sleep. Such was the cruelty of benzodiazepine withdrawal. The pint of gin she bought on the way home was purely medicinal. She needed to think, but her thoughts kept snarling into tangles she couldn't unravel, and she figured it must be that she was sleep-deprived.

She was relieved to find, when she got home, that her mom hadn't woken in the two hours or so since Maya had taken the car without permission. She poured herself a glass of orange juice for the vitamin C, then added about half the gin to help her sleep. She brought the drink to bed with her, quickly drank it, then sank into the pillowy mattress. Her hands and feet tingled as her blood thawed, and before long, she began to pass out.

She was tempted to ignore her phone when it rang, let it go to voicemail, let the gin pull her under, but then it occurred to her that she hadn't called her job this morning to tell them she was still sick. If that was her boss on the phone, Maya had to answer—she couldn't afford, on top of everything else, to get fired. Her hand shot out from beneath the blankets.

When she saw the caller ID, the relief hit her as hard as the gin. *"Dan!"* she gushed.

"Hey . . ."

"How—how are you?"

"All right, I guess. Halfway through exams."

He didn't sound as overjoyed or relieved as she felt. "I'm sure you're killing it," she said weakly.

"Listen, sorry I didn't text you back."

Her chest tightened. "That's okay, I know you have a lot going on."

He said nothing.

She didn't breathe. Maybe if neither of them spoke, the conversation would end, and they could go back to the way things were.

"What's going on with you, Maya?"

She wanted to tell him what she'd remembered tonight—she'd been carrying it too long on her own. But to tell him now would be to risk coming across as she had seven years ago, as though she were suggesting that Frank had cast some sort of spell on her, made her see things that weren't there.

It remained true that what he'd done felt like magic.

"See?" Dan said. "You don't want to tell me, do you?"

"Please," she said, her voice filling with tears. "I do, it's just that—"

"Right," he said flatly. "I'm sure you have your reasons, and look, I respect that. But honestly, this isn't what I signed up for. I don't want the kind of relationship where we feel like we have to hide things from—"

"I'm going through Klonopin withdrawal."

"I'm sorry, what?"

She'd been looking for the right time to tell him, always at some future point, but the moment had never come, and though the word for what Frank had done to her stayed mired in a strange, foggy soup, the rest of what was going on in her mind felt surprisingly clear as the words fell from her lips.

"Jesus," Dan said when she was done. "I don't get it. Why would you hide all that from me?"

"I don't know," she said. "It didn't seem important when we met, so I didn't mention it, and then I . . . kept not mentioning it until it started to feel weird. Like, why had I waited so long?"

Dan sighed.

"I wish we could talk about this in person," she said, wanting to hold him, but glad he couldn't see her this way.

"So that's why you got sick at my parents' house."

"Yes."

He fell quiet again.

"I'm so sorry . . ."

"I could have helped you through it."

"The thing is I was lying to myself too. I didn't *want* to be taking Wendy's pills anymore. I knew they were clouding my thinking, making me forgetful. I knew they were dangerous to mix with alcohol, but I've been doing that pretty much every night for years. And I didn't want that reality to be true, so I pretended it wasn't."

"Oh, Maya . . ."

"I'm sorry."

"You've been drinking tonight, haven't you?"

The disappointment in his voice stung. Of course he could hear the four shots of gin she'd just downed. She thought of explaining that she needed it to sleep but felt lucid enough to see that this was a poor excuse. "Yes," she whispered.

This time he was silent for so long that she had time to

THE HOUSE IN THE PINES

consider the two paths he might take. Seeing as how she obviously needed help, he might, on the one hand, choose to stand by her no matter what, help her through this.

Or he could say that it was all too much, that *she* was too much, throw up his hands, and walk away.

"You have a problem," he said slowly. "What are you going to do about it?"

Her tears were messy now, her nose running down her face, but her chest filled with gratitude because there was kindness in his voice. "I'll get help," she said. "I will. As soon as I get back to Boston."

"What kind of help?"

"I don't know, a psychiatrist? Or a therapist. Some kind of doctor."

"I have an uncle in AA. I think that's what you should do."

"But I'm not an alcoholic," she said, instinctively defensive.

"Really? You got drunk at my mom's birthday the other night. Now here you are again."

She couldn't argue with that.

"And all this week . . . Of course I knew something was wrong. And you—you hid it from me. You've been taking pills behind my back, making yourself sick with how much you've been drinking. You're hurting yourself, Maya. You can't hide it anymore."

Maya curled into a ball, drawing her knees to her chest.

"And anyway," he said, "those programs aren't just for alcoholics. They have them for all kinds of addicts."

The word made her wince. The first step of a journey Maya had no interest in taking. She didn't want to go to meetings, or find God, and when she thought about being sober all the time, she wasn't sure life would be worth living. She felt an urge to remind Dan that it was a *doctor* who had written her first Klonopin prescription—that this was *his* fault. Or that, until the last few days, she had cut back dramatically on her drinking. Or that she could—she *would*—straighten herself out on her own, no need for anything as dramatic as an Anonymous program.

But instead, she said, "Okay. I'll go."

The problem with the word *addict* was that it meant you were supposed to do something about it, as if Maya didn't have enough to deal with. But she had told Dan that she would, so after lying in the dark awhile, no longer tired, she searched for AA meetings on her phone. She found a chapter not far from their apartment in Boston and texted Dan to let him know. He wrote back with a heart, and she replied with ten, and told herself that she would go to meetings if it would make him happy. She would do a lot for him.

Even if she wasn't ready to admit she was an addict. She was physically dependent on medication. Wasn't there a difference?

The night was long, and she was acutely aware of the gin left in the bottle on her nightstand. She poured it down the kitchen sink. This wasn't going to be easy, but it was for the best. She had to stay sharp. She sat at the antique writing desk in her old room with the pen and flowery notepad her mom had left out for future guests and began to list what she had learned tonight, starting with what Steven had told her at Patrick's.

1. *Cristina was planning to move into Frank's cabin.* A chilling thought now that Maya knew the place didn't exist.

2. *He has clients of some sort.* She shuddered to think of what services he might provide. She'd look into this.

3. *His dad was a professor at Williams.* She still knew almost nothing about Frank's dad other than his name, which was Oren. She had searched for him online seven years ago but not found anything and given up after Dr. Barry convinced her to drop it. She hadn't thought much about Oren Bellamy since.

4. *Oren* . . . She recalled the apparent glee he took, the night she met him, in directing her to a cabin that he'd have known wasn't real.

Then hadn't Frank told her something about him in the clearing? Maya's brow creased. Her grasp of these newly recovered memories was tenuous, even more imperfect than might be expected of a night seven years ago. Yet somehow writing it down helped her think, helped pull the sunken past back up to the surface. *Oren* . . . she wrote, *was the reason Frank built the cabin.*

She remembered this now. Frank built his cabin to get away from his father.

She picked up her phone. Adding "Williams College" to her search for "Oren Bellamy" didn't turn up anything, but eventually she found references to two journal articles he'd published in the 1980s. One article was titled "Observable Personality Traits Associated with High Absorption Scores on the TAS," but when Maya clicked on the article, it had been taken down.

The other article he'd published had also been taken down, but back issues of the journal were available in print through the website. The journal was called *Experimental Neuropsychology*, and its website hadn't been updated in over a decade. Maya got her debit card and purchased Volume 17, October 1983, the issue Dr. Bellamy's article appeared in, typing her credit card info into a beige website that looked almost vintage.

So Oren had been a psychologist, and either Williams College had erased all connection with him or he'd never really taught there.

She searched for "Dr. Oren Bellamy," "psychologist," and, glancing over her list, threw in the word "clients," and there he was. Dr. Oren Bellamy, PhD, CHT. Not just his name but his face, a close-up of him in a plaid blazer, smiling at his desk with a bookshelf behind him. In the picture, he looked to be in his fifties, younger than when she'd met him.

The site was for a place called Clear Horizons Wellness Center. The website looked current, if not very professional. The design was shoddy, the font garish, and the logo—an orange sun on a blue horizon—looked like clip art. It was hard to tell exactly what kind of services the center offered.

Reading the "About" section didn't help much. Dr. Oren Bellamy's "proprietary therapeutic method" apparently had a 100 percent success rate when it came to curing a long list of "life-crippling ailments" such as addiction, phobias, anxiety, and depression, as well as facilitating weight loss, smoking cessation, and "moving past grief."

Several clients testified: "It isn't too much to say that Clear Horizons saved my life."—Carol M. "Finally, something that works!"—Mike R. "I never thought I could get over losing my sister, but then I met Dr. Hart!"—Susan P.

The final testimonial was a video. Maya clicked on it, and an elderly man began to speak. He sat in what looked like a therapist's office, in front of a window looking out on a forest. Serene music played in the background. "When my Diane died," he said, "I thought I might as well die too. Figured what was the point?" The man smiled, his eyes dreamy and unfocused. Maya felt her blood curdle. "I wouldn't be here if it wasn't for Dr. Hart," the man said. "Dr. Hart helped me go on living."

Nothing else on the website helped clarify the identity of Dr. Hart—though Maya had her suspicions—or the nature of the treatment being offered. All she learned was that Dr. Oren Bellamy's proprietary therapeutic method continued to be practiced at—and only at—Clear Horizons Wellness Center. Insurance was not accepted.

Maya read all of every page on the site, not sure what she hoped to find, but she kept looking. On the "About" page, she studied the initials after Oren's name and realized that she didn't know what *CHT* stood for. She Googled it, and the first thing that came up was "Certified Hand Therapist."

Hand therapist? Could that be right?

She added "psychology."

What happened next caused Maya to question if maybe something was wrong with her phone. A glitch in the screen. There was a certain phrase that appeared among her search results—two or three words, a professional title—that she couldn't make out.

"Certified . . . therapist."

She couldn't read the middle portion. Her eyes didn't seem to grasp it, like the letters kept slipping out from beneath her vision. No matter how she held her screen and regardless of what she clicked on, she couldn't read what came before "therapist."

Maya's vision had stumbled over words now and again in recent years, but it was rare enough that she would chalk it up to tired eyes and move on.

But now it was obvious that it was just one very specific word—or part of a word—that she couldn't read. She got out of bed, turned on the lights, and looked around. There was nothing wrong with her vision as far as she could tell. No dark spots or blurriness. Yet when she looked again at her phone, the problem remained. "Certified . . . therapist." It was like an optical illusion. Something was blocking her from seeing it. She felt sick. Nothing about this felt possible. Maybe she really was crazy.

She sank down onto the edge of the bed. Held her head in her hands. Then she had an idea and got back on her phone.

She created an online document. Copied "Certified . . . therapist" and pasted it into the document.

She selected the "Read Aloud" option.

What she heard turned her blood to ice. The middle of the word sounded garbled. She couldn't hear it any more than she could read it on her screen. "Certified *#@^-therapist." The warping was subtle—she might not have noticed had she only heard it once—but it kept happening. "Certified *#@^-therapist." Maya's heart raced. She slowed down the reading speed. Held the phone to her ear and closed her eyes and listened over and over and over and over. She listened until she heard. And a black sun dawned in her chest.

Oren Bellamy had been a certified hypnotherapist.

THIRTY-TWO

Maya still hasn't told Aubrey about the lost time. She's less sure of herself by the hour, and it's not like she can point to any injury, or say for sure that it wasn't her fault, so she didn't mention Frank after the Tender Wallpaper concert last night or before they went back to Maya's house and went to sleep.

But then she'd dreamed of the cabin. Not much happened in the dream—Frank sat across from her, the table set with bowls—yet terror had shrieked through the air and she couldn't move, couldn't open her mouth to let out the scream in her throat. The dream was so upsetting that, for the second morning in a row, she wasn't able to fall back asleep afterward.

She walks quietly to the kitchen. Her mom and Aubrey are still asleep. The window above the sink has been left open. The room is cool with morning. She pours herself a glass of orange juice and tries to shake off the dread of her dream, but then sees the number flashing on the cordless phone. Eight. Eight missed calls, and she knows who they're from. The call log confirms it—Frank's been calling her all morning.

The murky fear she's been holding at bay comes flooding back. It occurs to her that she has no idea who Frank really is.

"You're up early."

Maya startles.

Her mom sweeps into the living room in a cotton nightgown with roses on it, her blond curls a messy halo around her head. "Didn't mean to scare you."

Maya puts a finger to her lips. "Aubrey's asleep."

"She's here?" Her mom seems rested after a full night's sleep, a luxury in her line of work. She goes from room to room, opening curtains, filling the house with light.

"Aubrey! So good to see you."

Maya hears them in the hall. Aubrey must have been on her way to the bathroom, probably hoping to sneak back to sleep afterward, but now she's been caught awake. "Hi, Brenda." Aubrey's voice is sleepy but warm. She's spent a lot of time here over the years, including a whole month last year after her mom kicked her out of the house for sneaking a boy into her room.

Brenda makes them all French toast and serves it with local maple syrup, a splurge. The French toast is crispy on the outside and soft in the middle. The house smells like fried batter and the coffee that Maya has recently begun to join her mom in drinking with breakfast. She started largely because she wasn't allowed to drink it when she was younger, but she liked the way it made her feel and quickly learned to love its bitter taste.

She washes dishes afterward, and Aubrey dries. They talk over running water, the smell of Palmolive. "So about Frank . . ."

"Finally!" Aubrey says. "Thought you were never going to tell me."

Maya hadn't wanted to dwell on it last night, but now she needs to know how afraid she should be. "You were right. Total creep."

Aubrey would never say *I told you so.* She pouts sympathetically. "What'd he do?"

Maya lathers a fork as she tells Aubrey about the three times she seemed to black out around Frank. The first time, at Balance Rock, she assumed it was his dad's medical marijuana; that stuff is known to be strong. The second time, the night she kissed Frank, she'd been so giddy that she hadn't given the missing hours much thought.

"Hours?"

Maya, embarrassed, keeps her eyes on her soapy hands. "But how . . . ?"

"I have no idea . . ." She waits for Aubrey to dismiss her, and when she doesn't, Maya tells her about last night. The cabin in the woods. The missing minutes as she arrived and left. Walking in the rain with no idea how she got there. The phone calls. The fucking with her head.

"I'm going for a run," her mom says, suddenly behind them, dressed in shorts and a shirt that reads PUMPKIN FEVER TRIATHLON.

Aubrey nearly drops the plate she's been drying for the past two minutes.

"Geez, you two are jumpy." Her mom leaves the kitchen door open at her back.

Maya wouldn't have blamed Aubrey for being skeptical. But when she manages to look at her, there's not a shred of doubt on Aubrey's face. No judgment. She believes Maya, and it shows; she looks afraid. More afraid than Maya herself had felt up until this moment, until she saw the fear in her brave friend's eyes and the way she stands frozen at the sink.

"I knew it," Aubrey says quietly. "I think he did the same to me."

Maya stares at her.

"At Dunkin' Donuts, right before you ran into us. I felt like something weird happened that day, but then I thought . . ." She shakes her head. "I thought I was imagining it."

"Oh my god! Me too!"

Now they both look scared.

"It was after he set that book aside for me . . ." Aubrey seems to turn something over in her mind. "A biography about this doctor who lived in Victorian London. A mesmerist . . ."

"A what?"

"Mesmerism—it was a medical practice in the 1800s. Basically mimosas. This doctor became famous for performing it onstage. He had this patient, a servant, and he would treat her while people watched. Sort of like a magic show only instead of magic tricks, people paid to watch him minimize the poor girl, who was probably unconscious the whole time."

Maya furrows her brow, stuck on *mimosas*. "I'm sorry—what?"

"Which part?"

"Mimosas?"

"*Mimosas*," Aubrey says. "You know, like hippo sizzling."

Maya almost laughs. She turns off the water, and the room is silent. "Did you say . . ."

Aubrey's starting to look annoyed. "Seriously?"

Maya doesn't ask her to repeat herself. It doesn't matter anyway what book Frank lent Aubrey—she just needs to know what he did to her, what he did to them both. She shakes her head as if to clear it. "What happened at Dunkin' Donuts?"

"We talked about magic," Aubrey says. "He told me he practiced a little himself, sleight of hand, coin tricks, that kind of thing. As if he thought that would impress me."

Maya's face burns. She herself was easy to impress.

"He asked," Aubrey says, "if I wanted to see a trick. And he really sold it to me, you know?"

Maya knew.

"He told me the trick was really old and that very few people will ever see it. Well, of course I wanted to see it. I said yes and he took this *key* out of his pocket and set it on the table."

"Was the key weird? Like, did it look sharp?"

"Has he shown you the trick?"

Maya shook her head. "What did he do with it?"

"He said he was going to make it levitate. Told me to focus all my attention on it. He said I'd see the key rise off the table."

"Did you?"

"He never got to that part. He told me all *about* the trick first, like how it's never been written down and magicians have been passing it down by word of mouth for generations. Blah blah blah. I knew none of it was true. Magic tricks usually start off with a story of some kind. But his just went on and on and on . . ." A strange look comes over her face. "I kept listening, thinking something was going to happen. But it never did. The key stayed where it was, and I . . . stared at it . . . and then you walked in."

Maya stops washing dishes. She turns off the water.

"I walked home after that," Aubrey says, "and when I got there, I saw that I'd been at Dunkin' Donuts for more than an hour."

"Knock, knock," Frank says at the screen door.

They turn, eyes wide with fear.

There's no telling how long he's been there. How much he's heard.

Maya instinctively picks up a knife that had been lying by the sink. "What are you doing here?"

Frank eyes the sharp paring knife. She's not sure why she picked it up, and it feels like overkill, but she tries to hold it with confidence.

He raises his hands in a gesture of surrender. "I only want to talk."

"I told you I don't want to see you."

"I just want to clear the air about the other night."

Aubrey, standing closer to the door, faces him through the screen. She's an inch or two taller than he is and, unlike Maya, doesn't seem scared. "You need to leave, Frank. Now."

"This has nothing to do with you, Aubrey. Stay out of it."

"Or else what?" Aubrey stares him down. "*I know,*" she says.

A look of fear on his face, followed quickly by fury. His voice remains calm. "I don't know what you're talking about."

"I know what you did to us."

Maya can't tell if she's bluffing.

Frank lurches at her. Stops an inch from her face. "Like I said, I don't know what you're talking about." The words are edged with warning.

Alarm bells sound in Maya's chest. She wonders if Aubrey is telling the truth.

Either way, it's clear that Frank feels threatened.

"Leave," Maya says, "or I'll call the police."

"Call them," Aubrey says.

No one moves.

Maya's eyes dart to the phone on the kitchen wall, but someone has forgotten to return the cordless receiver to its base. She checks the living room, the knife still in her hand. She doesn't see the phone, so she hurries upstairs for her cell. Finds it in her room, in the back pocket of the jeans she wore last night to the concert. She flips the phone open and is about to dial 9-1-1 when she pauses to ask herself if she's really doing this.

What exactly does she plan to say? What is her emergency? A man she knows is talking to her friend at the back door? Frank isn't armed and hasn't done anything to threaten them. Maya takes the phone to the window and pulls back the curtain. When she presses her face to the glass and looks down, she can see Frank talking to Aubrey through the screen door. She can't see Aubrey, who's inside the house, but they appear to be talking calmly. Then he takes something from his pocket and holds it up for her to see.

The key.

Maya has no reason to think he's going to hurt Aubrey, yet her body reacts as if he has taken out a gun and is holding it to her head. Maya grips the knife tighter. Backs away from the window. She needs to get Aubrey back inside. Even if she appears to be fine. Even if all Maya has to go on is a feeling—she has to try. She rushes back downstairs, but her steps slow as she enters the kitchen.

She sees them through the screen door, Aubrey and Frank. They look relaxed, side by side but not touching. The sky is blue and birds are singing. Maya's hands hang at her side, the phone in one, the knife in the other. As she gets closer, she hears the low murmur of his voice. She can't make out the words but detects a strange, songlike rhythm. She's almost at the door when Aubrey tips over on her side. She makes no effort to break her fall. Her shoulder strikes the concrete, then her head.

Frank turns to her, a shocked look on his face.

The screen door slams open. Maya rushes out.

"What the fuck?!" Frank says. "What happened to her?"

Maya drops the knife and the phone and falls to her knees beside her friend. "Aubrey!? Aubrey! Wake up!"

"Does she have some kind of medical condition?"

Maya ignores him.

Aubrey's eyes are open as Maya grabs her by the shoulders and shakes her. "Oh my god, oh my god." Aubrey's head lolls against the concrete, lifeless as a rag doll.

Maya looks up at Frank. "What did you do?"

Frank looks stunned. "What are you talking about? We were just talking and she—she just—" He gestures at her body on the stoop, hinged unnaturally at the waist, green eyes refusing Maya's gaze, even as they stare at her.

"You can't blame me for this," Frank says, panic rising in his voice. "You can't."

"Aubrey! Wake up! Wake up!" Maya screams, her face wet with tears, as Frank slowly backs away.

THIRTY-THREE

It wasn't just that Maya hadn't seen or heard the word *hypnosis* in years. She hadn't thought it either, or considered what the word meant. The induction of a trancelike, highly suggestible state. It was as if the very concept had been deleted from her mind. But now that she'd managed to hear part of it—*hypno*—the rest of the word came back to her along with its meaning. And then it seemed obvious.

Frank had hypnotized her, not just once but repeatedly, then hidden the memories from her inside her own head. Looking back, Maya felt like she'd been circling this a long time, but it was as if the very idea had been garbled, and finally she'd grasped it. Now, as she read about hypnotism online, she learned of new research emerging from the field of neuroscience, new developments in the understanding of how what happens in the mind can have real effects in the body.

When she came to an article on posthypnotic suggestion, she felt dizzy. She rearranged the comforter around her
shoulders. She'd been too hot, so she had taken off her clothes,
but was then too cold, so she'd wrapped herself in blankets.
Her long hair clung to her sweat-damp back.

Suggestions made during hypnosis, she read, could af-
fect the patient's behavior in their normal life. The hypnotist
could tell a person who wanted to quit smoking, for example, that their next cigarette would taste like the worst thing
they'd ever eaten. For some people, this worked—a suggestion made under hypnosis, it seemed, had the power to alter
their perception later on.

Could this be why Maya's eyes had seemed to skip over
the word *hypnosis* and why her ears couldn't seem to hear
it? Had Frank implanted a posthypnotic suggestion in her
mind designed to keep her from figuring out what he'd done?
She could almost feel it there, alien, invasive. A seed that had
sprouted its pale tendrils through her brain.

Maya dropped her phone to the bed. She couldn't stand
to look at it anymore.

She wanted to scrub out the inside of her skull, could
almost feel his words worming through her. She had a word
now for what he had done to her.

But could hypnosis kill people? Was that possible? Even
with all the recent scientific research she'd found online, the
word made her think of stage tricks, a man in a suit making
hammy volunteers quack like ducks. It made her think of the
magic shows Aubrey had loved, which Maya had always
found cheesy. But this clearly wasn't the type of hypnosis

Frank's father had practiced. Steven had said he taught at
Williams College, and if this was true, the college, along
with both journals that had published his research, had
erased all signs of having been affiliated with Oren Bellamy.

Yet—according to the Clear Horizons website—he had
singlehandedly developed a "proprietary therapeutic method"
for treating patients, one with a "100 percent success rate."
Frank had said his father was brilliant yet dangerous, that he
had hurt people but not physically. Now Maya thought she
understood. Oren didn't have to touch anyone to hurt them.
He did it with words, just like his son. Frank learned from
his father.

Maya had to tell someone. She would tell her mom. Dan.
The police. She turned on the light, got back into her sweatpants and shirt.

Her mom didn't wake as Maya peeked her head through
the door of her bedroom. She slept on her back, mouth open,
blankets pulled up to her shoulders. The clock read 9:17.
Maya paused here.

Claiming Frank had hypnotized her would make her
sound as delusional as she had seven years ago. *It's like he
has some kind of power.* No one had believed her then, and
no one would now, not even her mom, unless she had proof.

She crept back to her room, thoughts tumbling. She
turned off the lights, then turned them on again. She rocked
back and forth on the bed, hugged herself. It wasn't enough
to point out that Frank's dad was a hypnotherapist. She had
to prove that Frank was too, and that the hypnotism they
had practiced was somehow deadly. She began to cry. It was

like a caged animal had been released from her chest. The truth that wouldn't let her sleep, that had lurked just beyond her grasp for the past seven years, was finally out in the open.

Either that or she'd lost her mind again.

The only person who knew for sure was Frank.

Steven had told her she could find him at the Whistling Pig most nights. The bar was less than a mile away. She downloaded a voice memo app on her phone. Tested it out, talking at different volumes with the phone tucked into her waistband, covered by her shirt, then beside her, hidden in her purse. The sound was best when she kept it in her purse. She found the cream-colored cashmere sweater she had worn to dinner with Dan's parents stuffed in her backpack; this would look better than the faded T-shirt she had on. She would pretend like she just so happened to be in town and decided to have a drink at the Whistling Pig. She would act like she was happy to see him.

Like it had never occurred to her that Frank might have killed her friend, or that it was him calling her on the landline the other night, perhaps worried that she was starting to remember. She went to the bathroom for more of her mom's cover-up, but the mirror told her there was only so much she could do. Her eyes were sunken, her lips bloodless and chapped.

Maya looked unwell, but she felt stronger than she had in years. She finally had the words for what happened to her. Frank had hypnotized her, planted his suggestions, then made her forget, causing her to think she'd blacked out. She might never know exactly what he told her during that time, but now she felt sure that her nearly instant infatuation with him, her blindness to the warning signs that had been so apparent to Aubrey, were all part of his programming. He'd cultivated in her the perfect companion for himself to dwell in the cabin in his head.

Or tried to, anyway. Though he appeared to have succeeded with Cristina, who, after all, would never leave him, never hurt him or let him down. Maya splashed cold water on her face, clenched her teeth to keep them from chattering. She appeared broken down and weak, even more vulnerable that she must have when he lured her in at the library.

But she wasn't.

This time her vulnerability would be a trap. She must have been an easy target for him then, hanging on his every word. Now she knew better. She wouldn't get sucked into one of his stories.

She wrote her mom a note on the back of an envelope. *Mom—if you find this, it means I need help. I'm at the Whistling Pig.* She placed the note on top of the alarm clock in her room, then set the alarm for midnight.

She slid a chef's knife from its block in the kitchen. She wrapped the gleaming blade in a dish towel and put it in her purse.

She closed the door quietly on her way out.

———

The Whistling Pig was on the ground floor of the old Berkshire Life Insurance Company, a stately gray building from the 1800s. The bar was tucked between a restaurant and a copy shop. She'd walked so that her mom would have the car if Maya needed rescuing. She paused to catch her breath before reaching for the heavy red door.

The bar was narrow and smelled like IPA. Weezer played on the speakers. Three men looked up from their table as she entered. The men were about her age, Irish-looking, guys she might have gone to high school with. The only other customer was a ruddy man in his forties, sitting alone at the bar.

A chalkboard menu listed microbrews and a few small-batch whiskeys. "Hi there," said the bartender, a local adopter of the man-bun.

"I'll have the lager," she said. The cheapest thing on the menu. She hadn't been to work in over a week, had rent coming up, and couldn't really afford this beer she didn't plan to drink, but didn't want to stand out any more than she already did as the only woman here. She gave the bartender her debit card.

The man sitting at the bar stared at her. He looked drunk, a defiant gleam in his unfocused eyes. Maya ignored him.

"Leave it open?"

"No, thanks."

She took her pint to a table at the back and sat facing the door so she would see anyone who walked in. She tore the napkin around her beer to pieces as the drunk man at the bar continued to stare at her. She pretended not to notice. She looked at the names and quotes patrons had chalked onto the walls, the pile of board games on offer. The cozy, shabby-chic décor.

She looked down at the pictures shellacked to the table beneath her elbows and saw they were all of half-naked women. Women in lingerie, in bikinis; women cut out of magazines. Close-ups of body parts, airbrushed, shaved. Faces covered by the bodies of other women. Maya stared at it a moment, then looked up to see the man at the bar laughing at her.

A smile played across the bartender's lips.

Maya could see why Frank liked this place. He must fit right in.

Her eyes flicked to the door as it swung open. A man in a dark, hooded jacket, his face in shadow. He nodded at the bartender, and the bartender nodded back, started pouring him a beer.

The hooded man sat at the bar, exchanged nods with the guy who'd laughed at her. The hooded man was Frank's size, but his posture was wrong. This man was bent over, weary-looking, but he straightened a little as soon as he had a beer in his hand. He lowered his hood.

It was him.

Frank looked tired. Leaner. Old. Older than he should have—seeing him now, it was obvious to her that he'd lied about his age. He'd told Maya he was twenty, but the math didn't work: this hollow-eyed, salt-and-pepper man was easily in his forties. No wonder he hadn't wanted to meet her mom.

Maya had come here unsure if she could face him, afraid she'd lose her nerve if he actually showed up, but now that she saw him, a red-hot surge of anger rose and she thought of the knife in her purse. She thought of sinking it into his neck. This pathetic little man had ruined her life.

She reached into her purse. Hit the record button on her phone, then set her purse on the edge of the table.

She approached the bar. "Frank? Is that you?"

His eyes went wide as he turned and saw her. His face fell. This time he would have no story prepared.

"Wow!" She smiled. "It *is* you."

"Maya! Good to see you. What are you doing here?"

"I'm in town for Christmas, felt like going out for a drink. Hey, want to join me?"

He stared at her. "You're here alone?"

She nodded, then watched him read her, the seven years added to her face, the bags beneath her eyes, the pallor. She probably looked as haggard as he did.

"Sure," he said.

Frank followed Maya to her table.

They sat across from each other. "Cheers," she said.

"Been a long time."

They clinked glasses, then fell silent, as if out of respect. The last time they saw each other was the day Aubrey died. In some ways Maya had never moved on from that day, stuck in her thick, foggy fear, but seeing him now, she understood that, in other ways, she'd become a different person. She was an adult, capable of seeing through the loser sitting across from her, desperate for love and thinking he needed to trick people in order to get it.

"You come here often?" she asked.

"Every once in a while." He shrugged. "Where you visiting from?"

"Boston. I stayed after college."

"Good for you."

"Boston's not all it's cracked up to be," she said. "And actually . . ." She let her expression grow pained. "The truth is I don't live there anymore. I recently left my fiancé. We were living together, he kept the apartment, so . . . yeah. That's the real reason I'm here. I'm staying with my mom." She smiled sadly.

Frank softened. "I'm sorry to hear that. Why did you leave him?"

"Long story . . . But tell me about you. How have you been?"

Frank sipped his beer. "I'm in the same boat, believe it or not. Just got out of a long-term relationship."

"Really? Wow, sorry to hear it." She felt him studying her, but she gave nothing away. "What happened?"

"Long story." A smile tugged at the edges of his lips.

"Must be going around," she joked.

Frank laughed like someone whose girlfriend hadn't just died, and for a moment looked like his old self again. Magnetic, fun. He took her in with his eyes. "Hard to believe it's been seven years."

"I know." She bowed her head. "I've thought about that day so many times . . ."

"Me too."

"Really?"

"Of course," he said. "I watched a girl die that day. Didn't know her like you did, of course, but still. Can't help but wonder if there's some way I could've helped her."

Maya's eyes shone with emotion as she leaned across the table. She wasn't a teenager anymore. "Oh, Frank . . . I thought you might blame yourself. After what I said—"

"You asked me what I did to her." He sounded wounded, as if he was the one who'd been hurt. "It's like you thought I . . ."

"I was wrong. I know that now." She touched the fingers wrapped around his beer. "I was scared when I said that, I wasn't thinking straight."

He moved his hand closer.

"I've been wanting to say sorry for a long time," she said.

"Thank you. That means a lot."

She smiled.

He settled back in his seat and she did the same. He appeared to believe her. To relax. Maya tried to relax too, but adrenaline surged through her veins and her heart beat like a war drum. Another Weezer song came on.

"What do you do these days?" she asked.

He took a long drink of beer. "What do I do?"

"You know, for work."

"I help people."

"Wish I could say the same," she said, "but I just work at a garden center. Customer service."

"Are you still writing?"

She shook her head.

"Why not?"

"I don't know. Lazy, I guess."

"You should get back to it. I bet you're good."

She smiled. "How would you know?"

"You have a good imagination." He held up his glass. Drank. It was almost empty.

Maya took a small sip. She needed to stay in control, but it would look suspicious if she didn't at least try her beer. "Speaking of helping people," she said, filling her voice with warmth. "Your father . . . I remember you were taking care of him. Is he . . ."

"Dead."

"Oh, Frank . . . I'm so sorry to hear that . . ."

He didn't seem too broken up about it. "It was his time."

"I only met him that once," she said, "the night I visited you at your cabin, but I remember thinking he seemed like a nice person."

A snarl curled the edges of Frank's lips, pretending to be a smile.

Maya pushed on. "What was it that he did again?"

Frank's expression grew steely. "What did he *do*?"

"Yeah, like, his job. Did you say he was a professor?"

He clenched his jaw. "You want to know about my dad."

"Yeah, I mean . . . just curious." A drop of sweat trickled down her ribs. She caught movement in the corner of her eye but held on to his gaze.

"Well, if you must know," he said, "my father was a psychology professor and a researcher. A brilliant man. Taught me everything I know."

"Wow, that's . . . wonderful."

His eyes burned. "Nothing wonderful about it." He spoke calmly, but anger simmered beneath the words. "My dad never meant to teach me anything."

Maya tilted her head. She glanced toward the movement at the edge of her vision and saw that it was his hand on the table, resting atop the collage of body parts. He was holding something small, turning it over and over in his right palm, like a magician about to do a coin trick.

The key—it had to be. She purposefully didn't look. The key to Frank's cabin was a blind spot—she still didn't know how, or if, it tied into his method. "So how did you learn?" she asked.

"The hard way. From the inside out."

His words confused her, his hand kept turning in the corner of her vision, but Maya didn't allow herself to be distracted. "What do you mean by that—from the inside out?"

"I was his test subject."

She swallowed. Every instinct told her to leave.

"He developed a method," Frank said, "a system of cues, most of them subperceptual."

The smile he gave her then was one that she recognized, the smile that did her in at seventeen. There was danger just beneath its surface.

"These cues," he said, "would induce a sort of trance in certain vulnerable personality types. The type to get lost in a book or a show on TV . . . the kind of person who needs to know how the story ends. Who's capable of blocking out everything else until they have the answer." His smile turned sad. "People like me."

THE HOUSE IN THE PINES

Her skin crawled.

"My dad never told me what he was doing," he said, "but I figured it out. I was ten when it started. He'd be talking to me, and the next thing I knew it was hours later and I'd be watching TV or eating dinner. And I saw the same thing happen to my mom. She'd always been so sharp, so bright, but around that time she started acting confused and weirdly passive. She stopped leaving the house or doing anything at all other than what my dad told her to do. Then one day I noticed him whispering in her ear. Talking and talking to her while she stared at the wall . . ."

His hand on the table began to move faster, as if he were growing agitated.

"I started breaking into his study at night," he said. "I'd go through his notes, read everything. I started to understand what my father was doing to me. His method. Over time, I learned how to do it too. It was the only way I could defend myself."

It couldn't be good, Maya thought, that he was telling her this. But she didn't stop him.

"I was better at it than he was," Frank said, as a smile crept into his voice. "More intuitive, much more subtle . . . When I used it on him, my dad was completely helpless against his own method."

Suddenly his churning hand went still. He unfurled his pale fingers, and Maya knew what she would see when she looked down. She knew, but she'd come too far to turn back, and she too was the type who needed to know how the story ended.

Her every nerve had been taut as piano wire since the moment she walked into the bar—and since before then too. Ever since she ran out of her pills. But at the sight of Frank's key, her whole body relaxed, a delicious warmth spreading through her, a feeling not unlike a high dose of Klonopin. The coziness. A heaviness of limbs. The sense that everything was going to be okay, regardless of the evidence before her eyes.

"I won," he said.

She almost laughed. She almost cried. But she lacked the conviction to do either. She stared at the key, its sharp teeth, and knew she was in danger but couldn't bring herself to care. The bar had gone quiet, and the table beneath Frank's hand had changed. Instead of body parts, she saw pine.

The only parts of herself she could lift were her eyes. She looked up.

She was in the cabin. There was the tall stone fireplace. The cathedral ceiling. The rustic wooden walls. Instead of stale beer, she smelled fire, and instead of Weezer, she heard the sound of the stream.

Frank sat across from her with the door at his back. "Talk now if you'd like," he said.

A voice deep inside of her screamed, but it was Frank who her mouth obeyed. "You . . ." Even her tongue felt heavy. Even her thoughts. "You hypnotized me."

He looked almost proud of her.

She thought of the knife in her purse. But her purse wasn't on the table anymore. Had he taken it? (Or had he taken *her*? And if so, where?) The voice inside of her screamed, but her mouth watered at whatever Frank had cooking on the stove. She smelled garlic. Fresh herbs. Cooked meat.

"Good for you for figuring it out," he said. "You remind me of myself."

"You . . . killed them."

He raised an eyebrow at the word *them*. "It was either him or me."

Maya realized he was talking about his father. Frank had killed him too. Her mouth hung open. Her jaw felt loose. And this felt good to her, like a long exhale, like the relief she'd been craving ever since being forced off Klonopin—or rather since starting on it in the first place. Ever since watching Frank kill her best friend, this tempting exhale, this heavenly unwinding, was all she had wanted. But now she fought against it as hard as she could. "Aubrey," she managed to say.

His smile fell. "You think I wanted to kill her? I didn't. But she figured it out. Can you believe it? I made the mistake of recommending a book to her about a famous mesmerist, and she made the jump to hypnosis. Pieced it together at the last minute. Aubrey was smart, I'll give her that. I only did what I had to."

"And Ruby?"

Frank looked as if she'd slapped him. "Don't talk about her. You don't know shit about Ruby."

Maya hoped her phone, wherever it was, was catching all this. "Cristina," she said.

"So you did see the video." His lips curled into a snarl.

"I talked to Steven."

"Fuck that guy. He didn't know her like I did."

"She wrote him a letter before she died."

The snarl fell as a flash of worry crossed his face. "A letter?"

"She . . . told him everything."

Frank's face grew uncertain. "What's that supposed to mean?"

Maya tried to stand, but her limbs felt made of concrete. She wasn't going anywhere; his control over her was complete.

He leaned in closer. "Tell me what the letter said."

She intended to evade, to drag this out. Keep him guessing.

Instead, to her horror, the truth marched obediently from her lips. She was an observer in her own body. "Cristina told Steven she was sorry for being a bad friend. She said she was moving in with you, into your cabin. He said it sounded like she was saying goodbye."

Frank relaxed. He sat back, and Maya did the same. They'd been sitting in the same position the whole time, but only now did she realize it.

"That should tell you everything you need to know," he said.

"She . . ." The answer came to her easily in this state of mind. "She knew she was going to die."

"It's what she wanted. I'd brought her to my cabin many times, and like you, she figured it out. She knew exactly what this place was." His voice was raw with love, though it wasn't clear if his love was for Cristina or his cabin. Or himself. "I only gave her what she wanted," he said.

Maya felt like she was sinking, her bones melting into the seat, the seat melting into the earth.

"She never wanted to go back to the real world. She'd spent her whole life trying to escape it. First it was through her painting—she taught herself when she was a kid. Said when she painted, the canvas would turn into an escape hatch. Come to think of it," he said, as if he'd just thought of it, "she kind of reminded me of you in that way. The way you would disappear into your father's book."

"Leave him out of this."

Frank acted as if she hadn't spoken, which made Maya wonder if she really had or if she'd only thought it.

"Then she discovered drugs," he said. "And getting high was an easier escape. More fun. Or so I'm told . . ." There was that smile again, the one that made her feel like they were in on the giddiest joke together, but now she knew this had never been the case. The joke had always been on her. She might have laughed if she wasn't struggling to hold her head up.

"The problem," he said, "is that you always have to come down. That was the part Cristina couldn't handle. Her heart. Her head. She felt everything too much—this is what that asshole Steven didn't understand. Cristina was *always* going to be looking for an escape, right up until the ultimate one. She was never at home in the world. Begged me not to make her go back to it, every single time, so I told her to prove it to me. Prove she wanted to stay here forever." He leaned across the table. "And she did." He ran a finger down the inside of Maya's wrist. "She tattooed the key to this place . . . right . . . here. She did it to herself, right in front of me."

"I don't believe you," Maya said. But a part of her did.

"It was her idea to die on camera at the diner," he said, "so that the world would see I never laid a hand on her. Because she knew how important my work is, how much my patients need me. I guide them back to the homes they carry inside. I help them build that space from the ground up."

She recognized these as words from the Clear Horizons website and understood that Dr. Hart was indeed Frank. She thought of the testimonials on his website and felt a flicker of hope—plenty of people had survived Frank's "treatment." They even said it helped them.

"Cristina knew this," he went on. "She didn't want me to get in trouble. Look, I don't have to tell you this, and I definitely don't owe Steven any explanation. But you should know that what happened at the diner was her final wish. I only gave her what she wanted."

Maya's head tipped forward, and she lacked the energy to haul it back up. "Please," she whispered. Her voice sounded far away. "I won't tell anyone, I promise."

"It's too late. You never should have come here tonight."

"Can't you make me forget?"

"Some part of you would always remember." His voice was thick with regret. "I know that better than anyone."

She sank further. Frank was right: he had won. But he was wrong if he thought she was just like Cristina. Maya might have shared Cristina's affinity for imaginary worlds and, yes, for getting high, and maybe it was true they both had been looking for an escape. But if there was one thing Maya knew—even if it had taken her until this moment to figure it out—it was that her home was with Dan and her mom and everyone she had, or ever would, love. Home would never be another world, some perfect cabin in the clouds, and Maya only hoped that if she ever made it back to where she belonged, she'd remember this.

"You've been suffering," he said. "You know you have, I can see it. You're tired of fighting."

She was tired of fighting. She felt her body slowing down.

"Close your eyes."

Her eyes fluttered shut.

"Listen," he said.

And she heard. The crackling fire. Babbling stream. The sound of water over stones. And beneath that sound, she heard something else, a sound she hadn't noticed before. Almost like a woodpecker pecking at a tree, but faster, and there was something unnatural about its cadence. In her usual state of mind, Maya would have known the sound at once, even if her age meant she knew it mostly from movies. But now it perplexed her, distracting her from the buried voice within. Drowning it out.

"Look," Frank said.

His word was her command. Her eyes opened. Her chin

lifted. He was smiling at her, and it was as if the past seven years had never happened. He looked handsome again, and full of life, suffused with that beautiful light that she'd only ever seen in his cabin, and in Cristina's final painting.

The door at his back was open now, and moonlight spilled through the crack. The sound was coming from outside. Something drew her to it, a longing she could neither explain nor act upon in her current state.

"Go on," he said kindly.

Her heaviness lifted and Maya rose from her seat. She felt like she was floating as she moved toward the door, passing Frank, who stayed seated at the table. She left him behind. The moonlight beaconed, prismatic, alive. She wasn't afraid as she reached for the door to the cabin. The sound grew louder.

The wooden porch creaked beneath her feet as she stepped into moonlight. The snow was gone, the surrounding forest lush with leaves. A summery breeze rustled by. She saw two rocking chairs made of the same gnarled pine as the rest of the cabin. A man sat in one of them, a typewriter balanced on his knees.

Pecking away with his fingers.

Maya hadn't known that it was possible to miss someone you'd never met, but now she felt the full weight of having missed her father all her life. It was as if that weight had been lifted. She walked slowly toward him. She recognized his face from the few pictures she had and because of how it resembled her own. The high cheekbones and dark almond-shaped eyes. The creases at their edges and the gray at his temples made him look about the age he would have been had he lived.

She reached out her hand, half expecting it to go right through him, but it didn't. His shoulder was solid. He looked up at her. Squinted as if trying to place her.

Then his face crowded with wonder, joy, and grief.

His hands shook as he set down his typewriter and stood to give her a hug.

Maya's legs threatened to give out, but her father's arms were there to support her. He was only a few inches taller than she was. She rested her tired head on his shoulder and cried on his sleeve. His skin smelled of soap and ink.

"Mija," he said.

"Dad . . ."

"Bienvenido a casa."

A low sob escaped her lips. She wondered if she was dead.

"Sit," he said, gesturing to one of the rocking chairs.

And it was only one word.

Sit.

A simple command, but it hit her like a brick. Her real father would have had an accent. His *sit* wouldn't rhyme with *pit*. It was only one word, a glitch in the illusion, but it was enough to let her know that this was *Frank* she was talking to. Frank who was speaking to her in the voice of her father. Frank who was once more manipulating her. And this angered her enough to reel back from his voice, from those words putting images in her head, words that had surrounded her, snuck in. Slithered through her being. She turned and staggered off the porch. Away from the cabin. Away from him.

She ran toward the dark forest, but her legs moved as if through water, and the trees seemed to get farther away—*Maya*—with every step, so she crouched low—*Maya!*—like an animal and hurried ahead on hands and toes—*Maya?!*—the way she only ever had in dreams.

What the hell is wrong with her?

The voice fought its way through the darkness.

No, you settle down, it said. *What the hell is going on here?* The voice was familiar. *Maya, come on. Let's go.*

Her mom!

Her mom was at the bar.

Maya gasped. She blinked a few times, then looked up to see her mom standing at the table, hands on her hips. Everyone at the Whistling Pig—the bartender, the drunk man, the three men sitting by the door—was looking at them. The sour smell of beer filled her nose. A jam band seeped from the speakers.

Her mom looked angry and afraid. "Are you listening to me?"

Maya let out a shaky breath.

Frank, across from her, was fuming. He glared at her.

"Hello?" said her mom.

"Yes, Mom. I hear you."

"Get up. We're leaving."

Maya touched her face. It was dry, yet she felt like she'd been crying. She felt like a sponge that had been wrung out.

Suddenly much lighter. Lighter even though she knew she should be afraid. Frank had done it to her again. She knew this, even if she couldn't remember.

She rose lightly to her feet, slung her purse over her shoulder, and threw Frank a withering yet curious look as she followed her mom out the door.

THIRTY-FOUR

f there's anything you haven't told me yet, now's the time," Detective Donnelly says. He sits across from Maya and her mom in a small white room at the police station.

Brenda gives her daughter a prodding look.

Maya shakes her head. She has explained as best she could, which isn't very well. Told them everything she could about Frank.

Detective Donnelly looks to be in his twenties, with a mustache and muscular arms. He sits up straight and leans forward when he talks. "Do you keep any controlled substances in the house, Ms. Edwards? Prescription pills? Sleep medication?"

"Nothing stronger than Advil." Brenda sounds like she's been crying. She had returned from her run two hours ago, just after Frank drove away, to find Maya cradling Aubrey's dead body on the stoop. Brenda had performed CPR until the ambulance arrived and two of her coworkers jumped out. But it wasn't enough. She couldn't make Aubrey's heart beat again.

"My partner's with Frank in the next room," Donnelly says. Frank had been asked to come in after Maya told the police he'd fled the scene. "You told us he did something to Aubrey, that he might have somehow killed her"—he glances down at his pad to quote her—"'just by talking to her.'"

Maya swallows. She nods.

"This is a very serious charge you're making. Accusing a man of murder. You know you can get in trouble for lying about this kind of thing."

"My daughter doesn't lie," Brenda says firmly.

"My partner's questioning him," Donnelly says, ignoring her, "but if you can't tell us what he did, we're going to have to let him go."

Maya's eyes burn with frustration.

"I'm going to talk to Detective Hunt," says Donnelly. "Wait here, please."

Maya turns to her mom. "You believe me, right?"

"I'm trying, Muffin, but you've got to tell me what happened. If there's something you're not saying, something you're afraid to tell the detective, you can tell me."

"I'm trying to!" Maya wipes her eyes with the back of her hand. "It's like he—he put us under a spell."

Her mom stares at her in disbelief.

Maya can see Detective Donnelly talking to his partner through the wide glass window. Detective Hunt, a woman in her forties, looks skeptical. She shakes her head.

"I know how it sounds," Maya says. "I can't explain how he did it, but I think I know *why*. Frank caught us talking about him. He showed up just as Aubrey was telling me about something that happened at Dunkin' Donuts. He said he was going to show her a magic trick . . ." Maya remembers the look on Aubrey's face as she'd described this, as if she'd just realized something. But what? The key hadn't levitated—but *something* had happened, hadn't it? Some other kind of trick?

"A magic trick?" her mom says. There are tears in her eyes, but her voice is strong. "Look, if Frank did something to you . . . or to her . . . then you need to tell me. But what you're saying, Maya, it's not making sense."

Detective Donnelly returns. He sits across from them. "My partner says Frank's story checks out. And it matches, more or less, what you told me."

More or less? Maya's stomach clenches. His tone makes her feel as if she's done something wrong.

"The two of you had a disagreement the day before yesterday," Donnelly says. "Frank went over to talk things out. You didn't want to talk to him, but there wasn't a fight—you agree on that. No one raised their voice. Then you left the kitchen—you say it was to call 9-1-1, but Frank says he wasn't aware that was your intention."

"He's lying—I said was going to call the police. They both heard it." Though even as she says this, it occurs to Maya that no one will ever know what Aubrey heard, or what she thought, or whether she'd actually figured out what Frank had done to them.

"Right," said Donnelly. "This is where you start to disagree. You say you went to call the police because you were afraid Frank was going to hurt you. But you can't explain *how* you thought he'd do it. And no call was ever placed to the police. Am I missing anything?"

Maya's shoulders sink. She shakes her head.

"Frank and Aubrey continued to talk through the screen door," Donnelly went on, "at which point she decided to join him outside. They sat on the steps, talked, and again, no voices were raised, no physical contact as far as you could tell."

Maya nods.

"The two of them had recently gone out for coffee," Donnelly said, "which was what prompted the fight between you and Frank."

"No! I mean—yes, sort of—but that had nothing to do with what happened."

"Did you not catch him with Aubrey at Dunkin' Donuts?"

"I did, but—"

"Were you upset about it?"

"At the time, but then I got over it."

Detective Donnelly checks his notes as if to make sure he's got the next part right; then he looks Maya right in the eyes. "Why didn't you tell me about the knife?"

The knife. She'd forgotten. "That had nothing to do with any of it."

A shadow falls across her mom's face.

"So why did you have it?" the detective asks.

"I just—I picked it up because I was scared—I *knew* he was going to hurt her. I wanted to protect us both against—"

"Against what?"

"I'm sorry," Brenda interjects, "but I think my daughter's in shock. We need some time, please."

"I understand, ma'am—I just have a few more questions—"

"No more questions," her mom says. "Not without a lawyer present. My daughter, she . . . she's clearly not well."

THIRTY-FIVE

Detective Diaz was different from Detective Donnelly.

She was older and didn't talk much, and though Maya never saw her smile, her face was kinder than Donnelly's. She wore her graying hair in a long braid. She had just listened to everything Maya had to say and gave no indication as to how she felt about it, whether or not she believed it. But she'd written it all down, including the date and time of the calls made to Brenda's landline. She sat across from Maya and her mom in a small white room very much like the small white room where they had sat with Detective Donnelly seven years ago.

They listened to the recording. The sound captured on Maya's phone wasn't as good as she'd hoped—Frank had spoken quietly, and most of his words were inaudible beneath the music at the bar—but they could hear some of the conversation.

After the part Maya remembered, she heard herself stop talking. Frank took over. His voice began to change. He grew quieter and quieter, as if someone were turning down his volume.

He slipped into that voice she remembered from the day Aubrey died. The cadence of nursery rhymes. Of spells. Even now, knowing what she knew, she found his voice bewitching. She heard *arms* and *legs* and *head*. Between two songs, they heard him say that her limbs were too heavy to lift. Then he drifted into a vivid description of the place he called home—*table*, *fireplace*, *loft*—and she understood that, although she had never been to Frank's cabin, a part of her had.

Detective Diaz took notes as she listened, jotting down the strange words that filled the room. Her calm face betrayed nothing.

Frank went on for several minutes, then fell quiet, and all they could hear was the music. A man laughed in the distance. Someone set down a glass. Eventually Maya began to speak, but her voice was almost unrecognizable.

Her words dribbled from the phone like syrup, low and slurred. Unintelligible. She sounded like she was drooling.

Her mom's mouth hung open.

"That's you?" asked Diaz.

"It must be, but I don't remember."

They kept listening as she and Frank went back and forth a few times—and Maya thought she heard herself say *Cristina*. She leaned forward, hoping to catch his response, but the music drowned it out.

"We should be able to clean this up," Diaz said. "Recover some of that audio."

Frank was still talking when the song ended, and they heard *relax* and *slow* and *breath* in a voice that was even more singsong. Maya quaked with fear. Brenda and Diaz stared at the phone, all their attention on the recording—and suddenly Maya was sure that his words had worked their magic on them. On all of them. Aubrey's blank face flashed through her mind, then Cristina's. He'd put them all in a trance.

"Let go," the recording said. *"Relax your heart."*

Maya looked at her mom. At the detective. They looked vacant.

Her hand shot across the table—she stopped the recording. "Mom," she said, panicked, terrified that Frank's words had stopped her mother's heart, just as they must have stopped Aubrey's, Ruby's, Cristina's—just as they'd nearly stopped her own.

Brenda stared at her.

"Are you okay?" Maya asked.

Her mom blinked. "You're the one I'm worried about. Are you okay?"

Maya exhaled.

"Would you like to take a break?" Diaz asked.

"No," Maya said. "I'm all right." She restarted the recording, and a moment later they heard her mom arrive.

"What the hell is wrong with her?" Brenda's voice was clear and loud. *"No, you settle down . . . Yes, Mom. I hear*

you." Maya sounded normal again. The recording ended a few seconds later.

Diaz looked at her notes. Her brown eyes crinkled at the edges in a way that was thoughtful, even as it was impossible to tell what she was thinking. "You said you had a beer there," she said. "Did you have anything else to drink?"

Maya sank. *Here we go again.* "I had some gin. Maybe two shots, but that was earlier. I wasn't drunk at the bar."

"Do you take any medications?"

Maya sank lower. She knew how this looked. Paranoia was a symptom of benzo withdrawal. She couldn't look at either of them. "I used to take Klonopin, but I quit."

"How recently?" Diaz asked.

"Last week."

The detective wrote this in her notes. Then she sat back, tapped her pen absently on the pad.

Maya wasn't hurt or angry at realizing that Diaz might not believe her. She was too exhausted for that. She wouldn't argue this time. If no one believed her, she would happily swallow whatever pills Dr. Barry prescribed—the more, the better.

While Diaz tapped her pen, Maya imagined spending the rest of her life hiding from Frank. Changing her name. Moving out of state. She pictured herself telling Dan why it was no longer safe for him to live with her. She imagined the pain she would feel, but at least she would be medicated. She'd have to be.

"I'd like a copy of that recording," the detective finally said.

THE HOUSE IN THE PINES

Maya looked up. Blinked back tears. "Of course."

"I've been in this job twenty years. Never heard anything like that." She shook her head. "I don't know what to make of it, not yet. But I'll clear up the sound, see what else I hear. And I'll look into that business you mentioned, Clear Horizons. I'd also like to have you talk to someone, a psychologist, about that med you were on. Get an assessment."

"No problem," Maya said, starting to feel hopeful. Diaz seemed to take her seriously. She asked a few more questions, then walked Maya and her mom back to the empty lobby of the police station. It was almost two a.m. and the station was quiet. A tray of Christmas-tree-shaped cookies sat on the front desk. "Let me know if he tries to get in touch with you," Diaz said.

"I will," Maya said. "Thank you."

A ray of warmth cut through Diaz's neutrality. "I'm sorry for what you've been through," she said.

———————

Brenda started the car, blasted the heat, and blew on her fingers, waiting for the fog on the windshield to clear. She was still in her pajamas, having run out as soon as she saw Maya's note. She had always done her best to protect her daughter; Maya knew this. Brenda was just afraid of the wrong things. She'd thought that she was helping when she found Dr. Barry and set up Maya's first appointment with him, and then when she brought home the meds he prescribed.

But tonight, she had saved her daughter's life. Even if she

didn't know it—even if all she thought she'd done was interrupt a conversation—Maya knew and she was grateful. She was alive.

"I'll take a sick day tomorrow," her mom said. "You shouldn't be alone."

"I'm doing all right."

This time Maya more or less meant it. It could have been relief, or the fact that she'd been awake for so long, or the hot air rushing from the vents, that made her feel as if she could finally sink into the kind of sleep that had evaded her since she quit Klonopin. The sleep of a baby in a car seat. She blinked, and the next thing she knew they were home.

She didn't notice until they were inside that her mom was crying, tears dripping from her chin onto her boots as she knelt to take them off. Maya rarely saw her cry and found it alarming. "What is it?" she asked.

"I should've believed you."

Maya sank onto the couch. She hadn't cried at the police station, but she cried now. They both did. They cried, then hugged, then laughed at themselves. Her mom draped a quilt around her shoulders and looked at her with such love and sorrow that Maya almost wanted to comfort her. Because her mom was Frank's victim too. Nothing hurt her more than seeing her daughter in pain.

"I don't blame you," Maya said. "The things I said didn't make sense . . ." She had talked of magic tricks. Of spells.

"I could have tried harder to understand. And even if I couldn't—I could have accepted that he . . ." A wave of anger threatened to burst from her mom's mouth. "He *hurt* you. I couldn't bear the thought of someone hurting you. The thought that I . . ." She'd never looked so broken. "I failed to protect you."

"You saved my life, Mom."

A shadow crossed Brenda's eyes as this sank in. To believe her daughter meant believing that Frank had killed Aubrey and that he had almost killed Maya. It meant believing that he still could.

THIRTY-SIX

'm not writing you a prescription for Klonopin," said the doctor at the urgent care center.

"I'm not asking you to," Maya said. She'd just finished explaining why she was here, and now the doctor had his arms crossed over his chest. He looked down at her sternly, as if he'd caught her trying to steal his wallet. She wanted to say that she wouldn't have gone back on Klonopin if he paid her, but as she had no regular doctor, and no insurance, she bit back her indignation. She needed the man's care. "I was hoping there was something else I could try? Something to help me sleep?"

The doctor wrote her a prescription for mirtazapine, an antidepressant that he said should make her drowsy.

Dan was relieved to hear that she'd seen a doctor, and Maya was relieved to hear he'd missed her. "Hasn't felt like home without you," he said to her on the phone. They made plans for him to pick her up the day after Christmas.

She'd start back at work on the twenty-seventh and was almost looking forward to it, the normalcy, the plants, even the customers, some of whom she'd grown friendly with over the years. Her boss had been understanding about the missed days, and the weight she'd dropped would lend credence to her story of having had the flu.

She slept for twelve hours straight that night in her old room on the new bed. The urgent care doctor had been right about the mirtazapine. It knocked her out like a frying pan to the skull. Her dreams were vivid, but as usual, she didn't remember them upon waking, and all she was left with was the muscle memory of fear. A tight jaw. Weary legs as if she'd been running. It was noon when she woke, and she was drooling on her pillow. She hauled herself out of bed.

Walking downstairs, she noticed for the first time how nicely her mom had decorated the small fir tree in the corner of the living room. Maya recognized all the shiny baubles and homemade ornaments. The plastic angel. A tiny snowman she'd made out of clay when she was eight. Growing up, she and her mom had always decorated the tree together, but as Maya hadn't come home for the past few years, the tradition had fallen by the wayside. She told herself it wasn't too late to start again.

Her appetite came roaring back at the smell of bacon. The mirtazapine, in addition to making her sleepy, made her ravenous. It was the day before Christmas, and they doused their banana pancakes with maple syrup. The sun was warm in the window. After breakfast, she sank onto the couch and began to fall back asleep.

"Let's go for a walk," her mom said. "It's gorgeous out there."

The crisp blue air cut through some of the fog in Maya's head. Ice crystals glittered in the snow. They walked past the houses of their neighbors, waving at Joe Delaney, out shoveling his walk, and Angela Russo, who, once upon a time, Maya had babysat, as she ran by with her dog. They passed the auto shop with its lot of sagging cars, and a few old industrial buildings, then walked beneath the railroad bridge to the neighborhood where Maya's grandparents still lived.

They arrived at Silver Lake and began to walk along its north shore on the path that had been built after Maya moved away. The lake had been the site of a massive cleanup in 2013, and though it still wasn't safe enough for swimming, and the fish still couldn't be eaten, people could now boat here or walk on the paved trail. New trees had been planted, and wildflowers. Maya wondered what Aunt Lisa would think of it, the notorious pond slowly returning to its natural state.

Still, it felt strange to walk so close to the water. Strange to see the old warning signs replaced by park benches. To not hold her breath. Every step felt like an act of faith in the lake and this town.

"I read that hymn this morning," her mom said. "'The Hymn of the Pearl.'"

"What did you think?"

Her mom was quiet for a while. Her breath was white. "Honestly? I liked the story better when I didn't know what it was based on."

"Why?"

"Guess I prefer stories that aren't trying to teach me something."

Maya hadn't thought much about the hymn's religious context, but she could see how her mom, who'd resisted converting anyone while on her missionary trip, might view it.

"What do you think it's trying to teach you?" Maya said.

Her mom looked thoughtful. Then she smiled. "What do *you* think?"

Maya fought back through her mirtazapine haze to what she'd read online, about how the hymn had been adopted by various religions. "People say it's about the soul," she said, "about how it starts off in this other place . . . wherever we were before we were born, I guess. But then we're born, and we forget about that original home, and our original parents." As she articulated this, both to her mom and to herself, Maya's reaction was the opposite of Brenda's. Knowing the hymn's meaning made her appreciate it even more. She could see why it had endured all this time.

"Exactly," her mom said. But she said it like this was a bad thing. They rounded a bend in the lake. "I don't agree with that. I don't think my true home is some other place. I think it's here."

The words resonated with Maya on a level she couldn't explain, as if she had said or thought them herself once.

"Look!" her mom said.

Maya turned to see that a dozen geese had landed on the lake and were gliding silently across the water in a graceful

V. "Wow," she said. She had never seen geese, or wildlife of any kind, at Silver Lake. "You think it's really safe for them here?"

"I do," her mom said. "I think we'll be swimming here ourselves someday."

THIRTY-SEVEN

D an hugged Maya so hard that her feet lifted off her mom's living room floor. She nuzzled her nose into his neck. She'd missed the musky smell of his skin mingled with the cedar and pine of his all-natural deodorant.

"I'm so sorry," he murmured into her hair.

She'd told him everything over the phone and sent him the recording from the Whistling Pig. Like everyone else who heard the recording, Dan had found Frank's strangely rhythmic cadence deeply sinister.

"I'm sorry too," she said. For breaking his trust. For the dinner with his parents.

He set her down and they took each other in. She had showered and washed her hair, and wore a yellow sweater that her grandparents had given her for Christmas yesterday. Dan looked like he hadn't slept well, and his eyebrows were tented with worry. "He hasn't tried to contact you, has he?"

"No."

"Any news from the detective?"

"She's looking into Clear Horizons Wellness Center and that therapy his dad developed." It felt good to be able to tell him this, that Detective Diaz had taken Maya and her theory seriously and was keeping her informed.

The recording from her phone had been cleaned up, and though most of Frank's words remained hidden beneath the music, the detective heard enough to convince her that he might have had something to do with Cristina's death. *It was her idea to die on camera at the diner,* he had said, one of the few full sentences caught on the recording. Not exactly a confession, but certainly suspicious.

Diaz had also traced the late-night calls placed to Brenda's landline. They came from Frank's father's house, which now belonged to Frank—and was also the location of Clear Horizons Wellness Center. The detective had helped Maya file a restraining order.

Dan shook his head in dismay. "I can't believe I let you confront that psycho on your own."

"You didn't know he was dangerous."

"I should have." He sounded angry with himself. "You tried to tell me."

Maya looked away.

She understood that it was complicated. Dan would have been lying before if he'd said he believed her. The murder accusation had seemed to come out of nowhere, and the only evidence she'd provided was the video from the diner—which had seemed, if anything, proof that Frank *hadn't* killed Cristina. That he'd been a bystander. Not to mention that Maya had been acting strangely even before all that.

It made rational sense that Dan had doubted her.

But would it ever make the other kind of sense? The kind she felt? Silence clotted in the air between them. Her mom was at work. The house was cold, and Maya had turned out all the lights as she was leaving.

Dan took her hands, brushed her knuckles with a kiss. And Maya reminded herself of the lies she had told him. The omissions. Maybe she had never deserved his trust anyway.

She looked up into his soft blue eyes, so full of worry and love, and wondered if their relationship could survive all the damage they'd inflicted.

She hoped so.

————————

Brenda had wrapped Dan up a slice of pecan pie from Christmas dinner, and left it for him with a note: *Happy holidays, Dan! Congratulations on your finals! Hope I'll get a chance to see you soon!* She'd signed her name with a smiley face.

Maya insisted on stopping by his parents' house on the way back to Boston. The longer she went without clearing the air, the weirder it would be the next time she saw them. She knew that now. She cared too much about Dan to let his parents think she was a mess.

His father, still on winter break, was reading the newspaper at the kitchen table when they walked in. "Maya!" he said warmly, standing to greet her. He looked almost as concerned as his son. "Dan told us a little about what happened. I'm so sorry. Are you okay?"

"I'm doing a lot better now," she said. "Thank you." She wasn't sure how Dan had explained the situation with Frank but knew he hadn't told his parents about why she was sick at dinner. They still didn't know why she'd run off so early in the morning, and she had worried they would assume it was out of shame.

But if Carl thought that, he didn't let it show.

"We just thought we'd stop by since you're on our way back east," Dan said.

Carl offered coffee and biscotti, and Maya gratefully accepted both.

"Is that Danny I hear?" His mom swept in from her office down the hall, draped in a turquoise pashmina. The delight in her voice gave way to a fleeting, involuntary frown the moment she saw Maya, but Greta was quick to recover. "What a surprise!" she said, looking questioningly at her son.

Then she turned to Maya, her sharp hazel eyes magnified by the reading glasses perched on her nose. "How are you doing?"

"Much better now," Maya said.

"Good," Greta said. "Good." Her face and voice were pinched. She brewed herself a cup of green tea and joined them at the table. When Carl offered her the plate of biscotti, she waved it away.

The four of them sat in the same positions as they had just last week, with Greta across from Maya, and although it felt like years had passed since then, and though her brush with death had really put things in perspective, Maya still felt nervous. She reached for her biscotti. "This is really good," she said.

"Wish I could take credit," said Carl, "but they're from the Black Sheep."

"You're looking much better," Greta said, gazing at Maya over the rim of her cup, her voice brimming with all the other questions she was too polite to ask. Like her husband, she seemed concerned, but perhaps less about Maya's well-being than about Maya in general. The fact that she was dating her son. The idea that Dan could be dragged into her mess.

"Thank you," Maya said. "I'm sorry for leaving in such a hurry last time I was here."

"Don't worry," Carl said. "The important thing is you're better."

Maya smiled, grateful. She saw in Carl his son's instinct to smooth things over. Now she knew where Dan got it.

It wasn't from his mom. "Were you able to see a doctor?" Greta asked.

"Yes," Maya said. She saw Dan's posture straighten, ready to shut the whole subject down if he needed to.

"So, what was it—if you don't mind my asking."

Maya had been hoping Greta wouldn't ask. She had wanted only to apologize, to clear the air, but of course she'd known his parents might have questions. Especially his mom. Maya glanced at Dan, who was looking at her wide-eyed, as if to say, *You don't have to do this.*

"It's what happens when you stop taking Klonopin," she said.

"Klonopin?" Greta didn't know what it was.

"Antianxiety medication. I'd been taking it for the past few years, and then I—I had to stop. And it ended up being pretty hard to quit, insomnia, anxiety, that sort of thing. That's why I wasn't feeling well that night."

"Ah," Greta said. "I was worried it might have been the daiquiris."

"Mom," Dan said.

"What? Your dad makes a strong daiquiri."

"It's true," Maya said, her face burning. "Probably shouldn't have been drinking so much either."

Dan leapt to her defense. "Maya's been through a lot lately."

Carl sipped his coffee. Dunked his biscotti.

"Of course," Greta said. "I can only imagine . . . What was it that your ex-boyfriend did exactly?"

"Now, honey," Carl said. "Maybe she doesn't want to talk about that."

"It's okay," Maya said. And it was. She understood why Greta was alarmed, and though the questions were uncomfortable, they were nothing compared to the crushing ache of holding it all in. Of pretending she was all right.

"When I was seventeen," she said, holding Greta's gaze, "I briefly dated an older man named Frank, and he—" She almost choked. "He murdered my best friend." It was hard to say, but then, once she had, Maya felt lighter. There was something freeing about stating it so matter-of-factly.

Greta softened. "I'm sorry that happened to you, Maya. I am."

Dan reached over, took Maya's hand. The moment was tense, but this was still going better than Greta's birthday dinner.

"I just hope," Greta said, "that my son—"

"All right," Dan said, "that's enough."

"I just want him to be safe."

Both Dan and his father sighed at the same time, as if Greta had gone too far.

"My mom says the same thing about me," Maya said.

Greta gave a slight nod at this, and her sharp eyes softened until they looked a bit like her son's. "I know," she said. Her voice filled with warmth. "I know."

THIRTY-EIGHT

Maya wanted to know more about the research study Frank's father had conducted back in the '80s, the one he'd gotten in trouble over. And now she had Dan on her side. He called in a favor with a friend of his who clerked for the district attorney's office and a week later handed Maya a police report. The report was from 1984. Oren hadn't been arrested, but he'd been brought in for questioning because of something that happened during the research study—the reason it was canceled, and his career ruined.

The purpose of the study—as summarized by Officer Finley, who'd written the report—was to test an experimental method of hypnotherapy proposed by Dr. Bellamy. The method built upon existing research into clinical hypnosis for pain management but had the potential to be much more effective. Dr. Bellamy claimed it would have been a major breakthrough for medical science.

It worked by employing a series of subperceptual cues, both verbal and nonverbal, to reach beyond the subject's conscious awareness and tap into the part of the nervous system that regulates processes not usually under the patient's control. The part of us that takes in information from the senses—like a burning hand, for example—decides what to do with that information, then sends a message to the hand—*Stop touching the stove*—without our needing to consciously think about it.

Dr. Bellamy's method, as Officer Finley understood it, took control of that whole system. It left the patient's mind and body—specifically the involuntary nervous system—open to manipulation in ways that traditional hypnosis did not. It was, according to Dr. Bellamy, "a trancelike state with enormous potential to treat ailments of both mind and body." He'd probably thought he was helping his son when he subjected him to this method, but he was also honing it on him, putting Frank into trances he was never aware of, and implanting suggestions designed to manipulate his behavior.

Like traditional hypnosis, it didn't work on everyone. The percentage of people who are highly susceptible to hypnosis is low—only one of the participants in Oren's research study had qualified as such a person. Forty-two-year-old Russell DeLuca had tested higher than anyone else on what was known as the Stanford Hypnotic Susceptibility Scale. DeLuca was highly hypnotizable.

Maya got a bad feeling when she read that. She Googled

"Stanford Hypnotic Susceptibility Scale" and learned that people who are highly hypnotizable tend to share other attributes as well. They tend to be imaginative. To lose themselves in movies and in books. To daydream.

Russell DeLuca died during a hypnosis session with Dr. Bellamy. The cause of his death was later determined to be a stroke. Because it couldn't be proven that the stroke was a direct result of the hypnotic trance he'd been under at the time, Dr. Bellamy was never charged with the death, but he lost his job and psychology license.

Dan agreed with Maya that this could turn out to be strong evidence in the case against Frank. In 1984, it couldn't be proven that Dr. Bellamy's method had caused DeLuca's death—but hypnosis research had come a long way since then. Imaging studies now confirmed that hypnosis causes changes in certain parts of the brain, which can in turn influence bodily functions like blood pressure and breathing. Now that doctors at major hospitals used hypnosis to treat gastrointestinal issues, the idea that something so effective could also be used to hurt, to kill even, seemed a lot less far-fetched.

What was needed, Maya and Dan agreed, was to show that Frank was also trained in his father's method, and that he'd used it on her.

This was where Clear Horizons Wellness Center came in. As Maya had suspected, the "center" turned out to consist of a single employee who went by the name Dr. David Hart. That was why Maya hadn't been able to find Frank all these years. He was going by another name and posing as a doctor.

The only name and face that appeared on the center's website belonged to Dr. Oren Bellamy. The center was the one place his "proprietary therapeutic method" was practiced. The testimonials page, all the happy clients, demonstrated Frank's efficacy when it came to his father's "technique."

Frank had taken the site down, but Maya had screenshots of every page and had sent them all to Detective Diaz.

She waited.

It wasn't long before the detective managed to track down Frank's mom.

Maya had tried to look her up in the past without any luck, and now she could see why: Sharon Bellamy had changed her name, not once but four different times since divorcing Oren and taking her son to live in Hood River. Sharon—who went by Dana Wilson these days—appeared to be in hiding. She'd moved many times over the past twenty years and had been in and out of institutions and diagnosed with paranoid schizophrenia.

But Maya doubted that Frank's mom was paranoid. And she understood why the former Sharon Bellamy had refused to talk to Detective Diaz. She hoped that, with time, Dana Wilson would be able to open up about the abuse she'd almost certainly suffered at the hands of her ex-husband, though Maya didn't blame her if she didn't. She knew how it felt to be called crazy.

The new dog's name was Toto because she resembled the terrier belonging to Dorothy, but this Toto was less adventurous than the one in *The Wizard of Oz*. This Toto shook with fear at loud noises. Her small bones had quivered with such intensity the first time Maya picked her up, she had worried something was wrong, but then, as she held the middle-aged dog to her chest, Toto had calmed down.

She likes you, the shelter worker had said.

"No!" Maya said now as Toto barked and bared her teeth at the mail sliding through the mail slot onto the floor. It was a Saturday afternoon, three weeks after Maya had gone back to work. She and Dan had been reading together on the couch, their legs overlapping in the middle beneath a soft blue throw she'd recently purchased.

Toto began to shake.

Maya picked her up and brought her over to the couch, its green velvet heaven on a lazy winter day. She put the mail on the coffee table, then smoothed the dog's shivering body with her hands, murmuring about how everything would be okay.

Toto had been with them for about a week, and it was obvious that Maya was better than Dan at calming her down. He joked that Maya was the dog's therapy human. He reached over, scratched Toto behind the ears. Toto huffed.

Maya noticed a large manila envelope among the junk mail and home furnishing catalogs on the table. She slid a finger beneath the envelope's seal, pulled out a vintage-looking scholarly journal.

Experimental Neuropsychology, Volume 17, October 1983. Her body tensed. She'd almost forgotten having ordered this online. The journal's cover was burnt orange, the white font from another era. Inside the cover, halfway down the list of contributors, she found Frank's father. She laid the journal on the coffee table so that she and Dan could read it at the same time. Toto settled at her side. The apartment was quiet, the only sounds the usual clatter of the street outside, the hum of the refrigerator, and, after a while, Toto's snoring.

Oren had published the article a year before the research study that left Russell DeLuca dead. It was unrelated to the study but also had to do with hypnosis. It was about what Oren called the "Bellamy Induction," a way of inducing a hypnotic trance in subjects who'd been previously hypnotized. It was faster, Oren claimed, than the popular Elman Induction, which many hypnotists currently used because of its ability to bring about a trance state in under four minutes.

The Bellamy Induction was based upon classical conditioning. Where Pavlov had trained dogs to associate food with the sound of a bell, Oren proposed that a subject, once induced into a trance, could be trained to associate that state of consciousness with an object.

Any object. A coin. A watch. A pencil.

Maya nodded knowingly. "A key," she said.

Toto twitched in her sleep.

Once the object and the trance state had been paired in the patient's mind, the sight of the object would induce the trance. It was practically instantaneous. Dr. Bellamy went on to stress the importance of selecting an object common enough so as not to be distracting while visually distinct enough that it wouldn't be confused with other objects of its type.

He concluded by suggesting a possible application for his method. It could be used, he said, to exert control over potentially volatile populations, such as prisoners or psychotic patients. Subjects could be restrained without the use of force. The Bellamy Induction was presented as a "theory," but Maya was sure it was more than that. Oren would have used the induction on his son, just as he'd subjected Frank to his hypnotherapy method.

And like the method, Frank would have learned the induction. He'd have perfected it until he was more adept at it than his father. Then he'd have combined the two procedures into what amounted to enormous power over anyone who happened to be hypnotizable.

Maybe Maya hadn't been so far off when she called what he did to them *magic*. He'd waved an odd-looking key at her and she'd fallen into a trance. He'd done this not only to her, but to Aubrey as well. And Cristina. And his own father. It was as if Frank had cast a spell on all of them.

Maya began to cut her mirtazapine pills in half as she neared the end of the bottle prescribed to her at urgent care; then she cut them into quarters. Little by little, she relearned how to fall asleep naturally, though it would be a while before her brain fully healed.

She'd been attending AA meetings for almost a month and couldn't tell if they were helping, if it was the mirtazapine, or if the truth was that she wasn't an alcoholic. But she hadn't had a drop since the night she confronted Frank at the Whistling Pig, and the only time she really missed it, the only time she felt like she absolutely needed a gin and tonic or she was going to lose her mind, was around dawn when she woke from another dream she couldn't remember and couldn't fall back asleep.

When this happened, her thoughts would turn to Frank. She might tell herself he'd be apprehended any day now— Diaz had all but assured her of this—but on mornings like this, so early that it might as well have been night, Maya would imagine other posthypnotic suggestions lying dormant in her head. An evil egg waiting for the right cue, the right word or image, to hatch and overtake her mind. She would picture herself slipping into a trance at the grocery store. While talking to a customer at work. While driving.

Or a floorboard in the hall would creak and she'd be sure that it was him. She had always been imaginative. She envisioned him slipping in through a window while she and Dan slept. Standing over their bed. Frank would never have to touch them as his words filled their room like poisonous gas.

On mornings such as this, Maya knew better than to lie in bed thinking, so she got up and crept to the kitchen. She turned on a light. Brewed herself a cup of coffee and stirred in a splash of milk. This was when she was most grateful for Toto. She heard the dog's claws clicking across the kitchen floor.

Toto stood with her head tilted, as if to ask what was wrong.

Maya stroked her soft head. "Shh . . ." she whispered. "It's nothing."

Toto followed at her heels as she went into the room formerly occupied by Dan's old roommate. Potted plants lined the windowsill. A futon for guests. The exercise bike stood in the corner.

Maya's desk was by the window. This was the desk where she'd written her first stories, back in middle school. She had brought it up from her mom's basement and installed it here, in what was now her office.

She sat in the comfortable chair, soft and close to the ground, and Toto curled up at her feet, giving off warmth.

Her father's unfinished manuscript sat on one corner of the desk, along with the marbled notebook containing the translation she'd written by hand at seventeen.

On top of that was a second notebook. The new notebook had a deep green cover. The color of moss, of jungle. The new notebook was filled with her messy writing, mostly notes at this point and ideas for scenes. She had her basic plot but was learning that this was only the foundation. The bones. The rest—the details, the flesh—would have to come from her. She had a lot of research to do. She wanted to get it right. She had begun to save money for the trip to Guatemala she planned to take in the spring. She would stay with her aunt Carolina. Maya was going to write Pixán home again. Toto began to snore at her feet as she opened the green notebook and picked up where her father had left off.

ACKNOWLEDGMENTS

Thank you to Jenni Ferrari-Adler for suggesting I turn my MFA thesis into a thriller. I'd always loved reading suspense, but I wasn't sure I could write it until you suggested I give it a shot. Thank you to Maya Ziv for your storytelling brilliance and deep insight into character. This book grew so much in your hands. Thank you to Lexy Cassola for your excellent notes, Mary Beth Constant for your copyediting magic, and Sarah Oberrender for the gorgeous cover. Thank you to Christine Ball, John Parsley, Emily Canders, Stephanie Cooper, Nicole Jarvis, Isabel DaSilva, Alice Dalrymple, and everyone at Dutton for helping bring this book into the world.

Thank you to everyone who read early pages in writing workshops at LSU. Thank you especially to Danielle Lea Buchanan and Hannah Reed for joining me in a pact to write five hundred words each day, and then holding me to it. Thank you to my professors and thesis advisors, Jennifer Davis, Mari Kornhauser, and Jim Wilcox, for your guidance throughout that messy first draft.

ACKNOWLEDGMENTS

Thank you to Jim Krusoe for your example, your famous surgical brackets around unnecessary sentences, and, above all, the beautiful community of writers you fostered at Santa Monica College. Thank you to everyone at 30B who listened to and commented on my writing, and to Monona Wali, who brought me into the world of teaching older adult writers at SMC's Emeritus College.

Thank you to my fabulous writing group: Catie Disabato, Anna Dorn, Jon Doyle, Maggie Murray, Robin Tung, and KK Wootton. I'm so grateful for all the feedback and for your friendship.

Thank you to my family. On the Reyes side: Gracias a mis abuelos, Hilda y Guillermo Reyes, por todo lo que han hecho para que sus hijos, nietos, y bisnietos puedan tener oportunidades como la que yo he tenido. To my aunt Hilda Reyes, in whose spare room I spent a lot of time editing this book: thank you for always making me feel at home. Thank you to my uncles. Gracias a Ana María Ordóñez Aldana, Gabriela Villagrán Ordóñez, Juan Pablo Villagrán Ordóñez, Jose Alberto Villagrán Ordóñez, Blanca Rosa Aldana De Alvarez, Wilfredo Alvarez, Carlos Muñoz Ordóñez, y toda la familia por hacerme sentir como en casa en Guatemala.

Thank you to my father, Paul Reyes, for sharing your love of history with me and being one of the kindest people I know.

On the Carey side, thank you to my late grandparents, Patricia and William Carey. Several of the Pittsfield settings in this book are places I visited with you when I was young. Thank you to my aunts and uncles for always cheering me on, and to the town of Pittsfield, where I lived when I was in fourth and fifth grade.

Thank you to my mom, Mary Carey, for talking about your hometown with me, for reading multiple drafts of this book, and for teaching me at a young age to value language and writing. Thank you to Brian Schultz for joining us in Pittsfield when I went to do research, and for doing all the driving.

Thank you to my brother, Nicolas Reyes, for talking about ideas with me and being hilarious.

Thank you, reader, for reading this.

And thank you, Adam D'Alba, for everything. There's nowhere in the world I'd rather be than on the couch with you, talking about stories.

ABOUT THE AUTHOR

Ana Reyes has an MFA from Louisiana State University. Her work has appeared in *Bodega, Pear Noir!, New Delta Review,* and elsewhere. She lives in Los Angeles with her husband and teaches creative writing to older adults at Santa Monica College. *The House in the Pines* is her first novel.